Nita Musgrave
US/Canadian AGM
September 2012

Shillingstone Press

or, The True Tragedy of
King Richard the Third

*The play on the life and death of King Richard the Third
that William Shakespeare should have written.*

Robert Fripp

Dark Sovereign

or, The True Tragedy of King Richard the Third

The life of King Richard the Third that William Shakespeare should have written

Copyright Robert Fripp 1988. This is the second edition, © 2011
Registered at the Canadian Intellectual Property Office, 1988

Shillingstone Press
125 Southvale Drive
Toronto ON, M4G 1G6
Canada

Cover and Interior Design: The Design Unit, Wimborne, Dorset, U.K.
Title calligraphy: Yaroslava Mills, late of West Nyack, New York

Notice of Rights

All rights reserved. No part of this publication may be reproduced, stored in a retrieval system, uploaded or transmitted in any form or by any means, electronic, mechanical, recording or otherwise without the prior written consent of the author. Short excerpts may be used in reviews; but no person, company or organization many offer this work, or any part of this work, for sale or reuse without the author's written permission.

First, private printing of 400 copies, 1991. No ISBN
This is the second printed edition, July 2011
ISBN-10: 0-9780621-3-2
ISBN-13: 978-0-9780621-3-2

Written between 1984 and 1988, *Dark Sovereign* takes the form of a play about the life and reign of King Richard III. *Dark Sovereign* is crafted in English as it stood during the life of William Shakespeare and his contemporaries: The 'Golden Age' of English literature lasted from about 1579 to 1626. *Dark Sovereign* challenges Shakespeare's depiction of Richard III as a moral and physical grotesque.

Cover: The Society of Antiquaries of London holds the Copyright to the Paston 'arched frame' portrait of King Richard III. Pamela Tudor-Craig, Ph.D., Lady Wedgwood, describes this portrait as having 'no trace of vilification'. She means that the majority of the nearly twenty known portraits of Richard III show that a hump or shortened arm were added after his death. The Paston family's portrait escaped. This likeness remains as the artist intended.

I DEDICATE *DARK SOVEREIGN* TO

CAROL, *WILL* AND *ERIC FRIPP*; TO *SATWANT GILL*;
AND TO PARENTS, GRANDPARENTS, FAMILY AND FRIENDS
WHO STRUGGLED HARDER AND DIED YOUNGER

IN MEMORY OF

EDITH WINIFRED NÉE *PARKER FRIPP*
WHO GAVE ME LIFE AND TOO SOON LOST HER OWN;
AND *KATE BRYAN*, '*NANNIE*', WHO SANG WELSH HYMNS
TO ME IN A PORTSMOUTH ANDERSON SHELTER
'TO BLOCK OUT THE DIN OF THE BOMBS AND ACK-ACK'

> *'When day droops into night, who then can light a brand*
> *so great 'twill show the hórizont? Nay, my lord.*
> *The face, the breath, the voice, the touch of hands,*
> *the quick — the very certain countenance of life*
> *rebuke our fond-imagin'd vizard of eternity.*
> *Had heaven wept good measure of my grief,*
> *the earth had wash'd away.'*

Dark Sovereign 2.4.7

CONTENTS

The Owner's Manual ix

Dark Sovereign:

Dramatis personae 2

Induction 1 4

Induction 2 9

Act 1 12

Act 2 40

Act 3 68

Act 4 110

Act 5 159

Epilogue 193

The Merchant scene 196

A scene by scene synopsis 201

Quotable quotes 207

King Arthur: surviving pieces 210

Carol Burtin Fripp, Her Verse 215

Books by Robert Fripp,
and contact information 216

THE OWNER'S MANUAL

IN 1983 I WAS the series producer of CBC Television's investigative weekly program, *the fifth estate*, a Canadian national current affairs series roughly comparable to BBC's *Panorama* or CBS's *Sixty Minutes*.

Investigative television demands a high degree of factual accuracy. Taking a reasoned approach to current affairs presentation requires that producers acknowledge this axiom: 'Television too often distils until it distorts'. The medium distils in two ways — first, through normal editing and shortening; second, by selecting for action and sensation. Hence a term too frequently implied in television newsrooms: 'If it bleeds, it leads'. That 'modern' approach reflects equally well on William Shakespeare's mauling of King Richard III.

A worn paperback was circulating in our production unit in 1983. Written under the pen name Josephine Tey, *The Daughter of Time* tells a tale that acquits King Richard III of murdering his young nephews, the Princes in the Tower. Ms. Tey set her scene by putting her principal character, a police detective, in a hospital bed with nothing to do but solve the case. He does this, acquitting King Richard and restoring his name and reputation. The author's motive for writing her book would have been clearer had she used as her title the full adage: 'Truth is the daughter of time' (from Francis Bacon after Aulus Gellius). Published in 1951, *The Daughter of Time* has been an influential primer, attracting newcomers to Ricardian studies for six decades (and helping broadcast professionals to focus). Ms. Tey's verdict may be correct, but her choice of sources can be challenged and her chain of evidence seems naïve.

In 1983, before reading her book, I knew only the generally unchallenged view of most Britons about King Richard III: that he murdered his nephews, the little princes, in the Tower of London, then ruled for just two years. In short, he was a 'bad' king, guilty as rumoured.

1983: KING RICHARD'S YEAR

News coverage was extensive in 1983. It marked the five hundredth anniversary of Richard's accession to the throne. Canadian newspapers printed features from the British press; and the Richard III Society went so far as to stage a mock coronation in Toronto's St. James Cathedral. Charles Ross, professor emeritus of history at the University of Bristol, whose book does not exonerate Richard, stated that Richard III was one of just two people who have been the subject of at least one major work in every generation through the past five centuries. This was intriguing to a current affairs producer. How to discover the facts and set the record a little straighter after so much time?

The winner writes history

Richard's body was barely cold before his reputation fell victim to the fact that the winner writes history. Richard, the last Plantagenet king, was defeated and killed in battle by troops under Henry Tudor (King Henry VII), whose tenuous claim to the throne made it essential that the memory of his defeated opponent be denigrated or obliterated. Even the fate of Richard's corpse was a mystery. When the victor took the throne as King Henry VII, he set about inflicting judicial murder on a number of people (I have read the figure nineteen) who had superior bloodlines to the crown.

The most damning assault on Richard III's character and reputation came a century later, when William Shakespeare wrote *The Tragedy of Richard the Third* for performance at the court of his patron, Henry Tudor's granddaughter, Queen Elizabeth I. In writing *Richard the Third*, Shakespeare distilled many scraps of Tudor propaganda, enshrined them and perpetuated a grotesque which has dominated the English-speaking world's perception of Richard Gloucester's life and reign through four centuries.

On a personal level I have no attachment to any given verdict. Was the last medieval king (or the first modern one) an ogre or a saint? He was neither; he was less than either. It is in the contradictions inherent to his very human nature that continuing interest in Richard Gloucester lies. The task I set myself in researching and writing *Dark Sovereign* was an intellectual challenge — to overturn a deeply-entrenched slice of received 'history' by substituting a more plausible version.

Challenging prejudice

My challenge was to overwhelm the prejudice built up and cemented through centuries. We find King Richard III's defenders emerging within twenty years of Queen Elizabeth's death. Several weighty biographies have countered Shakespeare's *Richard the Third*, but the public mind does not cleave to weighty biographies. The stigma remains. I came to realize that turning public opinion around demanded that a more accurate play be written in the English language as it had been available to the Bard and his contemporaries. Hence a steep-odds-against ambition: to write a play that would compete with Shakespeare's *Richard the Third* head-on, and do so in the English of the Renaissance.

> *'History, at least in its state of ideal perfection,*
> *Is a compound of poetry and philosophy'.*
> Lord Macaulay, 1828

Detachment and exaggeration

In 1766, the German dramatist Gotthold Lessing wrote an essay about a Greek statue depicting the Trojan priest of Apollo, Laocoön, and his sons, being torn apart by sea monsters. In *Laocoön, An Essay on the Limits of Painting and Poetry*, Lessing describes how the sculptor toned down the agonies of the men, leaving them muted, their facial expressions seemingly detached from their predicament. Understatement gives free rein to the beholder's imagination, Lessing opined. It is that force of 'compelled imagination' which must interpret all art.

William Shakespeare's portrayal of King Richard III falls the other way. *Richard the Third* offers small room for conjecture, little doubt and few shades of grey. Shakespeare's skill enshrined the Tudors' origin myth and continues to perpetuate farce. It is this that *Dark Sovereign* sets out to challenge. It does so by presenting its catalogue of human frailties with a human — not a demonic — face.

> *'Where History is vncertaine,*
> *reasonable coniecture must challenge precedency'.*
> Nathanael Carpenter, 1625

Challenge precedency, yes, but...

'Challenge precedency' it does, but *Dark Sovereign* is not wildly revisionist. Taking many ancient and modern histories into account, the play seldom accords King Richard's character more benefit of the doubt than the median value dictated by its source materials. *Dark Sovereign* is an exercise in modern dramatized journalism, albeit, by virtue of its language, one that is unique. *Dark Sovereign* seeks to explain, not to exonerate; to define, not to denounce.

> *'The English tongue is gorgeouslie invested in rare ornaments'.*
> Francis Meres, *Palladis Tamia*, Wits treasury, 1598

'Rare ornaments' or baggage?

Yes, English *is* 'gorgeouslie invested in rare ornaments'. It is also invested with the ability to express precision, and the language of *Dark Sovereign* is precise. It is written in the vocabulary, idioms and syntax prevailing in the interval from about 1579 (Sir Philip Sidney's *Old Arcadia*) to precisely 1626, (a cutoff date dictated by technical reasons involving Francis Bacon). This interval of forty-seven years — in reference to *Dark Sovereign* I call it 'the Period' — marked the renaissance of English letters. Every word in *Dark Sovereign*, each syllable, word-sense, expression, verb ending, tense and function, as well as word order, metaphor and patterns of construction are present here only because I managed to find precedents for them in written English before the year 1626.

> 'This period in our time seemeth to be the perfitest period in our English tongue
> ... there is in our tongue great and sufficient stuff for Art'.
> Richard Mulcaster, in
> 'The first part of the elementarie which entreateth chefelie
> of the right writing of our English tongue' — 1582

As a boy I won a choral scholarship to Salisbury Cathedral School, the probable model for William Golding's *Lord of the Flies* (1954). Golding taught and wrote at the school next door (and perhaps broke up fights across the common wall between the tribes). For my part, I learned survival skills while spending five years in the cathedral choir listening to, reading, chanting and singing the English of Cranmer's *Book of Common Prayer* (1559), the *Psalter* (1580s) and the King James' Bible (1611). The experience gave me an edge for this project, begun decades later. Even so, *Dark Sovereign* took about 9,300 hours to complete between 1984 and 1988. That's forty-five hours a week on top of producing network television. No one who has read the final text in typescript during the past twenty years has demonstrated an error in my use of vocabulary or syntax. The etymological research — much of it directed to establishing precedents before 1626 for each word and expression in the final text — covers more than 4,000 foolscap/legal hand-written pages.

1626 became my linguistic cut-off year for several reasons, the major one being that it marks the death of Francis Bacon, sometimes called 'the last great Tudor'. Bacon, an important prose author, ran up a large debt in his final years, resorting to rewriting and republishing much of his output to raise money. Only a specialist can tell what Bacon reworked in order to republish, and when he did so. Hence, choosing the year of his death as my linguistic cut-off gave me the freedom to use his full canon. (A lesser factor: Cyril Tourneur also died that year. Tourneur, or Middleton, wrote *The Revenger's Tragedy*, an unusual Period play and a fount of ironic wit. It was hard to resist the influence of a play full of one-liners such as: 'Virginity is Paradise lock'd up.' II.i.)

Delaying my cut-off year to 1626 made a difference. For example, Shakespeare seems to have used the neuter possessive pronoun 'its' just once, in his final play, *Henry VIII*, (1613). 'Its' was in wider circulation by 1626. (See the footnote at 1.1.154.) It is often the case in *Dark Sovereign* that the shorter any given word the more work went into establishing precedents valid in every respect. The odds against achieving the ring of authenticity in an antique tongue are enormous. Ben Jonson, commenting on Edmund Spenser's attempt to emulate Chaucer in *The Faerie Queene*, suggested that 'Spenser, in affecting the ancients, writ no language'. Hence the rigorous limits imposed on the language of *Dark Sovereign*.

WRESTLING WITH ENGLISH

In practical terms, the primary tool making this project possible was the optical reduction of the *Oxford English Dictionary*'s 16,000 pages into a two-volume set, published in the 1970s. (Had I started a few years later I might have used the CD-ROM.) *OED* sets out the evolution of the English language 'on historical principles', making it possible — although work-intensive and time-consuming — to establish: 1/ whether a given word existed or was being used in a particular sense before 1626; and 2/ the specific prepositions, conjunctions, verb endings, constructions or other baggage attached to that word during the Period. For example, the verb 'to look' always took an adverb, hence Shakespeare's 'The sky looks grimly', a usage that finds a place in *Dark Sovereign* as 'thou look'st too purely' (5.9.8). One did not refer to the 'foot' of a bed before 1626, but the 'feet', thus: 'And has the abbot's bed a piebald lozeng'd tapestry above it still? / and martlets on the written coffer at the feet?' (3.6.137). It's *'the* feet', you notice, not 'its feet', because, per my comment above, the possessive pronoun 'its' was just emerging into general use. Archbishop Cranmer is sometimes credited with the first use of 'its' as a neuter possessive pronoun.

Common or abstruse nouns (spawnling) presented fewer problems than the multiple shades of meaning inhering in such words as 'as' and 'so'. Furthermore, about half the nouns we use today took different prepositions — by, to, for, of, in, with — prior to 1626.

Shakespeare's borrowings

Figures of speech were often difficult to research. Both words in the phrase 'salt tears' date from Anglo-Saxon. But had those words combined in that phrase before 1626? I left a blank in the manuscript for months before finding 'salt tears' in a translation by John de Trevisa, circa 1385. (Months later it leapt from the text of *A Midsummer Night's Dream*.) The 1380s also bring the first cited reference, by the dean of St Andrews, to 'Lend me your ears', one expression among many incorrectly attributed to Shakespeare. This raised another problem: Since 'lend me your ears' was common currency in English for two centuries before Shakespeare, I could have used it legitimately in *Dark Sovereign*: it would have fit perfectly in two places. But since that expression is generally considered to be the essence of 'Shakespeare' I left it out.

Authors and editors

Other expressions confuse even scholars. Shakespeare uses the phrase 'shrewd turn' in *Henry VIII*. A scholar whose name attaches to an edition of Shakespeare explains the phrase as 'to do one a favour'. It means no such thing. It actually means 'to do one a grievous injury' or 'to play a dirty trick'. The scholar's definition is plausible in the context of the sentence in which the phrase falls — if Shakespeare intended irony — but makes no sense in the larger context of the scene as a whole. The *OED* supports my conclusion, citing an example from the 1520s.

Verbs, a special challenge

Verbs posed a special challenge. The third person singular has two forms — has/hath, reposes/reposeth. The Northern '-s' form eventually replaced the Southern '-eth', but not all '-s' endings moved south at the same speed. Verbs common in trade and conversation displaced '-eth' as early as the fifteenth century. But the more conservative discourse of law and religion preserved the Southern ending beyond 1626. Thus, 'No right reposeth in't; no wrong...' (4.1.85). Since much of *Dark Sovereign* is written in ragged iambic metre, the difference imposed by a single syllable (*gives* vs. *giveth*) is critical. Sometimes both forms coexist, but even here Period writers used them differently. For example, *hath* is employed for weak stress points and *has* for strong, especially at the end of a sentence. Thus Shakespeare's 'The earth *hath* bubbles as the water *has*'. (There are exceptions: 'Elizabeth has' trips off an actor's tongue more smoothly than 'Elizabeth hath'.) But, to finish my main point: In some cases passages in *Dark Sovereign* did not take final form for months until I had established whether '-s' had replaced '-eth' in a given verb before 1626.

Dialects: Mummerset, Northern and Posh

Exceptions to the above include parts for Gloucester (Richard III) and his consort, Anne Neville, which are written with a Northern bias, the better to be played in the accent of Yorkshire's North Riding. (Richard remains one of the few kings of England since Saxon times to have a Northern — as distinct from a Scottish — power base. Hence his inability to master the levers of Southern power in time to avoid disaster.) Thus, Richard uses 'wakeman' (Co. Durham dialect), instead of 'watchman', 'mine alone' (Yorks) instead of 'being alone'. One detects the difference between Northern and Southern style suddenly, in Act 1.1, where Anne, having not seen Gloucester for years, addresses him in 'Court English' until he, never deviating from Yorkshire, challenges her to revert to 'a Neville's Northern tongue'.

Then there's 'Mummerset', the ancestral form of South Western dialects spoken notably in Somerset, Dorset and Devon. Mummerset was common in Tudor farce. Shakespeare had a rare go at writing it in *King Lear*. (See notes at 3.6.106.) To my surprise, it was more difficult to write monosyllabic prose for low-life characters (Will, Kate, Ned and servants in *Dark Sovereign*), than to emulate the polished oratory of nobles, such as John of Gaunt's 'sceptred isle' address in *Richard II*.

Sources

I wrote that the *OED* was my primary reference. Perhaps I should have said that it was my *primus inter pares* source for validating each syllable and construction used in *Dark Sovereign*. Reviewing Scene 4.1, I counted precedents there deriving from 115 authors writing during the Period. Sources included such exotica as a vast volume of letters by Queen Elizabeth I. In fact, etymological research revealed deficiencies in the *OED*. For example, Francis Bacon uses 'voidance' to mean verbal evasion, a sense not cited by *OED*. And *OED* finds the first use of 'spawnling' in the 1690s. However, that citation turned out to be an unattributed theft from an earlier writer, Skelton, of 1612. Had I relied on *OED* I would have had no valid precedent for using 'spawnling'. Discovering its earlier source in 1612 allowed me to use it. *Dark Sovereign* contains thirteen words that the *OED* either missed or misplaced. The glossary gives these with their valid precedents.

Strange byways

Students of King Richard's reign have undertaken curious studies to support their researches, such as attempting to grow ripe strawberries in Holborn by mid-June. No need to explain that here: the 'cause-why' waits in the footnote at 4.3.34. However, such examples explain the diversions and sidetracks researchers confront.

Editors (good, bad, execrable), bowdlery and woodworm

At first glance the text of *Dark Sovereign* may seem older than that of plays actually written during the Period. That is because almost every play written during Tudor or early Stuart times has been subject to extensive editing through four centuries by editors of greater or lesser competence or fluency in the English of the Period. (I cite editors' changes at 1.3.180 and 4.5.98.) *OED* offers the same opinion in more guarded language, with such comments as: '... much altered by editors ignorant of its history'. Self-imposed limitations have prevented that happening to *Dark Sovereign*.

On the other hand, many of the better-known texts from the Period — especially works by the major dramatists — have benefited from more or less continuous written and directorial interpretations through four centuries. Other traditions may be brief, but influential: In 1944, Laurence Olivier introduced the 'modern' persona of Richard III as a power-mad Quasimodo. Olivier enshrined the ephemeral of performance into the permanence of cinema ten years later.

By contrast, *Dark Sovereign* has no history of interpretation unless one counts a two-day reading at the Stratford (Ontario) Festival. That is why my play is so extensively annotated. This edition offers guidance in footnotes (some are miniature essays) at every point.

Metaphor

These were among many linguistic and technical challenges posed in recreating a language that has not been written since the 'Golden Age' of Renaissance literature. Other challenges included choices of metaphor. For example, a century and a half after the work of Darwin and Wallace on natural selection, it is not easy to imagine Elizabethan concepts of Nature. Here is one: 'The crying puss cat is, as 'twere, th'imperfect work of Nature making lions' (3.4.26).

To reconstruct an accurate sixteenth century mindset one must understand the theory of imprinting infants' brains that commanded the human intellect from before the writing of Genesis (Chapter 30) to Jean-Baptiste Lamarck (d. 1829). Queen Elizabeth Woodville's decision to raise her sons at Ludlow, far from London, was a serious concern to her adversaries, the 'Old Nobility' party. They (Buckingham, Gloucester, Hastings, Howard *et al.*) would have seen her move as an attempt to mind-wash the twelve year old, future Edward V — 'The boy attends no instance foreign from our only cause, but ours alone' (1.3.162) — making both factions determined to possess the actual person of the young Edward V. This point must have been a major irritant between Queen Elizabeth Woodville's large family and favorites (the Queen's Party), and the Old Nobility. Hence the angry debate pressed on the Royal Council by Hastings and Howard: 'The common weal — moreover, the weal of our prince's soul — / hath nobler interest than that the king thereof / should wait on his kinsmen's trough!' (2.4.139). The struggle to possess the person of the boy-king Edward V triggered Gloucester's initial — and, I believe, reluctant — *coup d'état*.

Pruning, either judiciously or 'Cut to Hecuba'

Writing *Dark Sovereign* involved many unprecedented experiments running simultaneously through four years of work. One major unintended consequence is that *Dark Sovereign* may be one quarter again as long as *Hamlet*, making it by far the longest single-part play to have come to us in the English of the 'Golden Age'. *Hamlet* is seldom performed in full: the lapsed phrase 'Cut to Hecuba' refers specifically to chopping the stuffing out of its first and second acts.

Take it from the author, *Dark Sovereign* must also be energetically pruned for the stage. I publish it in its entirety because every syllable in this, the complete text, conforms to the same standard of precision, so that the play as a whole can be used as a teaching tool. (Even now there may be lines missing.) As an aid to editing, consulting the scene by scene synopsis may help. I made a start (several starts, actually) on essential editing: marks running down left-hand margins indicate a first generation of easy cuts. I invite directors to grab a machete and roll up their sleeves. Reading *Dark Sovereign* and its glossary will suggest many points and resolve a few. Beyond that, I welcome discussion.

I should apologize/apologise for my idiosyncrasies in modern English. When writing copy for business clients I'm fastidious about using Canadian, British or

American forms and spelling. My personal projects tend to be freestyle, combining North American spellings with British punctuation, getting the better of both worlds.

Did a rational mind write Dark Sovereign?

Yes, more or less. My research and reason in/spired (breathed life into) this work to a large degree. But exhaustion also played a major creative role. Exhaustion became the catalyst, the synergy that supported, sustained and invented creativity.

Philosophers, prophets and religious figures of every stripe have taken to wild places or induced starvation and deprivation to induce guidance visions or spiritual experiences: among them Jesus, John the Baptist, Siddhartha Gautama (Buddha), Mohamed and Merlin, to name a few. One can add countless anchorites, aboriginal peoples of the Americas (i.e. Black Elk), Australia, shamans from Siberia and northern Canada and southern Africa's Bushmen. Members of ancient Animist cultures have always understood a human's homing instinct to wild places for solitude and the intuitive insights it brings. Here is Igjugarjuk, a shaman of the Caribou (Willow-folk) Inuit from Canada's Barren Lands, west of Hudson's Bay: 'The only true wisdom lives far from mankind, out in the great loneliness', he told the explorer Knut Rasmussen, 'and it can be reached only through suffering. Privation and suffering alone can open the mind of a man to all that is hidden to others.' There is truth in that. So where did *Dark Sovereign* come from?

Crying in the wilderness:

Dark Sovereign emerged from many hundreds of fourteen to sixteen hour days of work, many of them sandwiched between my regular job in television production. Curiously, the first six to eight hours of writing sometimes produced little. Then exhaustion set in. At that point my conscious brain retired, bone-weary, from the fray. It let down its guard. When that happened, instead of repelling strange and alien words and concepts, it let them in. A larger, intuitive spirit kicked in — a shamanic state of consciousness — and I found my ink drying on words that appeared, and suited, and stayed under my hand. Yes, I wrote most of *Dark Sovereign*. But, as the Inuit and other shamanic peoples know, I had helper spirits, too. (*Spirit in Health* is my book on that subject.)

Acknowledgments

I owe thanks for assistance and research support to many people, several of whom are now departed. At the University of Toronto, Northrop Frye gave me advice on technique in the early stages, while John Meagher offered valuable comments, suggestions and a great review. N.H. MacMichael, Keeper of the Muniments at Westminster Abbey, provided details about the abbot incumbent in 1483. P.K. Seidelmann, Director, Nautical Almanac Office of the U.S. Naval Observatory, supplied information about lunar phases on key dates. Harry Kaufman, of Hunter College, City University of New York, presented his paper, *Basic Issues in Medieval Psychology*, at the ninety-second annual convention of the American Psychological Association (Toronto, August 1984). His paper supplied the theme for eleven lines in Richard Gloucester's soliloquy on the eve of seizing power (3.3.144–154). Michael Powicke, at the University of Toronto, steered me to 'reliable' older sources in the earliest days of the *Dark Sovereign* project. Yaroslava Mills, of West Nyack, New York, designed and executed the title calligraphy. Ron Freedman and Jeffrey Crelinsten have been wonderfully generous, donating office space at their company, *The Impact Group*, in Toronto. Janet Sandor, my friend and colleague at that company, has given freely of her many talents in communication and media relations. Decades ago, Messrs. Sutton and Vowles taught me English at Salisbury Cathedral and Canford schools respectively. My parents paid for that education, while Carol Burtin Fripp and our sons Eric and Will came close to losing the companionship of a husband and father during the four years it took me to write *Dark Sovereign*.

Robert Fripp © 2011
June 14, 2011
Toronto, Ontario
Shillingstone, Dorset
www.robertfripp.ca
http://eleanor.robertfripp.ca/ (*temporary*)

or, The True Tragedy of King Richard the Third

The play on the life and death of King Richard the Third that William Shakespeare should have written.[1]

---

[1] The title. Read *dark* in the title as *unknown*. It comes from the same sixteenth century etymological stable as *dark horse* and *dark star*, entities of unknown or untested qualities. Cf. 4.2.82.

DRAMATIS PERSONAE

I HAVE EDITED *Dark Sovereign* in many different, experimental ways. The result: it is possible to cut nearly half the play and present a lively, fast-moving plot. A vertical line running down the left margin of many scenes suggests some edits. There are many more, thus far unmarked, which I will be happy to suggest.

The following list of characters pertains to the full play. Given appropriate edits, many of these parts will vanish.

Murderer 1
Murderer 2
Princes in the Tower: The boy-king **Edward V** (12)
                        Richard, Duke of **York** (10) (Use a dummy)
Rumour (twin sister to Truth)
Lady **Anne Nevill** (**Q. Anne** in Act 5)
Richard, Duke of **Gloucester** (**King Richard III** in Act 5)
Councillor 1
Councillor 2
Councillor 3
King Edward IV
George, Duke of **Clarence**
William, Lord **Hastings**
John **Russell**, Bishop of Lincoln
Truth (twin sister to Rumour)
Queen Elizabeth Woodville (wife to Edward IV)
Anthony Woodville, Earl **Rivers** (Q. Eliz's brother)
Thomas Grey, Marquis of **Dorset** (Q. Eliz's son)
Thomas (varlet to Gloucester)
John **Morton**, Bishop of Ely
Richard, Lord **Grey**
John **Howard** (Duke of **Norfolk** in Act 5)
Archbishop **Rotherham** (Lord Chancellor, at first)
Humphrey **Percival** (privy servant to Buckingham)
Harry Stafford, Duke of **Buckingham**
Sir Richard **Ratcliffe** (henchman to Gloucester)

Sir Thomas **Vaughan**
John **Alcock** (Bishop of Worcester)
Ned, **Will** and **Kate** (three low persons)
The **Abbot** of Westminster
Brother Godfrey (a monk)
Servant 1
Servant 2
William Catesby (a lawyer)
Mistress **Jane Shore** (a whore)
An **Agent** from Lord Stanley
Thomas, Lord **Stanley**
Incubus (Gloucester's Id)
Elizabeth of **York**
Cardinal **Bourchier** (Archbishop of Canterbury)
John **Nesfield**
Bede (a cleric cum scribe)
Jasper Tudor, Earl of Pembroke
Christopher **Urswick**
Henry **Tudor** (Earl of Richmond)
Spirit

Many parts may be doubled, thus:

Murderer 1 (Ind. 1), to **Catesby** (begins in Act 4)
Murderer 2 (Ind. 1), to **Ned** (3.5, 4.4), to **Spirit** (5.9)
Councillor 1 (to 4.3), to **Person 1** (4.4), to **Alderman 1** (4.8)
Councillor 2 (to 4.3), to **Person 2** (to 4.4), to **Alderman 2** (4.8)
Councillor 3 (to 4.3), to **Person 3** (4.4), to **Nesfield** (4.8)
Lawyer (1.2), to **Brother Godfrey** (3.6), to **Crier** (4.4)
King **Edward IV** (to 2.2), to **Henry Tudor** (from 5.4)
Clarence (1.2), to Richard **Grey** (from 2.2)
Rotherham (until 4.3), to **Bourchier/Canterbury** (in 4.6)
Abbot (3.6), to **Bede** (5.2, 5.5)
Mistress **Jane Shore** (4.2), to **Elizabeth of York** (4.6)
Sir Thomas **Vaughan** (to 4.9), to **Jasper Tudor** (from 5.4)
Bishop John **Alcock** (3.2 mute, 3.4), to **Scribe** (4.4), to **Urswick** (from 5.4)

INDUCTION 1

The Tower of London. A summer night, 1483.
***King Edward V** (12), and his brother **Richard, Duke of York** (10), sleep in a great bed. A candle burns*

Enter **Murderer 1**, *a venal little man, holding a dark-lantern with a purse at his belt.* **Murderer 2**, *a simple giant, restrains him.*

Murderer 2: Hang back!
Murderer 1: Sayest thou me so?
2: 'Tis a desperate work, shall draw us on t' th'evil!
1: The sprite of the honest clown thou art commends thee.
   Mocking: Evil, a' says! A' were best contented, I durst wager,
   an' his pagan stomach had a purse.
2: If I were born to be hang'd, I'd hang well recompensed …
1: Well then, give over thy little manship to avarice …
2: They'll pay us home sweetly, sure!   2
1: … or shall thy cowardship die a leper's end?   10
   W'are well paid for our pains.
2: But here's a wicked thing doth prick at the heart.
1: 'Twould shiver Ulysses his bow to prick thine!
2: As how?
1: Mildness not grows t' th' nether millstone.   3
2: I speak my conscience!
1: Conscience, quotha! Besides gold, a' would own conscience.
   This is it that makes a lord!   4
2: Th'event is plain:
   Those shall bespeak us to hell before Peter's gate!   20

---

2   Ind.1.9. *pay us home sweetly*: To *pay one home* meant to reward in kind. *Sweetly* was frequently ironic in the Period, having the same sense as *dearly* in 'You'll pay dearly for'.

3   Ind.1.15. *not grows to*: doesn't match, doesn't go with. The *nether* (lower) millstone of a pair was made from harder stone than the upper one.

4   Ind.1.18. The inference is that lords can buy a clean conscience by hiring rogues for dirty-work.

1: Conscience! O, this is like the scurvy,
   signifies a poor man's ill; the rich not afford her, 5
   — and we shall be rich come the morning.
   Consider how the great employ such as we to port their sins,
   whilst they to shriving, unbloody, free of Satan stain as angels.
   Money makes an able sexton:
   A's oft employ'd to bury the corpse of Conscience.
2: These whelps is kings.
1: These kings is *pawns* of kings. 6
   As who are not set out for sacrifice; 30 7
   they buy their elders power.
   Thou mayest guess who bids that we skill of.
2: Hush! Be still. They'll wake.
1: They'll never wake.
   Screw courage to a deed shall live to time. 8
   Yon watch-candle will serve them for a lich light. 9
2: Damnation — 'tis like unburied death — droops hereabout.
   The very walls condemn us.
1: Strike down the Morals' modesty! 10
   There's no virtue in Virtue for any like to us. 40
2: Hark! Something stirs.
1: *Opens his dark-lantern, looks about:*
   Hangmen's leavings. Not but ancient ghosts …

---

5   Ind.1.22. *not afford*: don't waste time [having a guilty conscience].
6   Ind.1.28–29. *is*: was formerly used with a plural subject, but only when that subject was a noun, and usually when that noun was qualified by an adjective; perhaps because the act of qualification made the noun a special case, a singularity. When a plural subject was a pronoun, this figure was incorrect. OED notes that this 'usage is exceedingly frequent in the Shakspere folio of 1613 [sic] (though much altered by editors ignorant of its history)'. The Folio for *The Comedy of Errors*, III.ii.20 thus: 'Ill deeds is doubled with an evil word'. The confusion in modern editions is such that the Globe (1900) and Craig give: 'Ill deeds are doubled' while Cambridge goes the other way, making the subject fit the modern sense of the verb: 'Ill deed is doubled'. Had Shakespeare chosen to use a pronoun instead of 'Ill deeds', he would have to have written: 'They are doubled with an evil word'.
7   Ind.1.30. *As who are not*: As if they were not.
8   Ind.1.35. *to time*: for ever, through all eternity.
9   Ind.1.36. *lich light*: bier-light, corpse light. 'Lych gate' survives in modern English.
10 Ind.1.39. *the Morals' modesty*: moderation advocated by the Morals, a collective name in the middle ages for ethical writings by classical authors, notably Seneca and Plutarch.

Discovering the audience:
... and these, other spirits fetch'd from time,
not a long while come, full soon to follow.
Take no heed of them.
2: That be too young to play men's games
are younger than to die. Those twain not yet write man! 11
1: Childhood never touch'd thee before.
'Ods me! Thou dost not flinch to choke the life
of doxies' accidents. To wreak great villainy   50
I reck'd to have choos'd a great villain.   12
Belike an ill conjunction intends his influence upon thee.
2: We was cross'd since we was got. So 'twas lotted.   13
1: Dost fear, but thou diminish into fret?
As now thou art damn'd to a frantic
before thy night-seel'd ministry is done.   14
2: The linage of kings lieth there abed!   15
1: Now do I divine thy loathing: Thou dost not shrink
to spend their life; thou shrinkest to turn history.
Small man, thou fear'st from touching greatness!   60
2: There, where the stuff o' th' Lord's anointed lies,
e'en there, the divinities of kings would die.
The busi-ness pertains to lords, to priests,
to Mother Church. There's policy for you; here's no murder!
1: Wottst not physic? how every mountebank in England
riddeth martian agues with Venus gentler flowers?
And those at fall by ills o' the Great Lights: 16
are not their maladies redress'd
by powers vested in dark Saturn's herbs?

---

11 Ind.1.47. *not yet write man*: have not yet attained to man's estate.
12 Ind.1.51. *reck'd*: was anxious to.
13 Ind.1.53. *We was* (twice): Beyond dialect, *was*, in educated use from the 1500s on, was often the preferred plural in the Past Indicative. *Was* was also in general use with *you* (singular), no doubt to differentiate it from the plural. Cf. 5.9.163.
14 Ind.1.56. *night-seel'd*: Literally, night-blind; metaphorical, made invisible by night.
15 Ind.1.57. *linage*: lineage. The disyllabic form was common into the Period. Queen Elizabeth used it in formal correspondence.
16 Ind.1.67. *Great lights*: the sun and the moon.

	God's mystery is, that things oppose,	70	
	that two are ever twain. Though I say 't myself:		17
	"The poor shall be made judges upon the rich at Doomsday".		18
	By that were meet for two poor men to kill the great.		
	— or think'st the judgment of ill stars		
	not weighs back such as these?		

2: Worldly woes ne hardly dare weigh down such;
   but if their stars spell death, let them to write it!
1: Nay, but we are their instruments for the nonce,
   to serve the mighty architects of spiteful history.
   Beshrew us, but it's done. We shed mere blood.   80   19
   Who would shed ink — those shadows of man to come —
   They are not yet, that shall yet save or spill our age,   20
   and doom their verdicts.
   Come, let's to it and have done!
2: *Restraining the other*: You speak on Death as he were friend.
1: Their death is friend indeed that feeds us fat.
2: Is black th'alone colour in your mindsight?
1: Nay, his fellow is gold. A' must be won!
   *Running to the bed, he smothers **York** with his pillow.*
King Edward V, *waking*: Murder! Murder!
   ***Murderer 2** smothers the **King** to silence him.*
1: It's done. And 'twas well done. Their little ghosts
   been shot hence beyond earthly bourne, and there's an end.   90
2: What bloody work is there!
1: Doth noble linage assail thee still?
   Ponder on this: Die the great never so nobly,
   being dead, come all to common death.
2: *Praying*: … *cognosco iniquitatem meam* …
1: 'Sdeath! it was thyself reduc'd babies to clay!   21

---

17 Ind.1.71. *twain*: opposites, things or beings opposed.
18 Ind.1.72. *The poor ... Doomsday*: John Audelay, *Poems*, 1426.
19 Ind.1.80. *Beshrew us, but it's done*: Beshrew us if it is *not* done. Literally: 'except it be done'.
20 Ind.1.82. *save or spill*: make or break [a reputation].
21 Ind.1.96. *reduc'd*: in this context suggests restored to a former state. Perhaps Murderer 1 is subtle enough to intend irony, because *reduce* has also been used to mean 'bring back to life' (Lyly, 1580).

2: ... *et peccatum meum contra me est* ...
1: The whilst thy devilship stopp'd their breath,
   thine hallow'd touch bestow'd of them the *eis requiem*.
   Laughs: Quote the mortal miseries thou hast spared them of. 100
2: ... *iniquitatem meam dele* ...
1: Hast lost all wit o' mind?
   Mind how thou art, ere madness take thee off.
   Forces his purse on the other: Take hold on thilk scrip.
   Chi'l hold thee in hand thou shalt have more anon. 22
   To! Expiate thy bad conscience in a wench ...
2: *Libera mea de sanguinibus, Deus* ...
1: A slut shall purge thy woes; but though thou pay'st
   thy callet blood-gelt, have a care thou keep thy tongue.
   Immask thy mind. Many a one is damn'd of bedded whispers 110
   to these sweet confessors, woman ears. Have an eye to thy back.
   If our patron fail, Destin'll cross us the way.
   She'll crown us wi' a kingly ransom on our heads.
2: Lord, forgive!
1: A' may. I'll not! Yawl, an' thou darst feeze thyself. 23
   Judas, bide and damn! *Exit, running.* 24
   An arm swings down from a corpse, striking the floor.
2: Their ghosts rise! Had they, that too late speak from death,
   in life vouchsaf'd a word, then had I stay'd my hand.
   Hold. Here's money. Shall a cue suffice? 25
   Nay. To each a passage-penny. 120 26
   He seems to put a coin in the mouth of each corpse.
   Guard sure the toll. Now stilly cry wi' either voice;
   bid Charon have over, ye speedly to put o'er the Styx.

---

22 Ind.1.105. *Chi'l hold thee in hand*: For background on *chi'l* and related forms of *ich*, see the notes on Mummerset (3.6.106–153). *To hold [one] in hand [that]* meant to assure [one] of something.

23 Ind.1.115. *feeze thyself*: betray yourself, screw yourself.

24 Ind.1.116. *damn*: be damned. (Restricted to the Period.)

25 Ind.1.119. *cue*: variously, as a quarter of a penny (a farthing), or a quarter of a farthing.

26 Ind.1.120. *passage-penny*: It seems that in 1566 it cost a halfpenny to cross the River Styx to the nether world. Adlington thus: 'Deliver to carrion Charon one of the halfpence, which thou bearest for thy passage'.

Begone! Begone! 'Tis I as needs be gone. 123
He goes, running.

Lights: to black. The candle burns.

INDUCTION 2

Enter Rumour, in darkness. Taking up the candle, she examines the bed.

Rumour: Edward the fifth, child-king sans crown,
   that never more shall crown beget;
   and Richard, duke of York: *Requiescatis in pace,*
   — if ye truly be dead! Were these or agents
   for o'erween'd ambition rid ye this? 27
   or night-born phantasms do serve the time?
   th'occasions of my tongues? If these were ghosts,
   their work was woven of the many's mind,
   and you shall live long years beyond tonight.
   Be you in this world, or in another, brothers, sleep! 10
   It is not given me to understand
   whether this work were done, or no.
      *Lights: A spotlight reveals **Rumour***
      in a sequined, or reflective dress.
      House-lights come up.
   Ha! There are that hid their heads i' th' shade before.
   Replacing the candle, she is free to move.
   I know these company as you know me;
   for I, friends, am Rumour. Ye still still tell my fames: 28
   Men say! They say! 'Tis said! Holla, now you discern me:

---

[27] Ind.2.5. *this*: thus, (but only when *this* is in post-position). Cf. *Venus and Adonis*, 206.
[28] Ind.2.15. *still still*: on every occasion, all the time, endlessly.

I am each man his concubine, the envy and report of every she.
I am whatever company I keep.
    Am I not allective? Fair?   29
Pale am I, for Rumour doth thrive in darkness.   20
Note how light falls from me, broken,
shiver'd out to myriads of scintills,
full o' the rainbow's art withal.
    Thus and thus do my voices multiply: 30
At break of day I vest a tattle in one only lip
 — which whispers other ears — until my hum accrues
the sober susurrations of a hundred souls
at every matins chime. By the space of no long time
they spread, transforméd, from a thousand of prating voices
to a multitude at abay. At vespers bell, their addle fame,   30
compounded with ten thousand follies, doth all split,
like light that seeks out me to quash.
    Tantalus courted me, by the well-offering, for my favour,
secrets of the gods; whérefore he by them condemnéd was
to stand in water to the nether lip, always parch'd by thirst.
    My youth, that seems me well, is rather years,
for Rumour is older than the speech that was confounded
at the Tower in Babel. Adam and Eve took heed of me;
it was my serpent caus'd your forbears forth of Eden!
    As for this tale, wonder if be true.   40   31
I wot not if these carcasses reek vital heat,
or lie in death. Ne aught I care,
for Rumour's task is but to trumpet that I hear
till grey-beards write down me in learnéd books,
where I am taken for a gospel that is — *curtsies* — History!
Whereinsoever the presumption in me has no bounds.
    Like to a mill-wheel set in time's slow stream,

---

29 Ind.2.19. *allective*: attractive, alluring.

30 Ind.2.24. *Thus and thus*: In the manner indicated, in such a way.

31 Ind.2.40. Note the construction after *As for*, which was common in the Period. The pronoun one expects to find later in the sentence, *it*, is missing.

I, Rumour, latch the force of truth
to yoke th'engíne of mine invention.   50
And when I tire of sport, a noiseful,
seeming simple truth revolvéd is,
who lays claim to the mill-race.
    Know, that seeks for truth, I thwart wi' thee,
charming, with such Siren-sounds
as they should set thee to blind rocks.
Be ware, lest zeal-blind,
thou not run upon the stony shoal of falsehood.
    I take my leave of you.
The instance neither Rumour's time is, nor her place.   60
As cobs and crows that wait upon the plough,
so Rumour feasts it at the furrow left behind.
I leave this stroke to puzzle the sense
the while our toy unfolds.
Ponder, whether truth's fair thread
were spun with lies and other wonders.
    Princes, if ye live,
and that this was th'imagin'd tale of fools, hide close:
Keep far from Harry Tudor's iron heels.
Otherwise, if ye be dead by Richard's hand,   70
gently I bid you adieu.
    *She may cover the **Princes'** faces with bedclothes.*
    To the audience:
Ye wights to come, resign not your quest, for doubt.
Return we now upon a time eleven years before this night,

---

32 Ind.2.50. *engíne*: Notice emphasis on the second syllable. See note 3.3.49.
33 Ind.2.52. *revolvéd*: A valid sense of the word in this context might be *restored* (to its place).
34 Ind.2.56. *blind rocks*: submerged rocks, sunken reefs.
35 Ind.2.58. *thou not run upon*: The negative *not* is redundant, but was often added for emphasis after verbs of warning or threat.
36 Ind.2.63. *stroke*: an act causing death.
37 Ind.2.65. *truth's fair thread were spun*: The expression *to spin a fair thread* was always a figure of irony.
38 Ind.2.68. *and that*: and if. *That* was often substituted where otherwise a conjunction would have to be repeated, in this case *if*.

into an age from whence this act begun.
Then are we whither we may discover
how that this might be brought to pass.
Rumour *blows out the candle.*
    Lights*: All is dark.*
Until again, farewell.   77
Rumour *goes, in darkness.*

ACT 1, SCENE 1

A walled garden. Mid-winter, 1471–72

Lady Anne Neville *is discovered, dressed in mourning, heavily cloaked against winter.*

Sfx: *Sounds of horsemen arriving.*

Lady Anne, *speaking Northern*: Ha, Richard Gloucester comes at last!
  How must I receive him? Until as now I thought to hold back,
  for hate, cold as the frost that gripes this winter'd garden;
  to greet proud Gloucester wi' th' ice-dagger
  is the loathing of a woman dispossess'd.   39
  Pah! Instead of that, inly anger doth kiss me into colour;
  my cheek paints crimson and the like.
  My purpose to dissemble slips, beneath a vengeful scorn,
  the tear-fraught anguish of my loss.
    The space of a twelvemonth — two moons less! —   10
  twixt troth and mourning gowns. O might I loose
  th'embowell'd powers of Hecaté against that son of York
  which slew my prince at Tewkesbury! Lost! Give me lost!   40

---

39 1.1.5. *That* is omitted from the start of the line.
40 1.1.13. *Give me lost*: Give me up for lost.

My heritance; my Prince of Wales; and my ambition!
    Nay. Heart, be still; head, be in calm;
whatever pass, tongue say not nay, unless thou cast me
on a still more stony ground of my preparing.
    Our Lady, hear me! Take off my woman frailty;
instead whereof do on my heart an hedge of thorn
cloak'd all wi' flowers:
I'll treat this hell-fiend wi' fixen guile.
Or Lancaster, or York, it matters not.
It stands my life upon to marry to the royal house.

*Enter **Richard, Duke of Gloucester**, behind her.*

Winter wind, have mercy!
Quick, avaunt, to carry the blush of ire away.
My heart, be still'd. He comes.
Methinks great Gloucester has come.
Gloucester, *aside*: What stratagem is this? Her fellows henc'd,
    she stands to winter blast as 'twere fair June.
    She seems as though she would affect a summer flower.
Anne, *aside*: He not deigns to speak, but stands apart
    and stops his tongue. He would regard me rather
    with a curious eye.
Gloucester, *aside*: What careful snares she lays.
    Accoutred in her sighing weeds she chides at me.
Anne, *aside*: When shall he speak? how give me to discover him?
    La you, my lord, the lowest hell have not more hating in't
    than I for thee! My heart-grudge stops my mouth still.
Gloucester, *aside*: Perhaps those weeds denote but only piety.
    Half a year has gone about since Lancaster was brought to die.

---

[41] 1.1.14. *Prince of Wales*: King Henry VI's heir, Edward of Lancaster, Prince of Wales, was betrothed to Lady Anne Neville when they were seventeen, at Angers Cathedral (Wed., July 25, 1470.) See note 4.5.92.

[42] 1.1.21. *fixen*: vixen. Shakespeare was among the first to use the modern spelling. *Fixen* is phonetically stronger here.

[43] 1.1.33. *curious*: careful, calculating.

[44] 1.1.39. *sighing weeds*: mourning garb, dark clothing. Hence the expression 'widow's weeds'.

Anne, *aside*: Speak to me, Gloucester, speak! Hot temper
   born of action's easier borne than is th'expecting on't.
Gloucester, *aside*: I'll treat with her
   like one whose passage threads a mire.
Anne, *aside*: Speak, Gloucester, speak!
   I cannot bear silence out more.   45
Gloucester: Hem hem.
Anne, *aside, panic*: He will I should discover him!
Gloucester: Hem hem. My Lady Anne …
Anne, *turns, unruffled. Speaks Southern*: O, how doth your grace?   50
Gloucester: Well, madam. But I encroach upon your contemplation.
   I thought t'have found you in company of your ladies.
Anne: Poor silly slips, I chid them within-door,
   to chatter, at the fire. My heart was woe;
   'tis such an enemy a body needs will fight alone.
   She turns away.
Gloucester, *aside*: Gods a' me! 'Tis comfortable sorrow
   serves her better to friend than to foe!
   If she'd indict me of Lancaster's blood hereby,
   I'll scold but straightways I shall answer it.   46
   Speaks: So valiant an hearted prince than Edward seldom lived.   60   47
   Had Fortune smiled upon our opposites,
   then had that day have been reverse.   48
Anne, *aside*: Would God had would … !
Gloucester: How say you?
Anne *shakes her head. Aside*: Fate, dost thou despite me?
   or despise the time? I would know whether.
Gloucester: You shiver for the frost.

---

45   1.1.46. *bear silence out*: pretend to be silent; be responsible for keeping silent.
46   1.1.59. *I'll scold … answer it*: This represents one of the more limited constructions involving *but*, and a difficult one for modern perception. If *but* is taken to mean *even if*, and placed before the clause which it here follows, the actual sense will emerge. Modern English thus: Even if I have to scold (her) (by doing so), I shall reply right away. Note this construction in *The Merchant of Venice*: 'The villainy you teach me I will execute, and it shall go hard but I will better the instruction' (3.1.78).
47   1.1.60. *than*: was used in comparative contexts during the Period, instead of *as*.
48   1.1.62. *had … have*: Up to the early seventeenth century, *had* and *have* are sometimes found together in compound tenses where one or other is redundant.

I entreat we come within-doors.
Anne: I had rather stay, I thank you.
Gloucester: May I not see your face? 70
Anne: I crave a further moment of indulgence for my grief.
Gloucester: Your woman's reason bodies forth Lancaster's death.
   My very presence speaks it; which, as it did quicken you, 49
   lives yet inwardly, unless it be deliver'd from your brain. 50
   'Tis paradox: y'are with quick memories;
   and yet, wherein they feed time-was, 51
   they do supplant you of what life *shall* be.
   He died, my lady ...
Anne: *Angry*. My lord, you did him slay!
   Calm. How well your person I may fairly quit, 80 52
   but well the house of York shall stand to time 53
   attainted of his life.
Gloucester: What, will you have me to put it up without retort?
   Lancaster lacks not less innocence from blood! 54
   At Wakefield was my father slain; and more than so,
   my elder brother Edmund, earl of Rutland,
   — scarce had a' seen yet seventeen years.
   At York, their heads adornéd were with paper crowns
   and bodied with a stake.
   Small birds peck'd out the apples of their eyes 90
   as they were carcasses of rotted ravens, 55

---

49   1.1.73. *as it did quicken you*: Loosely, 'as if [your obsession with Lancaster's death] had developed a life of its own in you'.

50   1.1.74. *unless*: until. If *until* had been used, the verb following it would have had to be indicative. Using *unless* permits a less pointed subjunctive tense.

51   1.1.76. *wherein*: to the extent that.

52   1.1.79–80. After screaming line 79 at Gloucester, Lady Anne recalls that she hopes to marry this man! She delivers line 80 calmly, even apologetically, as a complete contrast.

53   1.1.81. *How well ... but well*: Although ... on the other hand.

54   1.1.84. *not less*: Though this usage of less is not identical to those in 2.1.15 and 4.1.6, comparison with those examples will help show how the word evolved through negative senses to the point where it actually seemed to indicate the opposite.

55   1.1.91. *Small birds ... rotted ravens*: The figure implies vendetta. In the medieval period, the raven, a bird of ill omen, was held to prey upon the eggs and young of smaller birds, which took revenge by pecking carcasses of dead ravens.

till at length the stink came up, obedient to the airs,
for worlds of men to smell out their dishonour.
Anne: In likewise fell my sire at Barnet,
and my prince at Tewkesbury.
Gloucester: These were not prick'd upon poles,
to be in death dishonour'd. Though Edward sits in throne again,
meseemeth, lo, this many years, a kind of madness reigns   100
throughout the breadth of all this England.
Anne: I pray for both parts; as Lancaster, so York.
Gloucester, *approaching* **Lady Anne**:
Would I might commend you to your prayers.
Howbeit, I may withhold th'imperate mind   56
no more nor I can stay the wind.   57
There needs no spur to a forward horse.
Interest, will we or nill we, doth press us apace.
Purblind, yet spurr'd like caparisoned horses of service,
int'rest doth mar whatsoever it pass.
Gloucester *stops close behind* **Anne**, *who flees*.
Your prince was dighted of the very womb   110
to do his duties and his complements. Nor could he else.
We are what our birth dooms.
In likewise, Fortune doth compel to struggle
whomsoe'er she lotteth high degree;
else, being dash'd, he falleth beneath vaunting hooves.
There are that tumble early, other late,
but needs perforce each must bear him alone,
his visor close, hemm'd all about,
not seeing nothing but for certain danger lies afore,
yet impotent to bear a rein upon his fate,   120
to draw aside, ne yet to stop.

---

56 1.1.104. *th'imperate mind*: a driven, compelled mind. Does Gloucester refer to his own nature as compelled or to the urgent demands of the times? The latter, surely. As I read him, drive was a forced rather than a natural feature of his cautious personality. Or is there more to it? After all, '…imperate acts [are those] wherein we see the empire of the soul' (Sir Matthew Hale, 1609–'76).

57 1.1.105. *no more nor*: no more than (Northern).

It is commanded of us, madam,
whatso stars of Destin frame.
Our period is all, where'er it lie. 58
Anne, *aside*: Mine angels, help! I cannot taint with misery. 59
Speaks: Speak to me, your grace, more soft and fair.
Gloucester: O Anne, if swords were harvest poppets
made of straw. If darts were thistle-down.
'Twas in your father's house I learn'd to war.
Remember wi' yourself, how I bethought was to play David 130
in Golias' armour; and whilst did you, a little golden girl,
sit out and pick pied daisies. For all we fought
as foes at Barnet, lov'd I your father well.
Never had boy a better master. Ah, sweet lady,
to be high-born in this England is a blesséd, curséd thing.
Anne: Your grace hath ridden far to call me to remembrance;
to instruct me in the politics.
Gloucester: Leave off affected Southern speaking.
If w'are not to perish for frost, then carry to the mark:
Vent far-hidden feeling wi' a Neville's Northern tongue. 140
Anne *turns to confront him. Speaks Northern*:
What wouldst tha then?
Gloucester: Why, what should I else? I would thee wed.
Anne: What mock be that?
Shall deep-affected night roll down her stars,
translating all to glorious day within a word?
Look well to my apparel, lord.
Thou! from forth malevolents, wert Edward's fellest foe.
Gloucester: This body mine alone can loose thee from thy bond. 60
Hess thou so soon forgot? Thy father, Warwick, is most dead.
Ever sithence, thy protection has devolv'd — so he holds — 150
upon your sister's husband, mine own brother, Clarence.

---

58   1.1.124. *Our period*: Our eventual fate; Where we end up. Our destiny is pre-ordained. Cf. 1.3.200.
59   1.1.125. *taint with*: lose courage or resolve because of.
60   1.1.148. *body*: Gloucester includes the word for legal reasons. See 1.2.70–71.

> *Imprimis*, your lands; *item*, your portion-money; 61
> — nay, *item*, your portion of the Warwick earldom,
> it right title, interess, and cares of state — 62
> all which, thy rightful heritance,
> George Clarence holdeth for his *chattels personals*,
> under colour of his match with Isabel. Be mine, my lady;
> or shall you rest my brother's *chattel reall*?
> Clarence shall give you to marriage how he will.

Anne: Out of which perdition you would raise me up 160
to mine inheritance!

Gloucester: I offer to horse thee again. 63
Or will'st thou to be bruis'd beneath shod hooves?

---

61 1.1.52. *Imprimis*: In the first place. First! Signals the start of an itemized list. Cf. *item* (Latin), pronounced *eetem*, 1.2.142.

62 1.1.154. *it*: its. The neuter possessive pronoun its was among late elements to take its present form in Mod. Eng. O.E. and early M.E. had been content with his (cf. German *sein*), or *her* as in 'each stone has his shape' or 'every bird has her nest'. According to *OED*: 'Already in M.E. *his* began to be replaced as the possessive neuter pronoun, substitutes being found in *thereof, of it, the*, and in the North West the genitive use of *hit* and *it* became common around 1600. *Its* is not used in the King James Bible (KJV) of 1611, which has *thereof* besides the *his, her* of old grammatical gender. The possessive *it* occurs just once in the 1611 edition, at Leviticus 25.5: "That which groweth of it own accord..." a verse altered to *its* in 1660. *It* was the preferred form when followed by *own* as in "Though in *it own* nature it be too moist" (1607). *The Tempest*, II.i.163 (Globe ed.) has "of it own kinde". That example has been altered in modern editions.'

The first edition of KJV was not slave to old grammatical gender. For example, Coverdale's Bible (1535) gives Jeremiah 8.10: 'The Storke knoweth *his* apoynted tyme'. Freed from grammatical constraints, translators of the KJV give 'Yea, the stork in the heaven knoweth *her* appointed times' (Jeremiah 8.7). The stork thus achieves in KJV the feminine gender of fertility.

Its had been colloquial around the London-Oxford axis since about 1550. Latimer may have used *it* in 'at its heels', but this example might be the work of a nineteenth century editor. *His* was still the literary neuter pronoun till after 1600. Gerard's *Herball* (1597) contains several hundred chapter headings along the lines of 'Peare tree and his kindes' or 'Cowslip and his kindes'.

Shakespeare was evidently uncomfortable with the modern its. *OED* states that the form never occurs in his works during his lifetime, although *it* and *it's* are not uncommon as possessive pronouns. *King Lear*, 1.4.218 (line 239 in Craig) thus: 'The hedge-sparrow fed the cuckoo so long, That it had *it* head bit off by *it* young'. On the other hand, all modern editions give 'My dagger muzzled, lest it should bite its master' (*Winter's Tale* 1.2.158).

It is often impossible to tell what was intended without reference to early editions. For example, the Cambr. ed. gives *Hamlet* 5.1.243: 'The corse ... did ... fordo *it* own life'. Other modern eds. give *its*. I have tried to use the several variants in the same proportion as I found them in Period texts.

63 1.1.162. *horse thee*: put you back in the saddle. To be more prosaic, 'put you back on your feet'. Were Gloucester intending to be coarse, one might take this figure as a *double entendre*, as in expressions such as 'to put the mare to the horse' or 'to take the horse'.

Anne *laughs*: You proffer her rare charity, whose troth of hand
   bestoweth on her husband four thousand pound yearly! 64
Gloucester: When you are mine!
Anne: Such husband as I choose have right!
   Thus much the so-commanding law.
Gloucester: The law's a sword, an iron thing, and cold.
   She cuts no deeper than the might of him who would uphold her. 170
   First, marry, an' thou wolt, by Clarence' bidding.
   Then, summon on thy part the clacks of crafty-headed lawyers. 65
   Thus much truth: To snatch the prize, thy corse,
   out of the jealous lion's jaws,
   an army of blind moles shall fare as well.
Anne: Perfidious York!
Gloucester: Softly, lady. Hear me. We are two younger shoots,
   whose each advantage us endows with common strengths.
   We shall have need t'apply the tother's power.
   Solely, we fall; but go we t' th' world together, 180 66
   we shall master all. Consent with me, and be my love.
   And if so be the soul have in it harmony,
   then may not we together find it twice?
Anne: Love is heaven-consolation to the base-begot.
   She falleth from our station. 67
Gloucester: Well then, let us raise her to 't. 68
   Not with hyssop, but with myrrh let each touch other's sprite.
   Thou canst love me a little and a little, and thou wilt. 69
Anne: You touch love's alchemy
   as if I were a serving woman, you a common ploughman. 190

---

64 1.1.165. Lady Anne Neville's share of the Beauchamp-Despenser estates has been estimated at £3,500 a year (Ross, p.26), making her by far the wealthiest heiress in England.
65 1.1.172. *clacks*: tongues.
66 1.1.180. *go we t' th' world together*: marry each other.
67 1.1.85. *She falleth from our station*: Love is beneath us.
68 1.1.186. *her*: Love personified usually took masculine gender, after French precedent. However, Shaks. uses *her* in *Love's Labour's Lost*, 4.3.380.
69 1.1.188. *a little and a little*: little by little, by slow degrees.

> Again: 'Tis the poor would owe love's solace; 70
> the great may not countenance love against life. 71

Gloucester, *aside*: Here's labour'd love!
> If so were that I did doubt this shrew her pedigree,
> now, for my life, all doubt is dash'd.
> Truly speaks a daughter to high Warwick's blood.
> *Speaks*: Little and long, or love me not. 72
> If thou would'st serve thyself, serve me.

Anne, *aside*: What hate so lorn, but melts?
> *Speaks*: But we are cousins, cousin. 200

Gloucester: The Pope shall grace us by dispensation,
> being we'll first grease him in the fist.

Anne: Then marry, let it be. As touching love,
> a fire well fuell'd gives forth his brightest flame.

Gloucester: How shall I love a one
> that stands a flight-shot back?
> *Approaching, he stops half-way, extends his hands.* 73
> Lend me thy hand; give hands thereby. 74
>> **Lady Anne** *approaches, but stops short.*
> Come hither, Anne, my bride, my love.
> I offer thee a token from my heart. 209
>> *Revealing her own hands,* **Anne** *moves to take his.*
>> *They go.*

---

70 1.1.191. *owe*: own. See note 1.2.86.
71 1.1.192. *countenance*: smile upon, support, favour, take the part of.
72 1.1.197. *Little and long*: From an English proverb given several forms since c. 1500: 'Love me little, love me long'.
73 *Stage direction*: Whether Gloucester extends one hand or both will depend on the interpretation of his presumed physical deformity. See notes at 4.3.92 and 5.1.35.
74 1.1.207. *give hands*: consent, v., give your consent.

ACT 1, SCENE 2

Council-chamber, London. Late winter, 1471–'72.

The royal Council awaits the king. Present: the dukes of **Clarence** *and* **Gloucester**; **John Russell**, *bishop of Lincoln;* **William Hastings**, *Chamberlain to King Edward IV;* *a* **Lawyer**; *two of three perpetual* **Councillors**; *others as may be.*

Enter **Councillor 2**, *late:*

Councillor 2: Wherefore are we met together so soon again?
— and that too at the urgence of the king?
Councillor 1: We ponder on war.
Councillor 2: Which self matter was before dispos'd!
Councillor 1: We are to hear the parts   75
twixt Clarence and the duke of Gloucester.
Councillor 3: I'll tell you, the king is sore vexed
at 's brothers. They, jealous, back each one a hot,
sharp blaze of riot toward either's strivings
to sequester Warwick's daughter from each other.   10
C1: They say eyes to Clarence espied Gloucester with the lady.
Whereon he caus'd her be carried into a far house,
disguis'd in manner of a kitchen drudge,
to vanish her the better.
C2: And she as stiff-neck'd as a quintain!
C1: Stiff-neck'd, i'faith. They stiff'd my lady Anne
in kitchen-fee and greasy aprons t' th' neck.   76
C2: There's a pretty contrariety.
C1: A pretty metamorphosis besides.
C3: All this avail'd Clarence nothing.   20
Haught-minded that she is, she play'd the ape
i' th' scullery, wi' hands as white as swansdown.

---

75 1.2.5. *parts*: sides of an argument.
76 1.2.17. *kitchen-fee*: fat, grease.

C1: Gloucester, that hath spies o' th' time everywhere,
   pick'd out my lady's scent. Discovering her
   from concealment, he hied her away.
C3: She present lies at Saint Martins the Graund … 77
C1: … keeping God's — or Gloucester's — sanctuary …
C3: … ensconc'd wi' Gloucester's men.

Enter **King Edward IV**, *angry:*

K. Edward: How now, my lords. And brothers! At a strife?
   Never any difficulty was, but some discourse might resolve. 30
   Endue our mind with that affair, which,
   ringing in our night-stopp'd ears,
   doth murder care-bestriding sleep.
   Wherefore, lest ye put us beside our purpose,
   we do set it aside — although it listeth us
   to touch weightier matter, grievouser unto our state.
       Lewis France, fain to war with us,
   seeks presently to raise the Scot for mutual aid.
   Lately went in embassy our trusted bishop John, Lord Russell,
   charg'd to make a league between us and our brother-in-law, 40
   duke Charles of Burgundy. By God his grace, and Burgundy's,
   we shall confound French tricks.
       This six months past,
   our Chamberlain recucéd Calais to our will.
   Waits Hastings now upon our pleasure to take ship,
   with men at arms, for France.
       All's made in a readiness;
   except it is not France doth blow the bellows to our weal;
   it is our brothers! Clarence. Gloucester.
   We do lovingly embrace you as our blood. 50

---

77 1.2.26. William Caxton, in *The cronicles of englond* (1480), gives the church as Saint Martins the *graunt*.
     A century later the spelling and perhaps the pronunciation had changed.

> But that ye fall, two fighting-cocks,
> the tone on tother, brings me out! 78
> > Submit it, lords! You shall argue forth before us:
> Got wot, we shall not make that matter longer forth! 79
> Let each hart royal expound his madded rut.
> It stands our will upon to fetch the right.
>
> **Gloucester**: My liege, the lady Anne is she whom my best love,
> my ready sense, commands me wed.
>
> **Clarence**: Brother, Gloucester throws his fondness in my teeth,
> to sever to himself the moiety of Warwick's fee. 60
>
> **K. Edward**: How fortunes that, to vex us, ye do strive,
> like drovers, for first favour of a strumpet at a bush? 80
> I charge you, answer: All London wags with tales,
> for your so long-held war is spectacle indeed;
> two royal dukes at wars about a woman!
> Every day recounteth lately-coin'd reports, 81
> of princes, urgent as a brace of hounds
> behind a rank bitch, proud in her heat. 82
> Your princely antics do too much besmear our royal house.
>
> **Clarence**: For that I am husband with the body of my wife; 70
> and for she, being heir to Warwick's body, is enrich'd; 83
> therefore my spousess conveyeth unto me
> the right of alienee upon the earl's fee simple. 84

---

78 1.2.52. *brings me out*: makes me mad as hell.
79 1.2.54. *make ... longer forth*: protract, draw out.
80 1.2.62. *bush*: tavern.
81 1.2.66. *coin'd*: made up, invented.
82 1.2.68. *in her heat*: OED does not find this expression before George Washington used it of a hound. The term is older, dating back at least to De Monfart's *An exact and curious survey of all the East Indies*, translated in 1615.
83 1.2.70–71. The curious use of *body* marks this as a legal debate, as explained by Blackstone (1768): 'As the word *heirs* is necessary to create a fee, so, in farther imitation of the strictness of the feudal donation, the word *body*, or some other words of procreation, are necessary to make it a *fee-tail*'. The Croyland Chronicler states that even the lawyers present on this occasion were impressed by the princes' ability in legal argument. Some scholars accept that Gloucester had legal training.
84 1.2.73. *alienee*: one who comes into property; one to whom property is transferred, whether by law or circumstance. § *fee simple*: OED thus: 'an estate in land, belonging to the owner and his heirs for ever, without limitation to any particular class of heirs'.

Stand I in 's face, I do deny my brother of right,
gainsay 's mere right, and contradict the colour of his match. 85

Gloucester: Clarence yields my lady but a paltry apanage.
No English law disheriteth the younger daughter.

Clarence: Who dieth in attainder dies intestate;
who dies intestate doth devise perforce t' th'eldest issue.

Gloucester: Brother, you misprize the Articles. 80
Touching whoso dies intestate, his abundance
is dispos'd of by his kindred and the Church.
The Great Charter would have it so.

Clarence: Eldership of birth (which state the heavens cherish)
doth invest our brother with the crown. The which respect,
enduring this gall-favour'd years, he owns of right.
In likewise Isabel takes Warwick's fee.
Whatever she have, all that is mine.

Gloucester: Thou — if thou'd convey thyself
as th'heir to Warwick — wert thrice blind. 90
Daughters not convey *heirs males* descent.
Moreover, though our brother sit in throne,
we want for neither honour nor high office.
Neither may your claim by eldership of Isabel
embar the puîné sister, Anne.
Twixt males, the eldest is worthy;
twixt females, their either is worthy of blood.

---

85 1.2.75. *gainsay mere right*: dispute that (another) has a right, as distinct from possession. § *colour*: legality.
86 1.2.76. *apanage*: Literally 'bread money', remittance, a provision made for noble families' younger offspring.
87 1.2.80. *Articles*: the Barons' Articles, the *Magna Carta* of 1215.
88 1.2.83. *the Great Charter*: the *Magna Carta*, specifically the Sarum (Salisbury) exemplar of 1215, clause 27, lines 32a–33a.
89 1.2.86. *owns*: The verb *own*, as in *possess* or *have as one's own*, dropped from use after about 1275, not reappearing until Shakespeare, who may have reintroduced it. The verb *owe* was current throughout the Period to mean the same thing, making it confusing to modern perception. *Dark Sovereign* uses both forms: *owns* here; *owe* in 1.1.191 and 4.1.129; and *ow'd* was changed to *had* for the sake of clarity in Ind.1.6.
90 1.2.93. *want*: lack. Note, *nor* here applies equally to the phrase preceding as following it.
91 1.2.95. *puîné sister*: the sister born later who, being younger, had less standing in law.
92 1.2.96–97. *worthy/worthy of blood*: eligible to inherit.

Clarence: Two parts of three convey'd by female line
   rest not therein: They tail by marriage or descent.
Gloucester: Aha! You yield a tierce.   100
   I am one third part richer than whilere.   93
Clarence: Will you my lady's top to wife?
   Her toes, with choice? Her trunk?   94
   I give it, Richard. Wed whichever part you will:
   The two parts remanent is mine.
Gloucester: Do we not take 't in scorn, my lords,
   to hear good English words bring succour to the French?
   My brother would compass a base reflection
   of the foisted Salic law, that not bears sway in England.   95
   Moreover, that Matilda had good right, the crown of France   110   96
   pertains to England from the heirdom of Queen Isabel.   97
   Two queens is precedent enow.
K. Edward: Whoa ho, brothers, ho! Ye put unto us a tidy knot
   would whip the froth out of a score pettifogging lawyers.
Clarence: Please your highness be remember'd
   how I am of Lady Anne most master, she most mine, of right.
K. Edward: Who'd fetch a path through drooping fog
   may find his way, where he that waits without
   sees giddy obfuscation.

---

93 1.2.101. *whilere*: a while ago. Frequent in antique usage, cf. Spenser's *The Fairie Queene* (1590).
94 1.2.103. *with choice*: by choice, as a matter of preference.
95 1.2.109 *Salic law*: a European law designed to bar female succession to the crown. In time it was debased to bar females in lesser suits, as, for example, to deny inheritance to women. OED gives a concise background under *Salic*. Shakespeare waxed eloquent on the subject in 1599, no doubt garnering Queen Elizabeth's approval. In *Henry V, 1.2*, he puts his longest monologue into the mouth of the Archbishop of Canterbury, whose sixty-two line speech describes the law and the English defence against it.
96 1.2.110. *Matilda*: Following the death of his son (1120), King Henry I managed to have his daughter Matilda accepted as his heir, marrying her to Count Geoffrey of Anjou, the progenitor of the Plantagenet kings. Stephen of Blois, the son of Henry's younger sister, Adela, asserted his own claim, leading to a protracted dynastic civil war in England which ended only in 1153, when Archbishop Theobald negotiated a compromise whereby Matilda's son (Henry II) would succeed to the crown upon Stephen's death.
97 1.2.111. *Queen Isabel*: The claim of fifteenth century English kings to the French crown derived from King Edward III's mother, Queen Isabella, daughter of King Philip IV of France. Estranged from her husband, Edward II, Isabella returned from Europe with foreign troops and, supported by the barons, took London. Edward II was murdered in prison; Edward III succeeded.

Clarence: My right is plain! 120

K. Edward, *aside*: W'are out of patience. Grant it!
  And may it do me grace, else comes the Devil to seduce,
  I'd fall away wi' wine and women to a merry-make.
  A pox of them that stay.
  George was ever the ingenuous knave, [98]
  despite of 's treasons. Were a' not my brother,
  I should prentice him to my fool!
To **Clarence**: Brother Clarence, by your argument,
  you shall cast aside the marriage use of Holy Church,
  instead whereof t'inspire into us the heathenesse
  of Mussulmans and Turks. 130
  Bishop Russell *crosses himself.*
  George, thou fleshly dog,
  thou wouldest sip of Anne and Isabel *both's* accommodations.

Clarence: My argument is mispriz'd.
  I claim the wardship of my lady, not to know her,
  being rather I shall bestow her as it becomes. [99]

Gloucester: It should seem that George would affiance
  the lady Anne toward some dark design or other,
  for and to take the better half of her possession to himself. [100]

K. Edward *to* **Gloucester**: You, which quote his articles
  to several ends, now you shall mark th'indifferency 140 [101]
  inherent to the Magna Carta.
  Item, no one may give an heir to one of lower state; [102]
  item, a widow shall not be compell'd to wed;
  besides, *item*, she shall not marry saving ourself do consent. [103]

---

[98] 1.2.124. *ingenuous*: ingenious, capable, talented — words often interchangable during the Period.
[99] 1.2.135. *as it becomes*: as is appropriate.
[100] 1.2.138. *for and*: moreover and.
[101] 1.2.140. *th'indifferency*: the neutrality, impartiality.
[102] 1.2.142. *Item, item, item*: The same word in English, pronounced as Latin, (*eetem*). The speaker ticks off a list of items on his fingers. Cf. *Imprimis*, 1.1.52.
[103] 1.2.144. *Magna Carta* (Sarum) clause 6, lines 13b–14a; also clause 8, lines 15a–16a. As late as the reign of Henry VIII, a law was enacted (32 Hen.VIII c. 46, para. 25) whereby 'King's widows' were subject to a fine for marrying without royal sanction.

Clarence: Take her, brother! Marry with the lady.
  What you will! I give her of my gift,
  as such a gift will prove the mettle of your love.
  The lady's thine; the lands rest mine.
Gloucester: Thou wouldst beggar me, Clarence!
Clarence: In love is no lack.   150   104
Gloucester: The Charter thus: Sans difficulty
  shall a widow have her portion and inheritance.   105
K. Edward: Cry hoo, brothers, hoo!
  Brother Clarence, and you, brother Gloucester,
  approach, you were best. We shall ordain an end,
  to all convenient, in speed and grace.

  *The **King** confers with the **Dukes**,*
  ***Hastings** & **Russell** with the **(Lawyer)**.*
  *The three **Councillors** whisper together.*

C3: Come, go, get we aside! Peruse their manners from afar.
  Though we of princes make our game, yet lay we this apart
  which otherwise shall drive us near;
  for here is a princes' game: let them alone to play.   160
  No good befalls whoever is catch'd withal.   106

---

104 1.2.150. *In love is no lack*: Proverb, Heywood, 1546.
105 1.2.152. *Magna Carta* (Sarum) clause 7, lines 14a–15a.
106 1.2.161. *Come, go, get we aside ... catch'd withal*: All writers get trapped from time to time into overworking certain words or constructions, sometimes for effect, sometimes from habit or exhaustion. Shakespeare was no exception. He frequently uses *which* as his mirror or fulcrum, building a sentence around it of matched or opposing themes. At its most intense, this construction occurs five, perhaps six times in the first seventy lines of *Richard II*, 2.3. At its least complicated, his construction is exemplified by 'that is not forgot *Which* ne'er I did remember'. This passage in *Dark Sovereign* builds a more complex construction along Shakespeare's lines:
  a. Come, go, get we aside!
    b. Peruse their manners from afar.
      c. Though we of princes make our game,
        d. yet lay we this apart
          e. which
        f. otherwise will drive us near;
      g. for here is a princes' game:
    h. let them alone to play.
  i. No good befalls whoever is catch'd withal. *continued over...*

C1: The sun will to his rest before their resolving is done.
C2: The age, to boot. High minds — *ambitio* —
   abate a headstrong wrath no other wise than that it must be spent.
C3: The stars will quit their spheres before such wonder hap.
   Whenas small reason catcheth passion,
   life it fleeting self is mortgag'd t' th' fight.
   Their púissance is their enduring will.
Lawyer: These can as well skill of argument
   as they had mooted half their lifetime in the Inns of Court.
   They show such fullness of the law.
Hastings: God graced their threesome threefold ableness.
   Could they but stay from greedy bickerment
   th'intrenchant might of York might never be sunder'd apart.
Lawyer: The more shame for them that it is so.
   The realm upbraids them with the waste.
Russell: Might man learn wisdom out of waste,
   how natural profit would attend us, all.
   Howbeit, is set down nothing but all which to God seems meet.
   That our princes' hearts and livers seldom meet
   in perfect temper burdens are, which, running in a blood,
   needs they must bear to prove and try them.
Hastings: And we that serve them.
Lawyer: Soft, they'll overhear us.

The word *which* in line *e* forms the fulcrum around which the passage builds. Lines *d* and *f* play on the opposing *apart* and *near*. Beyond the pure form of words in *f*, to *be driven near* suggests being forced to extremity, into a corner. Lines *c* and *g* play on combinations of *prince* and *game*. *Make our game* in *c* means *to make fun of*. In line *g*, *game* implies intrigue. Lines *b* and *h* comprise a tactful suggestion and its later repetition. Again, that is the mere form of words. The phrase *let them alone to* conveys the notion *They can be relied upon to* or *Trust them to*. Lines *a* and *i* represent the initial caution with its later complement. Compare the use of 'Come, go ...' in *Comedy of Errors*, 5.1.114, and *Romeo & Juliet*, 5.3.159.

[107] 1.2.168. *puissance*: is here a trisyllable, a pronunciation made popular by Spenser. Shakespeare uses both forms.

[108] 1.2.174. *intrenchant*: incapable of being cut. Peculiar to Shakespeare: *Macbeth* 5.8.9, 'intrenchant Ayre'.

[109] 1.2.180. *hearts and livers*: Temperament was seen as being formed and regulated by 'the principal parts, especially of the heart and the liver' (Crooke, 1615).

[110] 1.2.181. *running in a blood*: being an inherited trait.

Hastings: They'll hear of nothing save their selves.
    Each stops the ears against the thread of 's brothers' case.
Lawyer: Their chiefest enmities they hole within.
    Strange, intemperate humours course, familiar wi' their blood.
    What they may be, no man durst say.
Hastings: Nor durst he these gainsay!   190
Russell: It's jealousy, as mighty as the hell;
    and not so strange as true.
Hastings: By change, by turns,
    since my great grand-sire hath my line serv'd York,
    through all the last vicissitudal age.
    Seldom-when their furrow'd front betrays a judging mind.
    The rather do they chafe; they fret their hearts,
    like coursers rang'd to war.
Lawyer: Then nothing is chang'd with naught.
    Their father, holding safĕty in scorn,   200
    did sally from forth the walls of Sandal Castle
    upon a greater foe. Neither turn'd he back the bridle
    from his folly act, but forfeited his life,
    the promise of the crown, and eke his son.
Russell: Faith, then, York was father of these three.
    At every little prick they start.

C2: You have hit it, for York ever stood t' th' main chance,
    and perdition take the hindmost!
C3: Clarence is puff'd up wi' pride again.
    He seemingly knows not right and wrong asunder.   210
C1: Yet 's bethought to bear the person of the king on England.

---

[111] 1.2.185. *save their selves*: *save* becomes a quasi-preposition, releasing the following pronoun to the nominative possessive.

[112] 1.2.191. *jealousy, as mighty as the hell*: The sense of jealousy has been diluted in recent centuries. Here, it may even hint at a pathological condition. More so, since Russell draws the line from scripture, Coverdale's (1535) Song of Solomon, 8.6: 'Love is mighty as the death, and jealousy as the hell'. The impact was already reduced by 1611, when KJV gives: 'jealousy as cruel as the grave'.

[113] 1.2.210. *knows not ... asunder*: cannot discriminate between.

[114] 1.2.211. *bear the person*: take the powers of ... (as a viceroy); act for, impersonate.

C3: Husht! To voice the thought were treason.
C1: Did not a' take heinous arms with Warwick,
  outputting Edward into exile unto Burgundy?
C3: Then Warwick being slain,
  the king forbare for using Clarence cruelly:
  A' by and by restor'd him all his noble toys.
C2: Nor he hath taken in hand to attaint him.
C1: Instead whereof he winks hard at his self-conceit.
C2: 'Twas Gloucester reined the prodigal to Edward's side. 220
C1: Perhaps his dam fell Gloucester different
  from York's course of kind. [115]
C2: Stock, root and branch he is the sapling of his sire.
C3: And yet his tempers of the mind not speak him out; [116]
  they rather conceal him.
  Nor he'll not flash into his brothers' petulance;
  but affections of a house run in a blood.
C1: And cold withal.
  The moon intended influence at *his* birth-tide.
C2: Methinks *Saturnus* gave the stronger force.
C3: Were Gloucester Saturn, then Clarence had been Mercury, 230
  and the king had play'd great Jove.
C1: When Saturn is conjunct with Jupiter,
  he is made white and bright. But Gloucester harbours motives
  darkly as a cloudy star: A body may stare to see it;
  an eye wink after, a'll never find.

K. Edward: Give ear, lords! Our royal disposition thus:
  Our brother Clarence, with full soul and noble charity,
  doth well assent to grant the person of our cousin, Anne,
  for safeguard, to our brother Gloucester, which,
  his mind being bent to courtship, must wait so long 240
  to wive her 'til the forty lenten days are past. [117]

---

[115] 1.2.221–2. See footnote 2.3.94.
[116] 1.2.224. *speak him out*: distinguish him.
[117] 1.2.241. *so long ... until*: This const. emphasizes a reservation in an otherwise positive sentence.

As touching stubbornness of chattel law,
we put it to the issue. We shall appoint,
of these our lords, commissioners:
Those shall arbitrate our brothers' every several claims.
Clarence: No honourable man hath ground to settle arbitrage
twixt twain, where one only hath right.
K. Edward: Hold in, Clarence. Keep a care!
Clarence: Now dost thou abase thyself to root up law, 250
but even before thou madest reverence to 't.
K. Edward: Brother, you entreat my patience sore.
Clarence: Thou diddest fair pretence to have inheritance
in veneration. The self statutes thou wouldest now strike down.
K. Edward: Bite off your tongue!
You were better it were sever'd than your head.
Clarence: Thou puffest at my right of blood,
though when 'twas thine, thou mad'st no scruple
to attach the throne.
K. Edward: Thouest thou me, thou jackanapes?
Preserve thy wretched life an' thou hadst would. 260 118
Go hide thy head!
Exit **Clarence**.
Calling after: I knew thee for a swaddled infant;
nor I know thee from a swaddled infant still.
Even in the heat of thy distemper, ponder, noble duke,
to how a brother of the king is but a subject!
To assembled **Lords**: Us list, my lords,
to purge our too intemperate gere.
To fall t' ourself again, to lance the bitter choler
from our spleen, we would fain speak of more soft things.
And therefore shall we now treat war with France. 270

---

[118] 1.2.260. *an' thou hadst would*: if you choose to do so.

ACT 1, SCENE 3

***Truth** is discovered, sitting in King Edward's chair,
her garment similar to **Rumour**'s, but of coarse, unadorned fabric.*

Truth, *to the audience*: Their fury raged for a three years day,
    and all the while the carrion princes peck'd   119
    at Warwick's bones. All that estate they divided,
    and though their storm abated by little bits,
    methinks their envy minish'd never a whit.
    Rising: But stay, you are uncertain of me!
    You wrong me, mortals, every way. Bear me good mind:
    I am a spirit, whole, in most men's heart.
    I have you! Ha! About the eyes, whereat you speak,
    make I no doubt t'assign the doubt that I must answer: 10
    Your doubting answers to one only name.
    Such a one came at you in your way: She mock'd you,
    bid you quest to truth chastis'd with lies, wi' falsehood.
    Sweet didymists! W'are twins. She was my sister, Rumour.   120
    I am Truth. Where she is gaudy, I am plain.
    Where she would put impediment to history,
    I, without dissembly, answer truly,
    when the course gives me to understand.

*Enter **Queen Elizabeth Woodville**, embroidering.*

    Soft! Here comes one that can cunning
    equal with the Florentines.   20   121
        Since the fore-end of Edward the Fourth his reign,

---

[119] 1.3.2. *princes*: *Dark Sovereign* uses this term more loosely to include the royal dukes than does any play of Shakespeare's. As late as the reign of James I/VI, 'Prince' was a title extended only to the eldest son of the monarch. The longer formal title Prince of Wales being therefore redundant, it occurs less frequently in Period plays, although Shakespeare does use it in *I Henry IV* and *Henry V*.

[120] 1.3.14. *didymists*: doubters.

[121] 1.3.20. *Florentines*: Francesco Guicciardini, Niccolo Machiavelli.

Dark Sovereign 1:3 | 33

    this lady hath rent England into parts.   122
    Her kin have too much; other hath too little;   123
    most all have set their heart to enmity to her.
    And all because King Edward stew'd in coming passion
    of the male kind. Fourteen years ago he stole a marriage   124
    — with a lady some steps below —
    and she the widow to a knight, Sir John Grey, slain,
    for cause of Lancaster! at Saint Albans field.
    Moreover, her father and her brother bloody quarrel had   30
    to Edward the Fourth at Towton.
    Yet notwithstanding, here she stands,
    Elizabeth Woodville, wife to King Edward, queen of England.
Rumour, *off*: She's voic'd to be a witch!
Truth: Sister Rumour!

Enter **Rumour**.

Rumour: Sister Verity.
    Truth *&* **Rumour** *embrace.*
    Truth *places* **Rumour** *on her left.*
Truth: Stand by me, so. Thine advocacy's needful
    for each malapert and prating head.
    The part siníster shalt thou play.   125
    To the audience: Rumour ushers in the darkest clearness.   40
Rumour: There is as darksome truth as talk;
    more, rumour is oft the same that truth.   126
    All-telling talk will have the queen a witch,
    that, by art magic, snared the king; and she,
    well over-summer'd, is five winters elder than he is.

---

[122] 1.3.22. *parts*: rival factions.
[123] 1.3.23. *other hath*: Other is a valid plural form. *Hath* as a literary plural dies at the stake with Hugh Latimer, according to *OED*. However, it occurs in *Macbeth* III.i.109, and *King Lear* III.i.27. (The Cambr. ed. preserves both examples, but many modern editions alter to *have*.)
[124] 1.3.26. *stole a marriage*: married secretly.
[125] 1.3.39. *siníster*: The stress falls on the middle syllable.
[126] 1.3.42. *the same that truth*: the same as truth.

He wish'd to mistress her; but she, full ripe of woman cunning,
kept him from her bed, whereon, in 's lust, he burn'd.
When he besought her for her favour,
she did threat to thrust his dagger in her breast,
making vow as she would sooner die,   50
th'intemerate slave of chastity,   127
than Edward's other tool might prick her flesh.
Truth: Such a naughty talk of pricks!
Rumour: Please thee wit: There's more is just
in love than war, for love abides no chivalry.
Thy sister as I am, this is truth:
King Edward wedded her he would but bed.
Wherefore fames do noise abroad: The queen's a witch!
Truth: O, Rumour, pooh!
She chanc'd upon a woman's chance,   60
and 'twas her chancing, won a king.   128
If chastity be sorcery, then many a woman's a witch,
for many a man's bewitched withal.
Rumour *concedes defeat with a shrug*: The duchess,
his mother, took shame of their match, threatening him
that she'd denounce his kingly body for a bastard.
Truth: 'Tis of truth he fell a lip at counsel;   129
the king would not be rul'd. Could we the future,
then had we heard said: Who reigneth o'er the self
to rule his passion, he is the more king.   70   130
And yet is this lady so pleasing to her lord, she can no wrong.   131
Puff'd up with pride, and great of avarice,

---

[127] 1.3.51. *intemerate*: undefiled.

[128] 1.3.61. *She chanc'd ... won a king*: She chanc'd upon a woman's opportunity, and getting lucky, won a king.

[129] 1.3.67. *fell a lip at counsel*: sneered at or ignored advice.

[130] 1.3.70. *Who reigneth ... is the more king*: Truth retrieves this paraphrase from 'the future'. But then, she is spirit, and spirit is timeless. Cf. Milton, *Paradise regain'd*, 2, 466 (1671).

[131] 1.3.71. *she can no wrong*: In the context of the times, the expression is more literal than figurative. In modern use it is often ironic, but here it follows the legal maxim *rex non potest peccare*. Thus Starkey (c. 1538): 'Hyt ys commynly said ... a kyng ys above hys lawys'. *Oxford Dictionary of Proverbs*.

Elizabeth hath rais'd a flock of kin, joining them in marriage
t' th' noblest in the land ...
Rumour: ... or whether they would, or no!
Truth: Four sisters put she to the heirs of earls;
another to the duke of Buckingham, and Harry not past lad-age.
Her brother John, a stripling, did she to the dowager
of Norfolk ...
Rumour: ... a lady of that years that had brib'd Sergeant Death!   80
Truth: ... and she near three score years and ten!
Rumour: ... and ten again.
Truth: 'Twas but t'attach the portion ...
Rumour: ... and withal her quality. The house of Woodvilles
is as covetous as Joseph's brothers. And as rife.
Truth: And in this meanwhile, Clarence, loud as sounding brass,
proclaims his brother's queen and kindred's tree
in every way obscure.
Rumour: He takes no drink with her at meat,
publishing Elizabeth intends him dead.   90
The whiles she thinketh to be Judith to her kin,
the whiles the duke will have her Messalina.   132
The king's blood call her Lancaster's hedge cuckoo
in York's nest ...
Truth: ... whereon Elizabeth, to have her due,
maligns whom Edward loves. Great lords casts she aside;
nor spouses to their issues grow, for want of noble mates.   133
The Woodvilles fasten hands with all.
Thus Warwick raught to treason.   134
Rumour: But soft! I hear a footfall on the stair.   100

---

[132] 1.3.92. *Judith*: The widow who broke the siege of her home town by killing the Assyrian commander, Holofernes. § *Messalina*: The third wife of Claudius, who used her position to gratify her own ambitions, until brought down and executed in the year 48.

[133] 1.3.97. *nor spouses to their issues grow*: nor can their children obtain spouses. The verb *grow* suggests expectation by virtue of tradition or inheritance. Cf. 5.1.77.

[134] 1.3.99. *raught*: reached for, turned to.

Truth: Here comes the earl of Rivers, brother to the queen;
with Marquis Dorset, that's her first-born by the knight
that fell for Lancaster.
Rumour: Come away. We'll hear what they may say. *They go.*

*Enter **Rivers** and **Dorset**.*

Q. Elizabeth: Brother Anthony, and Thomas,
how gladly do I bid ye welcome.
Never a woman's heart so warm'd to touch her friends.
Rivers: How now, sister?
Why do we find our queen abash'd of melancholy?
Let England's core rather shine bright as Sol. 110   135
If the court be dark, why then, the whole dominions
waste in night.
Q. Elizabeth: Was ever queen so set against of foes?
I feel I am a leaky bark amid the boundless ocean toss'd:
now thrust aloft until the billows' top;
now plunging low, as if th'illimitable sea did part,
to split me on it slimy bed, and drown me in the deep. 136
Monsters, brother! Royal fish and monsters 137
compass our destruction all about.
Rivers: We rue to find thee out of heart.
Q. Elizabeth: I, his queen, they style me "witch" 120
on whom he got his sons!
I, the daughter of the line of Charlemagne,
they dub me with the name of "upstart" at his court.
I, whose duty is, and right, to be first raiser
of our house unto the quality of kings,
they clepe a "cuckoo" and a "serpent" in his bed.
Dorset: Leave to echo those!

---

[135] 1.3.110. *core*: The word plays upon *heart* (Latin *cor*) three lines before. This juxtaposition was common in the Period, eventually giving rise to Shakespeare's 'heart's core' (*Hamlet*, 3.2.78).
[136] 1.3.116. *it*: its.
[137] 1.3.117. *Royal fish*: Whales.

Rivers: Deny vile murmurings safe haven in your breast.
  Would thou conjure sprites, spit out their names.
  On a trice they shall run from the heart and the reins. 138
Q. Elizabeth: Buckingham! Hastings! Clarence! Gloucester! 130
  Straightway their fury, their false colour is pursued
  of lesser ones.
Dorset: Cast 'em out; be not possess'd of 'em.
Rivers: Let their envy their own ruin be.
Q. Elizabeth: Their malice is their envy written loud.
Dorset: Malice as like murder is as Nature's scorn to basilisks.
Q. Elizabeth: The heav'ns forbid it fall!
Dorset: That is the thought, this the deed. 139
  The tone is bodied by the tother.
  We were better crush their head 140
  before they lift their mouth to sting our heel.
Q. Elizabeth: England rages on us.
  The royal dukes pray all their gods to bring us low.
Rivers: Make Hastings be number'd with their company,
  who, pretending modesty, doth, in privy whispers,
  urge his own best-moving favour on the king, which, sober
  or in 's cups, should promise him the key of heaven.
Dorset: There's not a deaf ear but hath heard Hastings
  bear faith to York. Uncle, did not he, professing affection
  towards the king, snatch Calais from your grasp? 150
Rivers: The best preferment in all Christendom!
Q. Elizabeth: I am sensible to fear.
  Have I not gifted sons to Edward? daughters, too?
Rivers: Thou mayest not aspire fortune,
  except thou first assure the day.
  Rely no faith in time to come.
  Dame Fortune's smile oft-times is kind, always is fickle.

---

138 1.3.129. *the heart and the reins*: the heart and kidneys, considered prime seats of emotions.
139 1.3.138. *That ... this ...*: The former ... the latter.

If thou would rule the future, pray thy husband live
until thy son deserves the realm. Leave off to fear.
I know to keep the prince far hence, at Ludlow, safe from hurt,   160
from forth the far long fetch of London's strives.
The boy attends no instance foreign from our only cause,
but ours alone. When a' comes in good time to his crown,
I promise thee, Edward first and foremost shall a Woodville be,
a son of York thereafter.

Q. Elizabeth: Brother, if the future waits upon the present,
grant, of long experienc'd years, advice against the day.

Rivers: Defend our king. Keep troublous men from him
would hurt our case; say well of us;
whisper our upright demeanours in his ear;   170
and when thou liest quietly abed, advance our stratagem.
Many and great our foes; of friends have we but one,
for Woodville owes it vantage to thy king.
He, our lanthorn and our candle-light;
we, as dark as burnish'd brass
but if we might reflect his beams.
Now heaven forfend his light should shortly quench.
Our brazen face were black; we were undone.

Dorset: We must away. Farewell, my mother.

Q. Elizabeth: God by thee, Thomas, my first son.   180

Rivers: God keep thee, sister.
Our present hope and future fortune do depend of thee.

---

[140] 1.3.160. Rivers was appointed governor of the Prince of Wales' household at Ludlow, 1473.

[141] 1.3.161. *strives*: strifes.

[142] 1.3.162. *attends no instance*: gives thought to nothing.

[143] 1.3.166. *waits upon*: lies in wait for.

[144] 1.3.173. *it*: its.

[145] 1.3.174. *lanthorn and ... candle-light*: A London watchman's call.

[146] 1.3.180. *God by thee*: This phrase illustrates the difficulty of recreating antique language precisely. The word *by* is phonetically practical but not accurate. Editors seem unable to reach a consensus. An early edition of *Henry V*, 5.1.71 gives 'God bu'y you ...', *Globe* has 'God b' wi' you', *Craig*: 'God be wi' you', Cambridge: 'God buye you.'

Q. Elizabeth: Brother Anthony, on thee depends our heritance.
God speed thee. Hie to Ludlow, brother. Guard our prince.
Rivers and Dorset go.
The Queen resumes her embroidery.

Enter Truth & Rumour.

Truth: As night-dropp'd dew gives increase of the grass,
so turns this lady's fear, by subtle alchemy, to hate.
As toward the queen, the duke of Clarence hath no more wit
than a child has.
Rumour: There be that think him mad.
Some divine familiars go into the duke by night to fire his woe. [147]
Other say his contumation is the often lot of younger sons   190
writ over-large, for "jealousy is cruel as the grave". [148]
Truth: Well said. As Solomon foretold:
Elizabeth her jealousy speaks cruelty;
the duke of Clarence' jealousy shall be his grave.
Time-soon their war shall fall out thus:
One day, at Westminster …
Rumour: … 'twas dark midwinter tide …
Truth: … King Edward, being driven out of patience …
Rumour: … for and spurr'd to bloody vengeance [149]
with Elizabeth's entreaties …
Truth: … thinking long to make a period …   200 [150]
Rumour: … forbore no more.
Truth: The king bespoke the lords how George contriv'd
to cast him out, and utterly to waste his royal line.
Whereon he charg'd him for his "higher, more malicious,

---

[147] 1.3.189. *divine*: is a verb, not an adjective, as might appear at first glance. The modern sense: Some speculate (guess) that familiar (spirits) …

[148] 1.3.192. 'jealousy is cruel as the grave': See 1.2.191.

[149] 1.3.198. *for and*: moreover and.

[150] 1.3.200. *thinking long to make a period*: growing impatient to finish and have done.

    more un-natural and loathly treason" than ever the duke
    had have taken on him before.   151
Rumour: Condemnéd by the lords to die,
    the king caus'd Clarence from this world in spongy fashion,
    like a fish, for so ('twas said) he lived.
    Notwithstand no mortal eye discern'd his drowning mark,   210
    they drown'd the duke of Clarence in a butt of Malmsey wine.   211

*The **Queen**, satisfied by a private thought,*
stabs her needle into her sampler. She goes.
***Truth** & **Rumour** watch, then follow.*

ACT 2, SCENE 1

Middleham Castle, Yorkshire. About February, 1482–'83

*Enter an ancient varlet, **Thomas**, running …*

Thomas: *calls off*: Wine! Bring meat! Fetch wine!
    Duke Richard is come from London.
    He goes, running.

*Enter **Gloucester**, muddy, booted, cloaked.*

Gloucester: Thomas, what Thomas?
    Why varlet? Ancient, I say!
Thomas, *off*: Here, your grace.
Gloucester: Unboot me, Thomas!

***Thomas** returns.*

---

[151] 1.3.206. *had have*: The *have* is redundant. Cf. 1.1.62.

Thomas: Marry, your grace, the boots.
   ***Gloucester** sits. **Thomas** tugs at a boot.*
   Losing his grip, he stumbles back without it.
Gloucester: Bootless Thomas!
   I swear thou is a fool in all thy parts. 152
Thomas: So says my pardoner: 10
   "My son, I find thee perfect fool".
   Yea verily, quoth I. The fool am I
   by every measure of perfection, aye.
   Wherefore, in this world of fools,
   I'll never be without less foolishness 153
   than greater men.
Gloucester: Toil, thou. Hand my boot.
Thomas: They say he is a fool whose face will show his heart
   — in waking countenance — though not on sleep.
   Managing one boot, he tugs at the other.
   Do the wise dream wisely? while natural fools the while 154
   lie down to dream on foolish things? Nay, my lord. 20
   The meanest idiot is twin and equal wi' th' veriest sage
   when both them hath been brought asleep. 155
Gloucester: Then get thee to thy pallet.
   Make wise thou werest wiser. 156
   The second boot comes off. ***Thomas** falls back.*
   Thou wast ever benighted.
Thomas: I, sir? Shall I be knighted?
   Sir Fool. Sir Fool. Sir Thomas Fool.
   I'faith, your excellence, it sounds a pretty sound.

---

[152] 2.1.9. *thou is*: familiar dialect, Northern.
[153] 2.1.15. *without less foolishness*: Here, less may imply more. This is peculiar to Shakespeare, who reserved it for implicitly negative sentences. Cf. *Cymbeline* 1.4.23: '... be it but to fortify her judgment, which else an easy battery might lay flat, for taking a beggar without less quality'. Cf. note 1.1.84.
[154] 2.1.19. *natural fools*: born idiots.
[155] 2.1.22. *both them hath been*: Cf. 1.3.23.
[156] 2.1.24. *Make wise*: pretend.

Besides, the fool that wants the style and title of a fool
still more is fool.   30

Gloucester: Give me the boot.

Thomas: Nay, sir. 'Tis you gives me the boots.
Returning it. Swear and you'll not hurl it at my head?

Gloucester *taps the sole*: I'll be sworn on my sole.
Kneel down, dotard. Kneel.
   ***Thomas** kneels*. ***Gloucester** dubs him with the boot*.
I dub thee a fool, thy lord's most privy fool, to boot.
Sir Thomas Fool, arise.
   ***Thomas** stands*.

Anne, *off, calling*: Thomas? O Thomas!

Thomas: Alack the day! You lifted me too high.

Anne, *off*: What Thomas?   40

Thomas: Your grace inlorded me so high
I'm catch'd up into heav'n,
for of a sudden I descry the voice of angels.

Anne, *off*: Why Thomas?

Thomas: How? It fears me now to fall:
The highest fool's the greatest fool of all.
He runs to leave.
   ***Gloucester** flings the boot after him*.

*Enter **Anne, Duchess of Gloucester***.

Anne: Where is the little soul? Thomas!

Thomas, *aside*: Sir Thomas, an' it please you.
   Speaks: What will your grace?

Anne: Bring meat, fetch wine for your master!

Thomas, *aside*: Here's my self words come back again.   50

---

[157] 2.1.28. *wants*: lacks.

[158] 2.1.32. *'Tis you gives me the boots*: Beyond the obvious, this expression had another sense: 'It's you makes fun of me'. Cf. *Mother Bombie* (1594), 4.2.1482; *Two Gentlemen of Verona*, 1.1.27.

[159] 2.1.41. *inlorded me*: ennobled me.

It is of a truth, that the Ancient say:

    Thoughts scape from brains t'impress th'impressive air,

which, being impress'd, impresseth other brains.

Speaks: I away, your lady grace. *He offers to depart.*

Gloucester: Wait attendance, Thomas!

   *To **Anne***: I drank such store of wine to keep company with Edward,

   I had thought t'have founder'd, bursten, on my saddle-bow.

   I would fain rid the taste of venery.

   *To **Thomas***: Fetch small beer and fatted pork.

Thomas: 'Twill do your honour boot.

   Aside: Although it boot me not to fetch.

   On my grave they'll grave the epitaph:

             He fetch'd.

            And he fetch'd

          Until God did him fetch.

        Here lies Thomas, fetch'd up,

         His old life fetch'd again.

            *Exit **Thomas***

Anne: How chance this many months in London

   bind thee with a mask of shallow wit?

Gloucester: Why drawest thou a cloud before my sun?

Anne: An' thou diddest me to understand thy shining stream'd forth true,

   I'd not admonish thee. By this eleven years that I have been thy wife,

   I know thy proper sun as well as thou.

   Hide fox, I'll after: for my quarry hath thy face;

   he hath thy frame. Thy voice he has,

   yet stranger is this present voice

   than that it's truly thine. Where is my lord?

Gloucester: Why, here, at Middleham, with thee.

---

[160] 2.1.51. *the Ancient*: the Ancients. The word took a plural verb, despite its singular appearance.
[161] 2.1.53. Democritus suggested that thoughts leaking from other minds caused dreams.
[162] 2.1.60. *'Twill do your honour boot*: It'll do you good.
[163] 2.1.68. *in London*: Since early Mid. Eng., a distinction between *in* London, and *at* lesser towns.

Anne: As gypsies cun a smoky glass, so con I skill of thee.
Gloucester: The rack to careful inquisition
   is not liker than a wife.
Anne: The clouds before thy suns declare an instance
   wrought in strife. Tell that which gnaweth thee.
Gloucester: Three fathers hath my life experienc'd.
   My own too soon was slain,
   whereon our brother refuged George and me.
   Edward was our father; we, his sons;
   two little boys beneath his stately tree
   sought shelter from the heat and blast.
   After, worshipped I thy father, Warwick,
   that was master of my youth.
      York's red blood reek'd to win to York the crown;
   Warwick threw at all to rid the court of Grey and Woodville,
   setting 's state and honour on the hazard, lost his life.
   I show thee now the paradox mocks each his blood.
      Sweet England, that was Satan's hell of old,
   till Edward wrested government from mad Hal's feebled grasp!
   Of Edward, England knows more peace
   than very hist'ry did admit before.
   But now, now falling wi' th' weight of envy
   and disquietness again, she groans.
   No new day daws upon this king
   but Woodvilles count it for their gain:
   Their instrument to trample our corn
   and raise their chaff withal? Our house of York!
      That noble prince, whom I did as my father love,
   is lately become a rotted carcass,
   corrupt by lust-bred maladies. His queen,
   and all her dozen several of infamous besort besides,

---

[164] 2.1.82. *As gypsies ... skill of thee*: I read you as well as a gypsy reads smoked glass.

[165] 2.1.96. *threw at all*: gambled everything.

[166] 2.1.112. *besort*: the company one keeps, one's circle. Peculiar to Shakespeare, as a noun at 1.3.238 in *Othello*; as a verb in *King Lear*, 1.4.272.

(which loathly maggots generate their kind in flesh!)
engorge themselves with Edward's worldly weal within,
fall on his realm without.
    This is not my brother from remembering.
So comes he a no-king; he is rather their fatted bullock than a bull;
nay, he is their ox; they ring him to trot him about.
Whom reputation dubb'd the fairest prince in Christendom   120
is by these devils driven to a caesar's grave
prepar'd with bacchanalian feasts, as lewd as Priapus.
His light, which gloriously forth did shine,
now-a-days is dark. Ha! Edward is so corpulent,
were a' boil'd for render'd tallow,
he'd furnish a thousand of candles with his fat!

Enter **Thomas**, *followed by* **Servers**.

Thomas: Here's fatted porkling for your grace.
Gloucester: Out, out thy fatted porkling!
    Hence thee! Get thee hence!
    Again!   130
        Servers *drop dishes in confusion.*
        While they pick up ...
Thomas, *to* **Servers**: Here's a falling-off indeed.
    Master is from his wits. It makes no wonder that a wight
    whose blazon is the white boar should eschew porkling.
    The wonder is, that at a twinkling, Nuncle is absorpt
    wi' th' vital spirits from forth the swine o' th' Gadarenes!   167
    Exeunt **Thomas** *with* **Servers**.
Gloucester: I come to fear time-coming
    even more than I did fear it in times past.
    His moment hangeth o'er our heads, hois'd up, to fall.
    If Edward live, his peace shall broach on favour
    he dispendeth to his queen.

---

[167] 2.1.135. *swine o' th' Gadarenes*: Mark 5:1–17. Matthew 8:28–34 has *Gergesenes*.

> But 's life dependeth of a rotten thread, which,   140
> if it break, shall loose his hangers-on in law.
> Those shall raze the barons' rights   168
> and set their countenance to war,
> and to defile our blood.   144 169
>
> *They go.*

ACT 2, SCENE 2

***Attendants** bring in **King Edward** on a litter, followed by the **Queen** (mute), **Dorset**, **Richard Grey**, **Bishop Morton**, the three **Councillors**, **Lord Hastings**. Others as may be.*

K. Edward IV: Friends and my loves, belovéd you,
   in recent days my king of kings hath gave me note
   my latter end draws near.
   Whereto I bid you too frail welcome, and farewell.
Morton: Peace be to your grace.
K. Edward IV: Peace, aye, peace. My ever peace.
   But stay 't a moment more.
      Upon my death-bed have I ta'en such order with affairs
   as I may better recommend my one essential soul to God.
   My last will is this: Be it indeed I am in debt to any,   10
   whether by misprision or compáct, let him be given satisfaction.

---

[168] 2.1.142. *raze*: suggests erasure, as of a law or charter.

[169] 2.1.144. *and to defile our blood*: The *to* appears redundant, but was sometimes included in a sentence having more than one infinitive, when preceding infinitives (in this case *raze* and *set*) went without it. Cf. Berners (c. 1530): 'A good prince that wil governe well, and not to be a tyrant'. Also *Merry Wives*, 4.4.58, cited at 2.4.187.

After those receive their dues, the half of all my goods
shall be dispers'd among the poor.
>Say, Morton: Shall this extemporal intent suffice
to shrive my soul?
Morton: Trust thereto assuredly, my liege.
A like design suffic'd for Zaccheus,
whom Christ commended to his flock.
I not doubt 'twas not for 's deeds, rather right intention.   170
K. Edward IV: Then am I reconcil'd with God.
But man and man about my bed must each unto other reconcile,   20
before my uncompounded soul my body may the quietlier part.
I take 't on my last day: A single lively sorrow do I owe;   171
that all these nineteen years deep schism rives
our old nobility and these our queen her kind.
I entreat you — nay, we do command you of all love:
Do you *love* our son, the prince, as he were ourself!
Too soon for tender years he will be king.
If ye fall at dissension during his reign,
many here shall perish before England find peace again.
Wherefore, with these words,   30
the last that ever I am like to speak,
I exhort you and require ye set apart your griefs.
>Come, friends. Come all as one about my bed;
in common purpose, come! By these,
our waning offices of life and crown, we ye command:
Join hands, join hearts togethers. Each forgive other.
*The **King** collapses, lying on his right side.*

---

[170] 2.2.18. Evidently the Croyland Chronicler was not present during this bedside meeting. However, he was well informed regarding the contents of Edward's oral will. The biblical story of Zaccheus (Luke 19: 1–10) is written into the Croyland account as a churchman might think to detail it. Thus it seemed appropriate to return it to the mouth of another churchman, Morton, who attended Edward IV at his death. Francis Bacon takes issue with this convenient policy of posthumous charity. In *Of Riches* he observes: 'Defer not charities till death, for certainly if a man weigh it rightly, he that doth so is rather liberal of another man's than of his own'.

[171] 2.2.22. *I take 't*: I affirm, I confirm, I admit.

Sir Thomas More described the ensuing scene: "... Each forgave the other and joined their hands together". This concluded, the **Queen** *and* **Morton** *comfort the* **King**; **Dorset** *and* **Grey** *whisper together;* **Hastings** *confers with the three* **Councillors**.

Grey: We must intelligence the king's death to Rivers.
Dorset: Have a little patience, brother.
Grey: He must soon quit his clay.
Dorset: Patience perforce. We shall not strive   40
   to quell a storm whose force we can master.
   When Edward dies, we'll play the cat upon these mice.
   We shall rule this while without our mother's little king.
Grey: Liefer me were pray in aid of Rivers.
   Otherwise the barons shall destroy us.
Dorset: Let them conspire to play their game.
   Those shall not verdict us; they are the minim.
   We are the Council's better half.

Hastings: Note Dorset with 's brother, Richard Grey.
   O, might I catch the plots defile their lips!   50
Councillor 1: They seemingly mutter hurt nor favour.
Hastings: Resolve their eyen, how these unlick'd bear whelps   172
   conster wickedness. Mark how their ires flash.   173
Councillor 2: Would they were maidens to regard us so!
Hastings: God's light, my lords!
   Who peers in a cannon's mouth to watch the flash
   discerneth not the thund'rous glory from his end.
   Mock them and you will, but look you ware them still.
Councillor 3: Methinks it's they fear us.
   Cannot you smell to 't?   60

---

[172] 2.2.52. *eyen* for eyes was already archaic by the Period, but Shakespeare supplies precedent. He used *eyne* to rhyme with *mine* in *Midsummer Night's Dream*, 5.1.178. § *unlick'd bear whelps*: It was thought that bear cubs were born formless and licked into shape by their mothers. The expression is figurative, after Donne, *Elegie* XI, line 31, to describe something imperfect or immature.

[173] 2.2.53. *conster*: construe. *OED* reports its pronunciation as *conster* as late as the nineteenth century, long after the modern spelling became standard.

*The **King** cries out in pain.*
Councillor 1: I smell but tardy-creeping death.
Hastings: More shall die than Edward
    when Death brings him to his bier.

Dorset: Look to Hastings, how he lours upon us.
    It listeth him to bury us in Edward's sepulchre.
Grey: These conspire together even tendant upon the grave.
    Belike Hastings minds our fall. 174
Dorset: That thinks to play old fox is but a limping hare.
    We shall be lively-sprited beagles that will him waste at lair.

Hastings: These will not wield their baby king aright,
    but they must dab his Great Seal on complots 70
    to conjure estates away from better men.
Councillor 2: Nothing that they asked was ever denied to them.
Hastings: Not yet.
    The feral vices of their mother and her brothers 175
    require we wait on action. 176
    If these command the sovereign essence of the crown, 177
    the old noblesse shall be their special butt.
    When Edward dies, begins the fight. 78
    ***Attendants** bear off the **King**. All follow.*

---

[174] 2.2.66. *minds*: intends, has a mind to bring about.
[175] 2.2.74. *feral*: deadly.
[176] 2.2.75. *wait on*: anticipate, expect anxiously; hence, to prepare for.
[177] 2.2.76. *these*: the latter, i.e. their mother and her brothers.

ACT 2, SCENE 3

Middleham Castle, Yorkshire. Mid–April, 1483

Enter **Gloucester**, *with a letter.*

Gloucester: Vile spirits, from a starless inward dark,
   you mute, unquiet visitors, in fine I place you,   178
   — albeit too late.
   Each night you stole my quiet death of sleep
   to speak disquietly of death, to lead me to a world
   of far imaginings, beyond the usual frame.
      Sprites! that out of velvet sleep unstopp'd my eyes,
   to goad them wander ceaselessly the darkness of the bed;
   to bind me, wakeful, to the passing of the nights,
   you bad me note the hours by the watchman's tread.   10
      Long lay I in that fitful wake, until, to banish you,
   I drew aside the curtains. Nought avail'd.
   Your shadows gadded o'er the arras and the vault
   as they were moths quick'd by the candle's flame.
   Higher they sprang betimes, and faster,
   till the fire that spawn'd them chok'd his life.
      Misbegotten phantasms! Be you or part of me?
   or be you essences apart? How came you at these news?
   Unwary for my weariness, your light of nature
   spell'd a parable unknown: A life, like to a candle,   20
   burns ay downward to his grave.
      Dead. These two days since he's dead;
   howbeit he lived ghostly in me two days beyond his span.
   Till now. For now my king, that was of woman born,
   of words on paper hath been slain. You prescient wraiths,
   here is your writ of affirmation come at last!

---

[178] 2.3.2. *in fine:* at last, finally.

Enter **Duchess Anne**.

Anne: What hath ado?
  I heard the bruit of voices, where I come on thee alone.
Gloucester: The wind soughs under the mantel-tree.
Anne: They rais'd not sigh, but argument. 30
Gloucester: Daws war aloft the towers.
  They fight together in the chimney-tops.
Anne: What, hast tha not spoke?
Gloucester: 'Twas Hastings.
  Gives the letter to **Anne**.
  By this letter makes he sorrow: The king is dead.
Anne: Then let my grief comeddled be wi' thine.
  She unrolls the letter.
  This epistle turns over the leaf:
  T'expulse the years of old he writes the new.
Gloucester: The heaven forfend!
  This future fruit was riped i' th' devil's sun; 40
  'twere better expulse the new.
Anne: We stand athwart the threshold thou didst dread.
Gloucester: W'are come already within.
Anne: So Hastings: — *Reads. Then*: — I am sure it cannot be!
  Dorset, Edward Woodville and the queen
  have seiz'd themselves of treasures royall at the Tower.
Gloucester: They are that game with bones,
  like soldiers at the Cross.
Anne: *These* be familiar enemies that game at *thee!* 179
  Canst not thou set the dice upon them? 50 180
Gloucester: So wily a headed empty fox
  was never mewed up to guard such fowl.
  The Marquis keeps the office of the Tower. 181

---

[179] 2.3.49. *These ... game at thee*: These are foes within the family with designs against you.
[180] 2.3.50. *set the dice upon*: fix the dice, dictate to, control.
[181] 2.3.53. *The Marquis*: Dorset.

Anne, *reads*: A fleet is armed and put to sea.
  Edward Woodville is made admiral.
Gloucester: By which expedience they would overawe us.
Anne, *reads*: Rivers, dress'd i' th' worn authority
  of Edward's writ, beats up his drums to gather head in Wales. 182
Gloucester: Where York hath sown, these reap the corn.
Anne, *reads*: The earl intends the prince progress to London 60
  with an army at his back. Elizabeth and Dorset have wrought
  to bar your having voice in government, which point
  they do politically labour t' th' Council. Quoth Hastings:
  I have heard where they will anoint the boy in unseemly haste,
  thereby to void your office of Protector,
  that same that Edward will'd, in 's codicil,
  should unto you remain. 183
Gloucester: The grating harpy weaves her web of laun 184
  she spun aforetime.
Anne: Hastings bids thee heed most earnestly:
  Reads: I stand in certain peril for the tricks 70
  this throng and press of devils puts upon me.
  All rests in you, t'unloose this Medusaean knot of ill,
  to rid the isle from their iniquities. No more but so. 185
  She rolls up the letter.
  Elizabeth is overstrong!
  Canst thou not stifle up her commands?
Gloucester: Whereby I wot not.
  Now, Anne, do thou but wait: I will not sit on thorns. 186
  I shall to York, whereat sad mass of requiem
  shall will that soul to God which I did love.
  There too the northern lords and barons, 80

---

[182] 2.3.58. *to gather head*: raise an army.
[183] 2.3.67. No definitive record of King Edward's will exists in this matter, but it was widely accepted that he wished his brother Richard to act as Protector to his son during the latter's minority.
[184] 2.3.68. *laun*: sometimes *lawn*, the stuff of cobwebs.
[185] 2.3.73. *No more but so*: There you have it. That's how it is. A concluding formula used by Marlowe in *Edward II*, 5.2.34 (Tucker Brooke ed. line 2176) and *Jew of Malta*, 4.1.131 (T. Brooke, line 1637).
[186] 2.3.77. *sit on thorns*: sit around anxiously.

for the nonce to swear the prince their king.
Thence to London, mine office to repone:
I'll taste this future, what come may.
Anne: Hastings speaks how — albeit of his ancient malice —
that the queen would war thee.
Gloucester: Elizabeth hath gone about to war these seven years' day.
I shall so meet her, for at length the knife   187
under the smiler's cloak is bare.   188
   In time of mind, two dukes of Gloucester
by two English kings were slain.   90   189
This body shall not bleed to consecrate their couple
to a trinity! Rather old experience shall fend me
like a theriacal potion sure.   190
Anne: She doeth what Jacob did, that conjur'd even generation.   191
Doth not each dam conceive that she perceives?
Which creature, being got, must take again of qualities   192
he grows withal.
The queen hath destinied the prince's vital sense, that,
thinking only but on Woodville, sees none other interess.
How she soe'er commands, his sovereignty needs stray.
The prince cannot else but pluck on reprobate opinion.   100   193
Gloucester: To snare this queen, Elizabeth,
and eke t'attach her son, I'll set forth letters comfortable   194

---

[187] 2.3.86. *meet*: prepare to confront.
[188] 2.3.88. After Chaucer, *The Knight's Tale*, line 1141 in some eds.
[189] 2.3.90. *two dukes of Gloucester*: Thomas, d.1397; Humphrey, d.1447.
[190] 2.3.93. *theriacal*: antidotal.
[191] 2.3.94. This notion derives from Genesis 30, 37–43. The tale of Jacob, Laban and the spotted goats is the oldest recorded example of what later came to be known as Lamarckian evolutionary theory. Jean Baptiste Lamarck (d. 1829) suggested there was reason to believe that traits acquired in life could be passed to future generations. A comment in John Lyly's *Mother Bombie* (1594) credits this notion:
   Dromio: It may be, when this boy was begotten, she thought of a fool, yourself [the father] being very wise, and she surpassing honest.
   Memphio: It may be; for I have heard of an Ethiopian, that thinking of a fair picture, brought forth a fair [baby], and yet no bastard.
Shakespeare employs this principle in his 'woolly breeders' passage, *Merchant of Venice*, 1.3.78.
[192] 2.3.96. *take again of*: inherit genetically.
[193] Queen Anne believes that Elizabeth Woodville has been brain-washing her son(s) à la Genesis.
[194] 2.3.102. *set forth*: cause to be known, publicise.

will smooth it with the queen and Council both,
　　　and draw her in.
Anne: By these news I judge thou canst not gain of her.
　　　Consider how they did poor Clarence die:
　　　Upon his brother's head his brother's blood.
Gloucester: I have set down my period!
　　　Credit me absolutely this.
　　　Was not I litter'd under Libra? 110
　　　Then the case to certain justice shall be tried,
　　　and of it virtue fully put.
　　　We shall obtain our grace. 113
　　　Exeunt.

ACT 2, SCENE 4

The Council Chamber, Westminster. Mid–April, 1483.
*The Council assembles, in mourning. Present: the **Queen**, Bishop **Morton**, the three **Councillors**, **Howard**, **Hastings**, **Rotherham**, **Grey**, **Dorset** and **Russell**, with others as may be.*

Q. Elizabeth: We meet, my lords, upon a solemn time;
　　　we are his prisoners. What tortures had I endured,
　　　were I but giv'n to understand the king had peace.
Morton: Rest you easily, madam,
　　　in certain hope the king hath found eternal grace.
Q. Elizabeth: Certain, Morton? Certain?
　　　When day droops into night, who then can light a brand

---

[195] 2.3.105. *gain of*: gain the advantage over, get the better of.

[196] 2.3.108. *set down my period*: reached a decision, made up my mind. *Period* in this sense evolved to become the name of the dot denoting the end of a sentence in American English.

[197] 2.3.112. *it*: its.

so great 'twill show the hórizont? Nay, my lord.
The face, the breath, the voice, the touch of hands,
the quick, the very certain countenance of life   10
rebuke our fond-imagin'd vizard of eternity.
Had heaven wept good measure of my grief,
the earth had wash'd away.
Councillor 1, *to 2*: Why tears she thus before the Council?
Councillor 2, *to 1*: She thinks, beyond the king's death,
t'absolve in sorrow, sin compounded some time of 's reign.
Q. Elizabeth: That lies beyond, doth us appear
as 'twere th'uncertain comfort of a distant light,
spied far apart, across a wood of storm-toss'd trees.
Morton: We pray that your faith sustain   20
to flect your distresses, until this bitter cup
doth somewhat melt from you, into the balm of time.
Q. Elizabeth: Would 'twould salve death; yet sorrow,
like refiner's fire, yields best remembrance,
true, and undefiled.
E'en as now my heart's hand gives me up to take him near.
I thank you for your comfort, sir. I thank you all, my lords.
The three **Councillors** *converse among themselves.*
C2: Yon Morton does whited sepulchre rarely!
C3: A' was born to it: 'Tis just his skin.   30
C1: He was of Lancaster from Henry's time.
C3: Then he became, of Lancaster, a friend of York.
C2: Now is he chain'd creature from the house of Woodvilles.
C1: Better men fall foul, be so they soak up honour
with mother's milk. This bishop is a sponge;
him falls well supping plots.
C2: Pah. A cock aloft his midden crows as well as he!

---

[198] 2.4.8. *hórizont*: This spelling was already archaic during the Period. However, the final 't' ensures that the stress falls on the first and third syllables, not the second, as in modern English. That Shakespeare used the modern spelling with the old ictus can be seen in *3 Henry VI*, 4.7.81.
[199] 2.4.27. *my heart's hand*: This figure is explained at 3.7.85, *breasts of all hearts*.
[200] 2.4.30. *just*: precisely, exactly. Cf. 'just a pound of flesh' or 'just the fashion'.
[201] 2.4.32. *of Lancaster*: from Lancaster.

C3: None doeth as well, nor hath, as Master Morton Chanticleer. 202
The straight he maketh crooked; the crooked he maketh fork'd.
His life to an end, this prelate brings to end 40
the sum of his desires — and that most wonderfully!

Q. Elizabeth: To us, lords, is given to guide the prince.
As many as over-live the king are chargéd 203
to do on the frumpled brow of government. 204

Morton: *Vivat* King Edward the Fifth!

All, *noises of assent*:
All hail King Edward!
God save the king!
May he long become his throne. 205

Q. Elizabeth: Join we t'address the future.

Howard *to* **Hastings**: Wherein we'll scorch our arses 50
in the embers of their past.

Hastings *to* **Howard**: May God forfend!

Q. Elizabeth: A retinue is a preparing:
Rivers carries the prince hither from Ludlow.

Hastings: How many men come on, your grace?

Q. Elizabeth: They number, one and other, some few thousands.

Hastings: Some warlike thousands under the earl's dispose
make to an army. It shall be jeopardous to peace
the king to come so strong.

Rotherham: These wait, my lord, attendance upon their king. 60

Hastings: They rather dance attendance on the earl!

Rotherham: His progress needs must speak
the prince's majesty. *Clamour*

Morton: His train but serves the prince. *Clamour*

Grey: Soldiers witness quality befits the king. *Clamour*

Dorset: Men in harness dignify our brother's train. *Clamour*

---

[202] 2.4.38. Heywood's *Proverbs*: "'Do well, and have well', men say". This goes back in English at least as far as Caxton (*Dialogues*, 47), who takes it from a French source.

[203] 2.4.43. *As many as over-live*: All those who survive [King Edward IV].

[204] 2.4.44. *Do on*: don, put on [clothing, regalia; responsibility].

[205] 2.4.45. *OED* finds neither *Vivat* nor 'God save the king!' from the sixteenth century. However, both appear on the title page of King Henry VIII's Great Bible.

Howard: The very air's a cautel …
Hastings: … sly wi' plots.
Grey: Is't not meet the prince should lead
   his leal troop to London?
Dorset: What say you, Hastings? Bare your grievance.
Hastings: I would know if your Welsh be friend or enemy! 70
Grey: Treason!
Hastings: Honey'd loyalty drips rather from your lips
   than drives your hearts. Hah, and 'twere for a countenance, 206
   the inly man betrays his skin; your very fronts do flash out
   the ill advantage of your part.
Dorset: Set off ill will.
Howard: Is not our humour settled? Edward is our king.
   What needs for strangers in harness at his back?
Hastings: Or Rivers for troops at his beck?
Dorset: Your wilfulness makes t'exaggerate the seeming wrong. 80
   Our liege must with his retinue.
Hastings: By'r Lord, methinks these Welsh owe slight allegiance
   to their prince. Rivers hath made a base head
   to his baser dispose. 207
   The house of Woodville would this force;
   which, as heretofore, shall put the royalme on their rack;
   shall pill his body, drain his veins beyond distress …
Howard: … to venge old woes.
Morton: No. No. *Clamour*
Grey: Vile injuries! *Clamour*
Dorset: Take shame! *Clamour* 90
Howard: Whose line speaks loyalty to York
   shall lick no tyrant's shoe.
Hastings: I shall post-haste to Calais if you'd bid us arms.
   I had there liefer 'bide your shock.
Q. Elizabeth: I beg of you, lords, peace!

---

206   2.4.73. *for a countenance*: for the sake of appearances.
207   2.4.83. *head*: a force, soldiers, an army.

We were best descend within ourselves.
Let's treat of this in honourable ways.
Hastings: Small honour is, when Wales devoureth London.
Dorset: Have you no touch of shame?
Q. Elizabeth: Calm ye! Our way is to make compromise to jars.
I'll send t' th' king. How say you to the large limit of … ?
Hastings: Two thousand!
Dorset: Such trash were a woman's escort, unworthy for the king.
Fly to Calais, Hastings.
For fear of loyalty, go shit thy shame.
Hastings *must be restrained.*
Hastings: Fetch our mistress. Beg of her to fight thy quarrel!
Dorset *must be restrained.*
Come! Dost bid me arms? I'll stick you t' th' blood.
Q. Elizabeth: I'name o' th' king's living memory, be ruled!
Be bidden, peace! Two thousand men.
Let this be stifled and be done.
Howard: This lesser betokens a greater infection, your grace.
Q. Elizabeth: A greater thing, Howard?
Howard: The prince, since his infancy, is put in mind
to do his kinsmen's part; whereas the king his father
will'd this bias should be countervail'd.
Q. Elizabeth: No.
Howard: He late sought to grant prince Edward his ward
to his brother, Gloucester.
Dorset: These lies are nowhere written down.
Hastings: Thus runs the fame.
Howard: The prince, in nonage, takes the diadem:
No more may he with 's kin hold narrow friendship.
England is become his best becoméd family of the blood.
Dorset: The Household is more worth than other
to appoint his motives to a king.

---

[208] 2.4.95. *descend within ourselves*: reflect inwardly, consider quietly, calm down.
[209] 2.4.120. *in nonage*: during his minority.

Hastings, *to* **Howard**: Hark how he bears himself in hand.
    Those villains shame not lightly.
Morton: Lord Jesus had twelve only apostles.
    Yet loved he all mankind.
Hastings: Lord bishop, you would have the king of England
    sell indulgences, like priests!
Dorset: The nature of a king, no less than lesser men,
    accepteth certain persons, and abaseth others.
Hastings: Ha, he pleads it loud!
Howard: His mind, that rules the sapience of his tree;
    his heart, whence airy, fiery vital spirits flow;
    his threads of life,
    wherein attractive and repulsive powers run;
    those virtues in a king we hold most dear.
    The common weal — moreover, the weal of our prince's soul —
    hath nobler interest than that the king thereof
    should wait on his kinsmen's trough!
Grey: Call in the lie! *Clamour*
Q. Elizabeth: Retract the slur, do! *Clamour*
Dorset: Speaks Calumny's imp! *Clamour*
Bishop Russell: Pray, lords, calm the storm!
    Prithee, lend audience!
    Thus. (*Prose sets up a contrast here.*)
      Rash it would be, and feeble-brain'd, did we, full of
    native innocence, rely ourselves upon the atonement
    lately concluded betwixt factions at King Edward's dying.
    That remain are given to note that nothing doth so evidence
    our war-apparell'd state as this counter-affirmation doth,
    abundant in his fury.

---

[210] 2.4.125. *bears himself in hand*: deludes himself.

[211] 2.4.132. *accepteth certain persons*: In a modern context this might be called a 'Freudian slip'. Hence Hastings' terse rebuttal. A biblical Hebraism, in English since Wyclif, this phrase suggests corrupt practices such as conceding undue influences to favorites. Cf. Galatians 2.6, in part: 'God accepteth no man's person' — God doesn't play favourites!

[212] 2.4.36. *threads of life*: nerves.

[213] 2.4.140. *thereof*: Cf. 1.1.154.

No contract drawn out, hot at hand, in sorry grace, can
put men in mind to love one another, where accustom'd variance
is rooted in them, lo, this nineteen years. Since our hating
begun, the moon's *annus magnus* has come full about, pardie! 214 | 215
    The king is dead; but yet as well the king lives
as his realm. Our land is one; our only voice speaks several   160
parts. By that, the condition of the time changes the mode.   216
Solemn office is given us, or to fall the sword upon our head,
or to decide the peace.
    Hither, we were best be prudent. Needs perforce Gloucester   217
must arbitrate our discord, for that King Edward shall be
harmless, lees'd of sudden, jealous, wayward nor capricious
counsel — if such were verily his puissant father's will.   218

Dorset: The dead are not fit to rule the quick.
Thus, anciently, the Parliament.

Councillor 1, *to his fellows*: It were to be wished   170
that King Edward had written it down.

Russell: Moreover, that the duke doth greet her highness well,
his letters did declare the love he bears his nephew,
and this Council.

Dorset: Or rather bear a brain, lords!
This drift shall sort to woe.   219

---

214 2.4.158. *the moon's annus magnus*: The classical Great Year, or *megas eniautos*, was originally, and usually, applied to a cosmic cycle postulated in Platonic philosophy. Russell uses it here, loosely, to describe the moon's nineteen year cycle, after which it returns to approximately the same apparent position with respect to the sun. Later (1696) the phenomenon would be named the Metonic Year after the Athenian astronomer given credit for describing it (although there is evidence that this cycle was known to the builders of Stonehenge). On the face of it, Russell simply alludes to the fact that the state of quarrel and turbulence in England's politics has continued through a full lunar cycle of nineteen years. Implicit to his fifteenth century listeners is a suspicion that a Christian bishop could not voice: That a natural cycle was coming to an end, and that, for better or worse, things would change.
    Russell's passage is written in prose, to contrast with the preceding arguments.

215 2.4.158. *pardie*: verily, indeed. A mild oath, fit for a bishop.

216 2.4.161. *By that*: In consequence, Therefore.

217 2.4.164. *Hither*: To that end, For that reason.

218 2.4.167. *prudent*: No evidence links Russell to this speech. However, if Russell was the Croyland Chronicler, he used the word *prudent* to describe those at the meeting who subscribed to this policy. Clearly he agreed with it.

219 2.4.176. *sort to*: result in (Bacon).

Rotherham: Never did regent, of yore, give up his staff lightly.
  Who rules the king, is king!
Dorset: Whose nature is not grac'd with majesty, of God,
  corrupteth of authority.   180
Hastings: Dorset! y'are that cannot lack advantage
  on the young king's ear. The turn you walk'd
  on royal camomile is done.
Q. Elizabeth: We make to a divided house. Belike we are to fall,
  unless we do our diligence to cease from strifes.
Howard: Bid we then Gloucester do office,
  and to be Protector of the prince.   220
Hastings: Divers examples do precedent us
  i' th' like carriage of affairs.
Dorset: We have importancy, and powers enow, to govern.   190
  Ask England else. Bid Gloucester steal about
  his Northern barbary. Wales, and other England else,
  shall be our fee.
Hastings: Till war infest your head!
  You sweat ambition out for youthful sap.
  Ware, Dorset, like t'a tree grown over tall,
  ambition without 's root 's obnoxious to a fall.   221
Dorset: The king shall have his kingdom;
  England have her king; and we obtain the government!
Q. Elizabeth: We shall win nothing at blows;   200
  but much, and we were compromis'd.
  As modesty announce your virtue, Russell,   222
  so let modesties claim ours.   223
  I urge, that we send to Gloucester ...
Dorset: Here's harsh deliverance foisted upon us.
Q. Elizabeth: Howbeit, we shall not appoint the duke 'Protector',
  lest, as it is thought for, haughtiness possess him

---

[220] 2.4.187. *and to be*: An infinitive of intention. See this construction in *Merry Wives*, 4.4.57: 'Then let them all encircle him about, And, fairy-like, to pinch the unclean knight'. Cf. note 2.1.144.
[221] 2.4.197. *obnoxious to*: exposed to, open to, liable to.
[222] 2.4.202. *modesty*: moderation, spirit of compromise.
[223] 2.4.203. *modesties*: Shakespeare uses the plural when assigning this quality to more than one person.

    that a' might possess the whole.
    We had rather to furbish the style 'Chief Councillor'.
    Great Gloucester will not be one only over many,   210
    but as one among the chiefest subjects of his king.
Morton: A wise resolve, your grace.
Dorset: Large troubles come of naked promises;
    nor grows distress less vexing through such hap.
Howard: Renownéd queen, we do commend the compromise.
Q. Elizabeth: Our gracious lord of York, as Chancellor,
    do you, Rotherham, indite our Council's will,
    and put the Broad Seal to 't.
Rotherham: It shall be done, your grace.   219

ACT 2, SCENE 5

An apartment at York. Night, about April 20, 1483.

Enter **Thomas**, *running*.

Thomas: *calling off*: Please your grace, a pressing message
    was dispatch'd you from the duke of Buckingham.

Enter **Gloucester**.

Gloucester: To what purport?
Thomas: I nothing wot purports.
Gloucester: What words? what form? By whose hand borne?
    Which letters from the cross-row doth the unseen page compile?   224
Thomas: To me that am unlettered, letters signify but naught.
Gloucester: How chance the mention-making

---

[224] 2.5.6. *the cross-row*: the alphabet, so-called because it was customary to start and sometimes finish writing the alphabet with the symbol of Christ's cross.

    doth outstrip the he that bears it?
Thomas: Perhaps the tittle-est-Amen came before the row.   10
Gloucester: What trick of air words it to thee?
Thomas: Why, I show your excellence no trick.
    I tell my charge: Gallant Mercury is hither won
    upon the wings of his most valiant Pegasee.
Gloucester: Thou art sow-drunk again.
    Or hath a pothecary fuddled thee? Breathe upon me!
        Thomas *does so.*
    O God! No liquor this. 'Tis a vapour
    from the dung-hill of stopped-up bowels.
Thomas: Strike me a stroke an' I lie!
Gloucester: Not but an idiot descrieth thoughts,   20
    born o' th' air, that bestride a wingéd stallion.
    Thy mother borrow'd thy wits of *vacuüm*.
Thomas: Swart wizards fly; and witches too.
    But words fly faster.
Gloucester: Duke Harry's a born man in grace;
    but here's the sovereign'st force, when emanation of a thought moves air,
    now forging 's atomies to words, now stirs them hither
    through the starry front of heaven.
    Old man, in seventh age th'art wandering.
Thomas: They say Dame Rumour rides the expiration   30
    from twelve cherubs — those that blow the winds.
Gloucester: Speak plain-song, Thomas.
    Dark parables is stuff for clerks.
Thomas: I discover to your worship plainly as I know.
    Yond same Mercury — how is he bemoil'd! —
    tumbled off his jade i' th' court. He foam'd at mouth;
    he spitted froth; for and he blows shorter than his horse!

---

[225] 2.5.10. *tittle-est-Amen*: A modern rendition of this line might read: 'Maybe the alphabet came backwards'. OED gives the full mnemonic for learning the alphabet under *Christ-cross* entry 3 (1597), where Morley has 'Christes crosse be my speede, in all vertue to proceede, A, b, c ... w with y, ezod, & per se, con per se tittle tittle est Amen When you have done begin againe, begin againe'. Marlowe gives this figure to an illiterate, Robin, in some editions of *Doctor Faustus* (Penguin, 1969, 2.2.8).

[226] 2.5.37. *for and*: on top of that, in addition to that, moreover.

Gloucester: Unfetter'd dolt, what folly's this?
Thomas: Why, his name is Percy-well.
Gloucester: Percy-well? 40
Thomas: And indeed he 'pears most passing well.
    Old Maggie minister'd her simples:
    Knitback to his bruises; Setwall, for his sympathy thereto.
Gloucester: Hath thy pedlar's French the ending?
Thomas: I'faith, he spurr'd post from forth of Wales,
    and rode to York, benighted but a night.
Gloucester: Is't true, Thomas, flesh and fell?
    or be this throughly fable?
Thomas: My fable's true. A's wrought thereof by contraries,
    on muddy flesh, that oft-times fell. Your ending's evident. 50
    He waits without.
Gloucester: How? Without?
Thomas: Why, Percy-well — he that's henchman
    from the duke of Buckingham. He waits upon your grace without.
Gloucester: Then bid him wait on me within!
    Thomas goes.

*Enter **Humphrey Percival**, dishevelled.*

Percival: God save your grace.
Gloucester: And you, dark stranger;
    though like an ímpious imp you scour about the pit of night.

---

[227] 2.5.42. *simples*: herbal remedies, medicines.
[228] 2.5.43. *Knitback*: a Northern name for Comfrey. In North Yorkshire it would have been *Symphytum tuberosum* rather than *officinale*.
    Setwall: a common name for Valerian. Gerard's *The Herball* (1598), describes 'The Vertues' of Valerian (p.1078): '… it hath been had (and is to this day among the poore people of our Northerne parts) in such veneration amongst them, that no broths, pottage, or physical meats [medicinal foods] are worth any thing, if Setwall were not at an end: whereupon some woman Poet or other hath made these verses: "They that will have their heale, / Must put Setwall in their keale" '.
[229] 2.5.44. *pedlar's French*: nonsense, gibberish.
[230] 2.5.47. *flesh and fell*: a mortal truth, a real threat.
[231] 2.5.50. *oft-times fell*: This use of *fell* (from a horse) completes Thomas's play on the word. Contrast this usage with *fell* (terrible, dire, real) three lines earlier.
[232] 2.5.58. *ímpious*: Stress falls on the first syllable.

Percival: My name is Humphrey Percival, privy servant
   to Duke Harry. I come stilly to say my master's mind. 60
Gloucester: Your grim looks speak that urgence spurr'd you.
   Let's have the tale.
Percival *gives* **Gloucester** *a letter*: This letter of credence
   approves me earnest spokesman in his grace's cause.
Gloucester *reads*: This bearer, *et cetera* ...
   The message is pick'd bones.
Percival: For the rest,
   the pith and the infolding carry I inly. 233
Gloucester: Then labour it forth.
Percival.: The duke, that speaks in my behaviour, did admonish me, 70 234
   your person your alone, may be the key unlocks my tongue.
Gloucester: Stands here your key.
   Let your cipher by your motive be unlock'd. 235
Percival: Duke Harry swears allegiance by me to your nephew,
   Edward, Prince of Wales, and earl of Chester.
   God bless King Edward the Fift!
Gloucester: And make him long to reign.
Percival: However —
   the world is new, whereof, in his green age,
   this boy attainéd hath the top of sovereignty. 80
   Duke Harry, incens'd with high devoyer, bids — just as 236
   the perfitest fortune of our verdant commonwealth requires —
   that your grace must be to seek to be protector of the king.
   My master's put in fear unless his sister snatch the sway: 237
   Wherefór she readies her; her green-ey'd envy's sire
   to cunning malice, which, by course, she puts t'accustom'd power.

---

[233] 2.5.68. *infolding*: Francis Bacon, in *Of the advauncement of learning* (1605) II, xvi, para. 6, uses this word to describe either the means by which a message is encoded, or the encoded message itself. *OED* does not find *infolding* until 1873, assigning an unrelated meaning.

[234] 2.5.70. *that speaks in my behaviour*: who speaks through/for me. Cf. *King John*, 1.1.3. Also *Dark Sovereign*, 3.4.112, 'Chide him in my voice...'

[235] 2.5.73. *motive*: tongue (peculiar to Shaks.). He used the word for moving parts of the body, per *Troilus & Cressida*, 4.5.57. In *Richard II*, 1.1.193, *motive* refers to the tongue.

[236] 2.5.81. *high devoyer*: duty, devoir. The spelling is phonetic.

[237] 2.5.84. *sister*: sister in law, Queen Elizabeth Woodville.

For her parentage, the upshot can be alonely this:
She will vent monstrous policy.
Gloucester: Sith Harry's tree is noble, and that he sired fruit
on Woodville stock, what matter's in't? 90
Fortunes few be they that ride such brace of fates.
Percival: I but hold my master's stirrup. I may not conjecture
's purpose, although meseems your grace doth look beyond him,
except to tell, there is matter in it; which did, perhaps,
eye to his grace as he had com'd on the parting of two ways.
Gloucester: Yet chides he me to strive a vie with Elizabeth
who shall claim the right. Power, Percival!
Power is a fickle mistress; vicious are her parts.
Like t'a pleasing strumpet, Power slaves who thinks to hold her.
I can live without it. 100
Percival: Then am I commanded say:
Whoever commands the king commands the crown;
whoever commands the crown commands his sovereignty;
whoever commands the sovereignty commands the right.
Gloucester: Would Harry, by your office, else?
Percival: But only this: By still practice, an astronomer,
full expert of his art, discerneth of sweet influences,
evil aspects, of the stars, as he, in measure,
were endow'd with some celestial force.
To latch England's ear so just, 110
to win good willing of the king, is all.
And if that boon be not soon wrested out, for spite,
noblesse shall fall under disgrace and forfeiture.
Gloucester: Such news is loud. I'll know his inner thought.

---

[238] 2.5.87. *For her parentage*: Given her ancestry.
[239] 2.5.90. *what matter's in't?*: What importance attaches to this?
[240] 2.5.92. *hold my master's stirrup*: I do what I'm told; I say what I'm told to say. The expression rather suggests loyalty than servility.
[241] 2.5.93. *look beyond*: misunderstand, project an unintended meaning
[242] 2.5.106. *still practice*: constant practice § *astronomer*: astrologer.
[243] 2.5.242. *loud*: common knowledge.

Percival: By my loyalty! and lest I pass my bonds,
   I may not move the inmost of my master's heart.
   Howbeit, his grace is famed a hate-wife,
   that doth deadly hate his wife the duchess
   for the lowness of her kind.
Gloucester: Marry, then it is as always was! 120
Percival: I am bidden in sum to say:
   Whither your grace shall lead, thither the duke will follow.
   And a thousand men withal to do your will. So far my master.
Gloucester *calls*: Thomas!

Enter **Thomas**, *behind him.*

Thomas: Aye, sir?
Gloucester: Meat, drink and featherbed for Master Percival.
   To **Percival**: I shall answer you tomorrow such an answer
   as will spur you forth to Brecon. Good Percival,
   rest quiet while you may. I give you fair'st good night. 130
   Thomas *and* **Percival** *withdraw.*
   Harry Buckingham sets his nobility aloft as 'twere his banner,
   his gentle line as 'twere his lance. But thou, Elizabeth,
   mad'st him to wive thy sister; with thy blood
   thou diddest Harry's haughtiness besmirch.
      Wicked one amidst our royal house,
   which wert unworthy Edward should be thine,
   in thy summer of ambition caredst thou little
   how great hating stalk'd behind thy back.
   Here's now thy winter fell. 140 244
   That gav'st for husband to thy sister this ...
   ... this too proud boy become a prouder man,
   reap down the harvest thou didst sow.
   Dark angel, fall from grace! *Exit* 144

---

[244] 2.5.140. *fell*: terrible, cruel. This adjective, used here in post-position, may be mistaken for a form of the verb *to fall*.

ACT 3, SCENE 1

An inn at Northampton. Afternoon, April 29, 1483.

Enter the **Duke of Buckingham**.

Buckingham *calls*: Sola, sola!
  This swine-sty's hollow emptiness. Hollo? Hollo?
  What's gone amiss? Is this our meeting, Percival?

Enter **Percival**, *following*.

Percival: It is assuredly, your grace.
Buckingham: The appointed day?
Percival: On Tuesday, yes.
Buckingham: Are we not timely?
Percival: Aye, 'tis yet long first. ²⁴⁵
Buckingham: Then Gloucester slips the hour.
  Perhaps he passed this by. How will the moon tonight? 10
Percival: A bare straw sliver of her crescent's light.
Buckingham: As how?
Percival: Till her last end, before the dark.
  The old moon dies tonight.
Buckingham: Take honey at the changing, Percival.
Percival: Yea verily, your grace.
Buckingham: It is far days already. The duke nor another
  shall call, if he comes not for't soon at night.
Percival *looks off*: The instance is the sooner for your thought.
  Look where he comes, with Ratcliffe too. 20

---

[245] 3.1.8. *long first*: before the appointed hour, in good time. Knowing he is early, Buckingham then suggests that Gloucester is late, *slips the hour*. The comment says more about Buckingham's personality than the nature of time.

Dark Sovereign 3:1 | 69

Enter **Gloucester**, *attended by* **Ratcliffe**
and several "**Gentlemen of the North**" *in mourning black.* 246

Gloucester: God save you, Harry Buckingham.
Buckingham: Now, Gloucester! and indeed's well y-met.
  Percival hath quite worn my horses to bring us to Northampton.
Percival: The cause why is worthy pains, my lord protector.
Gloucester: Pray you say sooth. It is to wear that title
  in my style I do oppose the queen her compact of iniquity.
  Where lies the king?
Percival: They had like t'have chamber'd hard by us,
  but of a sudden hasted to post hence.
Buckingham: Ha, th'unwelcome mystery. A' leaves a bitter tang. 30
Gloucester: Whereof needs opinion must float. 247
Percival: A penny to an ostler bought a quart;
  a ha'penny more spill'd his intelligence.
Buckingham: Base brazen pence!
  How basest metal doth adulterate the noblest coin.
Gloucester *to* **Percival**: What did your chuff bewray? 248
Percival: Rivers, with the king, had not so soon made alto, 249
  but Lord Grey came spurring hard from London;
  whereon the royal body hurried, not long sin,
  to night at Stony Stratford. 40
Ratcliffe: I am clear in it; that they hope to go beyond us. 250
Buckingham: Well fighteth that well flies. 251
Ratcliffe: They are fain to keep the king
  o' th' windy side of us.

---

[246] S.D. *mourning black*: The apparel of his entourage notwithstanding, Gloucester himself entered London with Edward V some days later wearing purple, a colour of mourning garb which English tradition reserved for the monarch.
[247] 3.1.31. *opinion must float*: we can't draw a firm conclusion, we must keep an open mind.
[248] 3.1.36. *chuff*: low fellow, rustic.
[249] 3.1.37. *made alto*: stopped for the night (Mil.).
[250] 3.1.41. *go beyond*: circumvent, evade, go around.
[251] 3.1.42. The proverb, after Menander, was first cited in English c. 1250, thence to *Hendyng's Proverbs* in the fourteenth century. A parallel evolution in French results in: *Reculer pour mieux sauter*.

Gloucester: Were we but body strong enough!
  So an awful wrong we'd right, and never strike a blow.
Buckingham: The whilst we whine, cur-like, at their hard heels,
  their progress speaks us doom'd their trash.
  These are that nod at every crime,
  and snatch each hufty-tufty beck, fawning on' t. 50
  Only but those shall answer England.
Gloucester: What incantation had you I should reach against them?
Buckingham: Why, take the king; which taken, take authority.
Gloucester: 'Sblood! Hard matter entertainéd too long deep
  hath turn'd to ill suppose. Besides,
  these are the substance of an army, we the shadow.
Buckingham: This self time that friendeth them, to us is foe.
  A sennight hence our nephew will be crown'd,
  the office of Protector outlaw'd,
  and the Council turn'd another way. 60
  Our kingly lad's Great Seal shall prove his charact
  of indentures with his dam. Was never so innocent headsman!
Gloucester: Think you our human handful
  might appease the malice of fierce Mars?
  I might as well charm Sol; slave silver Luna to my car;
  drag Saturn of his everlasting dark; take flight on Mercury.
  I come at this to seek up remedy.
  What name your profit, Harry?
Buckingham: Why, remedy.
Gloucester: How excellently I apprize your profit; 70
  though not a syllab glean'd from Percival,
  whose loyalty speaks silence like the tomb.
  Like lips, like lettuce. Give it form!

---

[252] 3.1.51. *Only but*: except that. § *answer*: give a satisfactory explanation to.
[253] 3.1.55. *ill suppose*: malign intentions.
[254] 3.1.73. *Like lips, like lettuce*: Like meets like. Frequent in the Period.

> I'll hear you shape forth the intent
> would make this conquest its.
> Mark, if you dissímule, I shall not dissemble it!

Buckingham: Then I'll not leave to say't: I hate!
> I hate with hating without end.
> Now, because hatred is a notion mark'd with contrarieties,
> and that it chalks his passage broadly i' th'intent, 80
> therefore needs perforce it must, at last, possess the brain.
> Whose inner man must hate is like t' th'ancient worm, which,
> consuming up his tail, is of his end devour'd.

Gloucester: Meseems you tell the length of your foot,
> and his last, to boot.

Buckingham: You will, I take it, I should count my woes.
> Sum up each Woodville. First and foremost, they put me
> to my wife before my littlest member, riping to
> his stiff-grown age, might raise himself to prove her.
> Secondly, of Edward's gift and copious favour, 90
> Rivers rules my fee in Wales.
> Lastly, that my lands, which, from the house of Bohuns
> fell to me unto the fourth degree, King Edward took away.
> His son, our king and nephew, claims my property.
> What would your grace beside?

Gloucester: I would I wist half so well th'intention of my foes. 96

Exeunt omnes.

---

²⁵⁵ 3.1.74. *intent*: suggests state of mind more than intention.
²⁵⁶ 3.1.75. *its*: OED finds only one instance where the modern neuter possessive pronoun, without an apostrophe, finds its way into a Shakespearean Quarto during the Bard's lifetime: *Henry VIII*, 1.1.18.
²⁵⁷ 3.1.76. *dissímule*: The stress falls on the second syllable. The line suggests: 'If you deceive (me), I shan't overlook it'.
²⁵⁸ 3.1.80. *in th' intent*: See 3.1.74.
²⁵⁹ 3.1.82. *th'ancient worm*: One of the more fabulous creatures in medieval bestiaries. The Urovore, Urobore, Orovore consumed itself by devouring itself tail first. It is represented as a snake describing a perfect circle with its tail deep in its mouth.
²⁶⁰ 3.1.84. *To know the length of (one's) foot*: to understand a man well enough to know his weaknesses.
²⁶¹ *his*: its.
²⁶² 3.1.93. *unto the fourth degree*: through four generations.

ACT 3, SCENE 2

The Rose & Crown, at Stony Stratford. The same afternoon.

*Enter **King Edward V**, **Rivers** and **Richard Lord Grey**. The retinue might include **Sir Thomas Vaughan** and **John Lord Alcock**, bishop of Worcester and tutor to the king.*

King Edward V: What inn is this?
Rivers: It's called, your highness, the *Rose & Crown*.
King Edward V: You choose well, uncle. Very well.
 'Tis just the name fitting to a king.

*Enter a **Messenger**.*

Messenger, *to **Rivers***: Two hours since, my lord,
 Gloucester, wi' th' duke of Buckingham,
 raught Northampton.
Rivers: How many men?
Messenger: As I deem,
 not above the twice three hundred agreed on. 10
Grey: They bide by the terms.
Rivers: It should seem so.
King Edward V: Uncle, why do you impute them
 for willing us ill?
Rivers: The times are fatal,
 which beneath unconstant colours come.
Grey: Trust not other than your near companions,
 brother.
King Edward V: Richard Gloucester is our uncle;
 Harry Buckingham besides. 20
Rivers: Some innocence doth credit you.

---

[263] 3.2.7. *raught*: reached.
[264] 3.2.10. The rancorous negotiation which settled the size of the king's escort at two thousand men, (2.4.108), also resolved that the dukes would bring no more than three hundred men each.

>   Would that his land lack'd less guile 265
>   than his king does.
> **King Edward V**: Why did we post to Stony Stratford,
>   when our uncles attend us at Northampton?
> **Grey**: Why, let me see, it was to make room enough
>   for the dukes to take up their inn.
> **King Edward V**: They might not but imagine
>   that we hold them carelessly;
>   that, disdaining them, we steal'd away. 30
> **Rivers**: I have yet day enough.
>   By your leave I'll reverse,
>   to bid your uncles welcome in your highness' name.
>   *To* **Grey**: Do you, Richard, bide with our company.
>   Command to these country cloynes about
>   to satisfy their king.
>   I'll on, without delay. 37
>   *All go,* **Rivers** *alone.*

ACT 3, SCENE 3

The dukes' inn at Northampton later that evening.

Enter **Gloucester, Buckingham** *and* **Percival** *(mute).*
Enter **Ratcliffe**, *meeting them.*

Ratcliffe: Methinks the sun hath gone aback,
    or I be from my wits for stonishment;
    Earl Rivers keeps way hither!
Buckingham: And how many men?
Ratcliffe: But few.

---

265 3.2.22. *less*: See note on 2.1.15.

Buckingham: The earl is made the stale
    to take us in their seeming tender snare.
Gloucester: Peace, Harry, peace.
    Albeit Rivers is a cunning fox, he's honorable.
    Of his strength he doth contemn us; therein his weakness lies.   10
Buckingham: He contriveth to discover that he may.
Gloucester: Then shall we set a false glass to his gaze,
    and so discover him. Feign we to hide our misery in forc'd content.
Buckingham: So be't. The duke of Buckingham
    not drinks off sorrow wi' a Woodville.

Enter Rivers.

Rivers: I give you, lords, hearty welcome to Northampton
    in King Edward's name. My lord protector,
    know how woe my heart is for the king your brother's death.
Gloucester: The folded brows, in manner of a sexton's dole,   20
    is instance of calamity felt sensibly as spoke.
    If sorrow did cun thank, Rivers,
    I did repay 't as fully with mine own.
Buckingham: Come in, do, before we take diseases
    of some chilling exhalation of the air.
Gloucester: Let's to the table all to dine:
    We'll strew about some cheer instead of griefs.
        They move to sit at table.
Buckingham: Within there! Ho, tapster!

*Enter a **Tapster**.*

    Wine! Fill 's bowls of sack, and Borage for his courage.

---

[266] 3.3.6. *stale*: decoy.
[267] 3.3.29. John Gerard's *Herball* regarding Borage:
    'Pliny calleth it *Euphrosinum*, because it maketh a man merry and joyful: which thing also the old verse concerning Borage doth testify: *Ego Borago gaudia semper ago*: I Borage bring alwaies courage'. An Elizabethan play, *A new and mery enterlude called the Triall of Treasure* (1567), includes the line: 'Drawer, let us have a pint of white wine and Borage'.

In deepest rivers let it flow; the earl requires reason. 30
*The **Tapster** goes.*
Rivers: I thought to find more curious sympathy
under black attires.
Buckingham: Death's a malady no powder can resolve.
We can but stay him a short while wi' wine and good fellowship.
Gloucester: Life smites fire too slight to smother it with woes.

*Enter the **Tapster**. He serves, and goes.*

So, so, Rivers, we shall do you right.
All drink and murmur together.
***Lights** dim into night.*

*Enter **Truth**.*

Truth: The chroniclers of old be severally agreed:
The dukes receiv'd the earl full lovingly ...
Buckingham: Light, there! Fresh pottles!

*Enter **Tapster** with candles and jug. He serves; he goes.*

Truth: The company gave Rivers countenance,
and with true face bade him make cheer. 40
Wherewith, till long within night, they conviv'd.
In fine took they their leave, one of another,
giving each the goodnight "very familiar, with great courtesy".
Thus the earl of Rivers came his ways betimes,
to lodge beside this very inn.
*Exit **Rivers**. **Ratcliffe** and **Percival** make to go.*
The dukes remain'd the coming of the day, whereon bald wish

---

[268] 3.3.30. *requires reason*: a drinking term, *reason* being a euphemism for alcohol.
[269] 3.3.31. *curious*: cautious.
[270] 3.3.35. *do you right*: a drinking term.
[271] 3.3.39. *gave ... countenance*: gave the appearance of amity.
[272] 3.3.46. *remain'd*: waited for.

took root and solid resolution of this slip of opportunity.
Exeunt **Percival** *and* **Ratcliffe**.
Now, the indigést sensations of their cares and wishings
breed their own engíne, until, within the pregnant hour,
the snarling creature of one's hating and the tother's fear
is bodied forth and born. For the rest,
we'll steal behind the arras, and to give these dukes the gaze.
Exeat **Truth**,
leaving **Buckingham** *&* **Gloucester** *slumped at table*.

Buckingham: The noble earl toil'd out his wits to win our policy.

Gloucester: A man may delve to hell
and never fathom notions where is naught.

Buckingham: As to speak of questrists,
we fared worser than the earl: The worst success was ourn.

Gloucester: I am at the latter end of care.
Sleep's toil enfolds me.

Buckingham: Fetch yourself again, or fetch the earl!
He'll dispatch us, for pity, to a deeper sleep, sans cares.

Gloucester: He counter'd with us by jibes and jests.

Buckingham: In right grace and gentle courtesy.
"Lord Protector" quoth he,
but as to let us see their policy, the earl stood mute.
Altissima flumina quaeque minimo sono labi. Bah!
Note how two drops of spongy cheer
dissolve in buckets of despair. We sat,
three bowsy buckets in a well — filling other, aye —
but minding only echoes of the plash.

Gloucester: No matter for that. When all's cull'd out,
or heav'n or hell take their occasion of us all.

---

[273] 3.3.49. The sentence scans in iambs if *indigest* and *engine* take Period phonetic values. OED finds *engine*, stressed on the second syllable, as late as 1632: 'High press thy [Etna's] Flames ... But higher moves the scope of my Engine' (Lithgow). But Marlowe (1588–'9) uses the modern ictus in *Faustus* 1.1.94 (line 123 in Tucker Brooke's edition; Scene I.99, in Folger, Washington Square ed.).

[274] 3.3.65. *To stand mute*: to refuse to plead (Legal).

[275] 3.3.66. The line plays on Rivers' name and reluctance to be open about the Woodvilles' intensions. *Altissima ... sono labi*: The deepest rivers flow with the least sound. Still waters run deep.

Buckingham *revives*: God worshipp'd might he be!
    The very earl gives us occasion to lay hold upon occasion.
    So a worldly-wise man never offer'd eviler occasion to his foes.
Gloucester: The devil he did. How so?
Buckingham: Take we the earl tonight.
    Then betimes to Stony Stratford: We shall attach the king.
    'Twas Rivers styl'd you "Lord Protector".
    No one about the king pretendeth power to resist,   80
    excepting none but him.
Gloucester: You bid me, lonely, pluck Ambition from his top.
    Nothing were so simple, nor so greatly charg'd with fate.
    It sympathies not with reason.
Buckingham: Needs we must fight, no remedy!   276
Gloucester: Whoso take an ill advantage, he leads on a press
    as cannot go aback, but blindly wendeth up a winding stair.
    So strives Ambition, heady, to find heav'n above the clouds,
    except the stair sometime takes end,
    where such as reach Ambition's tricks are cast in jeopardy.   90
Buckingham: Emulate Warwick!
    Took he England and ruled, i' th' name of mad Hal.
Gloucester: And after claim'd it in Edward's name,
    and died attainted.
Buckingham: In sum, Warwick could not prevail
    upon the late-achievéd unity of York.
    Consider that, and speedly, before th'engendering of doubt
    bemire you in old Occam's trap. Th'occasion that's lost,   277
    being scarce, breeds manifold regret.
        Sfx: *A cockerel crows.*
    Drink hath well o'er-ta'en us. Comes now the dawn.   100

---

[276] 3.3.85. *no remedy*: There's no alternative, unavoidably.
[277] 3.3.98. *Occam's trap*: Also 'Occam's Edge' after William of Occam/Ockham. Occam's Principle refers to the sometime human tendency of making things more complicated than they have to be. The original form states: *Entia non sunt multiplicanda praeter necessitatem*, or, loosely, 'Things need not be more complicated than they need be'. So, when confronting a number of different possibilities, start with the simplest. Cf. Lao Tsu, *Tao Te Ching*, 63.

Gloucester: False bird to herald the deceiving light.
The rising of the lark stays yet an hour.
Buckingham: Ware, Gloucester, unless the real morrow
prove as false! Our hurt's not small;
no more is the common griefs of England. Spare for no cost,
no more than if it were the cause of all.
    A time and times the Rose that bare you
wept death-wearied tears for York, which,
claiming England's dear-bought majesty,
did quit it debt with dearest blood.   110
'Twere the devil's undeserving profit, did your father
— his three sons withal — untimely fall in grave.
For nothing!
To sway the diadem doth mitigate abominations.
To lose the rule were death. And treason.
Standing: I'll take me out a pissing while.
I'd purge the wine of fellowship on daisies.
He goes.
Gloucester: Alone. At last alonely and alone.
The nighted hours pass, a quiet wilderness without,
contráry to the noise keeps coil within.   120
How should I think? nor why, with voice of word,
lend mettle and substantial form to thought?
Springs up this maund'ring from a sudden fury of the night?
or wells it from a lock'd up inly fount?
I might as well with plummet sound the bottoms of this cup
as plumb the well of conscience.

---

278 3.3.101. *deceiving light*: zodiacal light (Brit.). False dawn (U.S.).
279 3.3.107. *A time and times*: time and again, time after time. § *the Rose*: Gloucester's mother, the duchess of York, known for her beauty as the Rose of Raby.
280 3.3.115. *treason*: used loosely here in two senses: First, Buckingham suggests that Gloucester's seeming reluctance to act forcefully is sure to betray their family's interests; second, as the charge which would be laid against both dukes in the event of a Woodville supremacy.
281 3.3.120. *noise*: is used as it appeared in the original Folio edition of *Richard III*, 5.3.104: 'I'll strive with troubled noise to take a nap'. The 1597 Quarto and modern eds. have thoughts instead of noise.
282 3.3.126. *conscience*: state of mind, consciousness.

Certs, it is the Málaga that speaks. 283
    'Tis said the soul is fed with charity, 284
but charity contendeth ever to prevail upon base fearful parts.
The mind of man is wax, wherein old use sets to his seal.   130 285
I'faith, it is his learn'd experience breeds each his habitus. 286
This man, this *habitus*, is phoenix-like his gather'd self,
but wanting Charity's pure phoenix-fire
came to his years unpurified.
Seldom suck'd I Charity wi' nurses' milk.
How the devil can I express her?
    Whence welleth thought? and whither flows?
Being mine alone, I speak to me alone. But which self speaks? 287
and whether, as Another I, doth arbitrate his thought, 288
I may not know. Some humour feeds the tongue,   140
which, being feeding, moves noise, so.
Other chooseth out th'opinion ears give audience,
and which reject, as they were darts turn'd by a buckler.
    Lights: *Dawn breaks.*

Enter **Buckingham** *silently. He listens.*

    Speaks Reason to my Will?
or doth proud Will to Reason speak?
The Comedy did anciently set forth how wayward Will 289
strove with his government, the passive voice of Reason.
O, would I wist which captain order'd thought,
prescrib'd it me, dictated every deed.

---

283 3.3.127. *Málaga*: White wine (sack) from Málaga.
284 3.3.128. The line is John Wyclif's.
285 3.3.130. *old use*: a life's experience. Also 'old experience', Shaks.; 'long experience', Spenser; 'learned experience', Bacon; 'the powder of experience', Gabriel Harvey. Here's the sentence as a whole: The mind of man is wax that becomes impressed/influenced by life's experiences.
286 3.3.131. *habitus*: nature, character, disposition. After Cicero. Cf. Shaks.: 'How old use doth breed a Habitus of a man'.
287 3.3.138. *mine alone*: alone, by myself (Northern).
288 3.3.139. *Another I*: A second self. Also 'Another myself' since 1577.
289 3.3.146. *The Comedy*: Dante Alighieri's *Divine Comedy* (*la Divina Commedia*).

> Whether doth the Will or Reason urge me fasten on occasion   150
> of this night to sway the rule on England?
> If either door gaped wide, mankind would wholly righteous be
>   — or damn'd. How stony is the way 'twixt Reason and the Will,
> to judgment.

Buckingham *pretends a noisy entrance*: A wink ago
  I catch'd th'odd ends "To judgment". Clear dawn is sprung,
  and time's no more by night delay'd.   290

Enter **Percival** *and* **Ratcliffe**.

> The question's so brief, needs the answer were briefer:
> Shall you sit in judgment? or be judg'd?

Gloucester *does not turn*: So, so, it falls to that.   160
  All hangs by this betide. *Sweeps a mug to the floor*   291
  with the back of his hand. Calls: Ratcliffe!

Ratcliffe: Aye.

Gloucester: Summon up the meinie.   292
  Do captains with our inwards presently attend,
  in stockings, lest they rouse the house.
    Ratcliffe *goes*.
    Buckingham *signals* **Percival**, *who goes too*.
  We make the devil's means to fasten a good intention.

Buckingham: To brook our name without reproach.

Gloucester: Nothing brook conceit!
  Imaginations smack of women's longings.   170

Enter **Ratcliffe** *with Gloucester's* **"Men in Black"**;
Enter **Percival** *with Buckingham's* **Retainers**.

---

[290] 3.3.157. *time's no more by night delay'd*: Beyond the literal meaning, the line plays on to *delay time*, meaning to put off, to procrastinate.

[291] 3.3.161. *betide*: event, chance, opportunity.

[292] 3.3.164. *the meinie*: household, followers, retainers. In some cases the word has been lost in modern editions of Renaissance texts, being confused with a homonym, *the many*. Compare the equivalent use of *Household* in 2.4.123.

Buckingham: Pluto's shades! we make a dark, infernal company.
Gloucester, *standing, turns at last*: I give you "good morrow"
  of more than ordinary courtesy. May good befall us every way.
Buckingham, *more excited than drunk*: We not ceas'd t'invoke
  our every art of argument the whole night long;
  plied Rivers wi' that honeyedness at whose hest
  solemn humours stretch like cheveral skins, and melting,   293
  speak, professing unwise Truth — not a whit less foolishly
  than Reason does — whose each sworn enemy is drink;
  wherewith brains want not to give licence to the lips,   180
  who, by large drinking, no more seek to brains,
  the rather take it. No. Nor Lethe mist,
  nor Morpheus' inly wont dimm'd Argus' careful eyes;
  nor aught effected they to expedite the intercourse of state.   294
Gloucester: In sum, though Buckingham breathes after orat'ry   295
  as if he were the living inspirations of Demosthenes,

---

293 3.3.177. *cheveral skins*: Cheveral leather is so pliant and stretchable that it came to figure in expressions like 'The lawyers have such cheveral consciences' (Philip Stubbes, *The anatomie of abuses*, 1583). The notion is frequent in the Period, passing into *Romeo and Juliet*, II.iv.87, and *Henry VIII*, II.iii.32.

In the 1920s, Edgar Innes Fripp used Shakespeare's frequent references to cheveral (and other leathers) to support his argument that the Bard had once worked at his father's leather trade. He probably did, but Fripp's argument, in so far as it rests on the cheveral figure, represents a circular logic all too common in literary analysis of character and background. It fails to recognize the idioms of contemporary language. The pliant property of cheveral was widely used as a metaphor since the 1570s, and owes nothing to Shakespeare or his origins. Quite the reverse. Scholars often fail to recognize Shakespeare's debt to the rich common fund of English.

This tendency is best illustrated in the expression 'Lend me your ears' (*Julius Caesar*, 3.2.78). No other line in his canon is so quintessentially 'Shakespeare'. But the use of *lend* in this sense goes back to fourteenth century Scotland. Once again it is Philip Stubbes in *The anatomie of abuses* (1583) who uses the expression more than a decade before Shakespeare plucked it from the voices around him to use in *A Lover's Complaint, Julius Caesar* and *Hamlet*. Stubbes' line reads: 'The sweeter the Syren singeth, the dangerouser is it to lend hir our eares'.

That Shakespeare is mistakenly credited with the authorship of very many common English phrases complicated the task of writing *Dark Sovereign*. In at least two places (3.7.1, 4.8.1) this play could have used something like 'Lend me your ears'. But that figure and several others were never used, lest they be construed as plagiarism.

294 3.3.184. *We not ceas'd t'invoke ... intercourse of state*: A play written in Period style would be negligent if it failed to include at least one passage combining a complex Shakespearian sentence with Christopher Marlowe's interminable lists of classical example and metaphor — and Ben Jonson's love of the abstruse. This passage, Buckingham's address to the retainers, is as close as *Dark Sovereign* intends to come.

295 3.3.185. *breathes after*: aspires to.

    Rivers told us nothing.
    No spark of 's policy might we discern.
Buckingham: From hence conciliation's banish'd [296]
    with the rags of night.   190
    Clear dawn arrays our fasten'd mind wi' harsher stratagem.
Gloucester: We seek a bloodless upshot, yet, fall what will fall,
    the power on England shall be restor'd in blood. [297]
    But 'tis a victory must be won by sleights and cunning tricks.
    Edward's meinie overbears us three and more to one. [298]
    Harden your heart as it were an hammer forg'd at the fire.
    Be you loath to do 't, or do your heart reproach you
    to the quick, rip compassion's dart from each his breast,
    else we shall perish, they prevail.
    It shall go hard with us but we our cause sustain.   200 [299]
    To a **Captain**: Take the earl where he lies.
    Look weapon nor word diminish your resolve.
    Th'adventure is but lost an' if Rivers wins to the king.
        Exit the **Captain**.
    To **Captain 2**: Take horse enough; go ride toward Stony Stratford.
    Let none pass, save by my only writ. No desperate message
    from Rivers must fore-run us to the king. *Exit* **Captain 2**.
    To **Captain 3**: Inform the watch upon every gate:
    Lock up Northampton! None shall enter, none goes out.
    Do it! *Exit* **Captain 3**.
Rivers, *voice off*: Ho!   210
Gloucester: What's the matter there?
    Off: *Sounds of strife*.
Rivers, *off*: Give over to handle me! My life is humbled
    but to the king. Never I'll be humbled to iniquity.
    Unhand me, there! I will see Gloucester.

---

[296] 3.3.189. *From hence*: In consequence, For which reason.

[297] 3.3.193. *restor'd in blood*: restored to the rightful blood-line.

[298] 3.3.195. *overbears us*: outnumbers us.

[299] 3.3.200. *but*: unless.

Enter **Rivers**, *guarded by "Men in Black".*

    Ha! The very fount and front of treason!
Gloucester: Remedy, my lord. Otherwise there is none.   300
    To the **Escort**: Do the earl to breakfast, sirs.
    Leave not to put him in comfort. Good cheer, Rivers.
Rivers: Dearth reward the doing of it; death revenge the act;
    the devil pick the scraps!   220
Gloucester: We shall treat upon it later. Courage yet.
    All will be well. *To the* **Meinie**: The rest, come all to horse.
    Before the forenoon has climbed away we'll overget the king.   223
    All go, variously.

ACT 3, SCENE 4

The Rose & Crown, Stony Stratford. Later that morning.

Enter **King Edward V**, *attended by* **Grey**, **Vaughan** *and* **Alcock**.

King Edward V: Wherefore is the earl?
    The dial declares two hours of day.
Vaughan: He linger'd yesternight with your uncles at Northampton.
    To agree at the table is a melting dose
    as full of slumber as to quaff a sleeping cup of dwale.   301
    I warrant they but tarried over-long.
King Edward V: Now tarry they over late to day!
Alcock: They'll be here presently, your majesty,

---

[300] 3.3.216. *Otherwise there is none*: plays on 'There is no remedy' or 'No remedy!', meaning 'There is no way out of it', or 'There is no alternative (except to…)' cf. 3.3.85.

[301] 3.4.5. *dwale*: sleeping nightshade. *Solanum soporiferum* Turner (1538); sleeping nightshade, Gerard (1597). *Dwale* was applied to several herbs with soporific properties, including Black and Woody Nightshades, *Solanum nigrum and Dulcamara* (Linn.), and Deadly Nightshade, *Atropa belladonna* (Linn.).

according well-a-fine in one.
They have not visited each other oft before. 10
King Edward V: The queen will we should haste towards London.
Our privilege dependeth of our duty, lords,
our duty from our state; whereof we go.
To **Grey**: Give order, brother. To horse! We journey.
Uncle and his dukes must catch us that catch may.
They make to go.

Enter **Gloucester**, **Buckingham** *and their* **Retainers**.

King Edward V: Uncles! for so I guess you; whom to disguise,
inchoate mem'ry drawn from childhood doth compound
with our too long remove.
Gloucester *kneels*: God give your majesty His grace.
Buckingham: God give your grace good morrow. 20
King Edward V: Welcome, uncles both, with all my heart.
Gloucester: May He endue your highness with your subjects' love,
to the largest profit of your state.
King Edward V: Prithee stand up, uncle.
Gloucester *remains kneeling*: If words were troops,
were phrases báttailons, such drums have I struck up, 302
such cornets wound, to marshal their dark sentences
that spell my woe upon your father's death …
King Edward V: We thank you, uncle,
that are blood and party in our griefs. 30
Gloucester: … to none effect,
for death forbeareth no fit epitaph, save life is rais'd anew. 303
'Sbody! every inch you are to Edward son.
King Edward V: Uncle, I beseech you, stand. Where is Uncle Rivers?
Gloucester *kneeling*: The earl's detain'd, nephew,
safe-chamber'd to Northampton.

---

302 3.4.26. *báttailons*: the word, though English, had come recently enough from French that Period spelling suggests a French pronunciation with the ictus on the first and third syllables. The more recent English *battálion* resulted from transposition (metathesis) of *i* and *l*.

303 3.4.32. *forbeareth*: makes no allowance for an epitaph.

King Edward V: With what disease detain'd?
  I'll know, my lord, straightway!
Buckingham: No sickness troubles him,
  saving he impos'd him some slight surfeit,   40
  too irreverently for his too reverend age.
King Edward V: You maze me, uncles, cruelly.
  We'll know what this note signifies.
Gloucester: The Earl of Rivers' plots
  hath fetch'd him in his proper snare.   [304]
Grey: Riddle me, riddle me, what is this?
Gloucester: Your father, from a child, wore the pious exemplar
  of King Harry in his bosom. So well he liv'd, unbeblot,
  as he did reign; until in 's latter days the vices of his flatt'rers
  overbore his noble spirit, scouring his resolve …   50
Vaughan: Never, never, never was it thus.
Gloucester: … whose worse than vile affections
  counsell'd worser deeds: The which drew in your sire,
  all too unwitting, toward that corrupted appetite
  doth feed temptation.
  Your inwards, Rivers and the Marquis chiefest among them,
  inveiléd thus their king whom they would master.
  These were his pretenc'd companions in their vice.
Alcock: No, sirs!
Grey: He lies in his throat.
King Edward V: What my brother Marquis is about I cannot say, 60
  but in good faith I dare well answer for my uncle Rivers
  and my brother Grey, that they be innocent of any such deceits. [305]
Grey *to the King*: And if you yield, brother,
  you yield us to their wrath.
Alcock: Their face is set against us;
  and more than so, their company is hideous to see to.   [306]

---

[304] 3.4.44. *proper*: own, of his own making.
[305] 3.4.62. Some passages in this scene derive from an early translation of More, adapted to Period date and style. Seward, *Richard III*, p.94, gives More's dramatization of the event.
[306] 3.4.66. *and more than so*: and more than that: Cf. 3 *Henry VI*, III.iii.l03 (Cambridge).

Vaughan: These deadly fear me. If your highness fail,
   they look as they would put us out of life.
   For a surety these dukes be death writ twice.
King Edward V: Good uncles, these were true servants   70
   to our father's peace. I cannot be secur'd
   but that in likewise they'll serve mine.
Gloucester: Nephew, in their heart they rail at thee.
   Sweet Edward, strong sinew'd, prosperous in each resolve,
   lies rotted. These same that claim for England
   in thy tender name are those as went about
   to do your father die.
Vaughan: Swallow that ordure down!
Gloucester: Above the rest, I lay this fulsome thing
   most nearly to their charge.
King Edward V: These are even the same comfortable companions
   to my youth.   80
Gloucester: They have confin'd thee from the court.
Buckingham: It is to deny to suffer them their plot
   the earl of Rivers lies detainéd prisoner.
   'Twas not his grossest crime, though grossly rash,
   to sever Gloucester's office of protector of your majesty …
Gloucester: … That was your father his ay-living Will.
   Standing: Whereby do I possess mine office while now denied.
Grey: Which style the royal Council did resolve was abrogate.
   The better part brought to effect to signify your grace
   chief councillor, among the rest.   90
Buckingham: Speaks here the even advocate
   did plead the justice on't. Shall Grey and Woodville
   rule as Warwick wrought on wretched Hal?
King Edward V: Good my lords,
   upon the queen my mother's counsel, and in these, I rest.

---

[307] 3.4.71. *secur'd*: persuaded, convinced.
[308] 3.4.79. *most nearly*: especially, particularly.
[309] 3.4.87. *while*: until (Northern).

Buckingham: It is not women's bus'ness to govern. 310
Gloucester: I, for my part, nephew, do content thee,
    that to do my diligence I'll nothing fail,
    nor shall neglect that appertains a subject
    loyal to your majesty.
King Edward V: Great words suffice no more to clothe intent. 100
    The bare of truth is you have ta'en me prisoner.
Gloucester: 'Tis neither so, nor so. Thou art my king, 311
    my brother's blood, whom I acknowledge and to guard
    from wayward, froward and mischiévous counsels
    of thy mother's kin.
    To his **Men**: Arrest these of their treason!
        The dukes' **Men** *move to arrest the king's* **Party**.
Grey: Proud lords, you do exceed the compass of authority.
Buckingham: The prouder fool, you reap but as you sow'd.
Vaughan: Who wears the highest crown, protect the king!
Alcock: God keep your highness!
    Jesu nostri miserere: tu nos pasce, nos tuere. 110   312
    They go. Weeping, **King Edward** *is surrounded*
    *by other "***Men in Black***", and led away.*
    Ratcliffe *remains with the* **Dukes**.
Gloucester *to* **Ratcliffe**: Hie it to the captain of the Welsh.
    Chide him, in my voice, if he'd see Severn more, 313
    disband his troops and turn their foreign backs from England.
    And if, unmannerly, they lay rebellious ears upon your English speech,
    do them to wit the lord protector speaks;
    who them constrains straightways to Wales.
    Give them remove, today.
        Exit **Ratcliffe**.
    Why so, it's done. The end was here begun.

---

[310] 3.4.96. *bus'ness*: The word still had three audible syllables in the Period. Bourchier (Canterbury) uses it that way in 4.6.42. Drayton gives *business* (line 30) to preserve metre, in *The Moone-calfe* (1627).

[311] 3.4.102. *'Tis neither so, nor so*: Frequent in the Period, to refute a string of allegations.

[312] 3.4.110. *Jesu ... tuere*: 'Jesus, have mercy on us: sustain us and preserve us'. From *Lauda Sion*.

[313] 3.4.112. *in my voice*: in my name. Cf. 2.5.70.

Buckingham: How chance swart furrows hath effac'd
    the lately-purchas'd laurel from your brows? 120
Gloucester: You mark a queasy conscience stomaching
    which liefer me were swallow down than choke with it. 314
Buckingham: If Conscience virtue has,
    'tis that she bindeth up the weak to aid the strong.
    The crying puss-cat is, as it were, th'unperfect work of Nature
    making lions. Does your lion weep to seize the lamb?
    Or doth a mighty cry salt tears to fall upon his prey 315
    that in his turn would turn to fall on him?
    High Nature naturing — or God —
    hath natur'd His each creature with it fang or claw. 130
    Come away, lord; unwish nothing.
    Compassion's Nature's fools' cloth: 316
    Never it shall be the stuff of Nature's politics.
    Be acknown of this: Of strength comes victory; 317
    and knowing that, be strong. 135
    They go.

---

314 3.4.122. *swallow down*: retract.

315 3.4.127. *a mighty*: a powerful man.

316 3.4.132. *Compassion's Nature's fools' cloth*: Compassion is the mark (uniform) of Nature's fools.

317 3.4.134. *Be acknown of this*: Be apprised of this. Realize or recognize this. Make yourself understand this. This expression is more usual in a negative context.

ACT 3, SCENE 5

London, that evening. April 30, 1483.

Enter **Howard** *and* **Hastings**.

Hastings: Cannot you smell it, Howard? feel?
    discern the lightening impress'd in night?
    Suffer me joy'd! The dukes heal England's chame.   318
Howard: Pray the news holds for true, Hastings.
Hastings: I'll wager Calais upon it. 'Tis such sweet news
    as doth unburden England of her queen.
    Hardly can I check myself from laughing.
Howard: How unburden'd, yet untreasur'd too: 319
    Sir Edward is laid off to sea
    with that the Marquis emptied of th'Exchequer.   10
Hastings: God grant their villainy destroy them.
Howard: God rather grant our treasure home.
    Meanwhile 'tis bobbing by the lump
    in leaky bottoms on th'inconstant deep,
    crying mercy of French pirates and Lord Cordes.   320

---

318 3.5.3. *chame*: a variant of chaum, meaning crack or fissure. *OED* cites it once (1559) as cracks in skin, which might disqualify it here; but the word appears in early editions of *Richard II*, II.i.63: 'England ... is now bound in with chame, With inky blots, and rotten parchment bonds'. Globe and Cambr. eds. render the word *shame*, although there is no instance of *shame* taking an initial c later than the fourteenth century. Elsewhere in that passage the words *shame* (line 106) and *shameful* (line 66) both take modern spelling. Which makes the early emendation of *chame* to *shame* in line 63 inexplicable; it is inappropriate with respect to key elements — 'inky blots' and 'parchment' — in that sentence. A chame or fissure in 'rotten parchment bonds' would seem more consonant to the intent of Shakespeare's expressed thought. Parchment is skin, and liable to crack. Surely that is the original intent of his line. The variant, *chaum*, was used by Holland (1601) in: 'chawmes, and gaping gulfs'.

319 3.5.8. *How*: However.

320 3.5.15. *Lord Cordes*: The French commander, Philippe de Crèvecœur, seigneur d'Esquerdes (1418–1494), appointed Marshal of France in 1486. As Maréchal des Cordes, he was feared for his attacks on English shipping and south coast settlements.

Hastings: These Jacks-out-of-office do defy the verdict.
    They set Fortune's very spite at naught to do their kind.

Howard: I'faith they take no little recompense.

    ***Sfx**: Noise off.*

    Precious coals! How's this?

*Enter **Ned**, drunk, supported by **Will** and **Kate**.*

Ned: Walk slow, brave Will — I prithee, gentle Kate.
    Though all the surly world wag up and down
    and throw his shag both to and fro,
    yet a body has his station to uphold.

Will: Although he be a whoreson
    and a scullion's prentice to the Marquis, aye.

Ned: Did not I tell … ?

Will: Many a many time.

Kate: And ofter!

Ned: A sennight since told I the Marquis loud:
    Thy kingly bab shall never come a king to London.
    The Fates, quoth I, resolve his voyage royal to terminate.

Kate: If divination were descried of hydromancy in an ale-jug,
    all the Wisdom of the Father would be your.

Ned: Nay, sweet Kate, 'twas not a penny jug,
    but plain as you to them 's are wise to know.

Will: Stiff your tongue, Ned. Here's gentles here.

Ned: Gentiles? An' they take up us, I'll swagger wi' 'em.

Howard *to **Hastings***: Curse these loobies, how they stink.
    This rabble knows not persons.

---

[321] 3.5.17. *to do their kind*: to be true to their character.

[322] 3.5.34. *penny jug*: may be played as mere response, or as an insult, depending on the emphasis placed upon 'but plain as you' in the next line. *Jug* was diminutive for Joan or Joanna, coming to be applied to whores, or other women low in the social order.

[323] 3.5.36. *gentles*: persons of good birth, gentlemen.

[324] 3.5.37. *take up*: confront, swagger; quarrel.

[325] 3.5.39. *to know persons* implied recognizing and respecting persons of quality.

Hastings *to* **Howard**: It speaks to our advantage so. 40
    If they have anything to tell, let them tell it here, in Gath.
Ned *shouts*: Look to the Twins!
Will: These ge'men be no *gemini*, chy not grant.
Kate: Twins is that his drunkard sees,
    a foggy, merry world, scry'd twice.
    Uphold, rascal! Hogshead, stand!
Ned, *looking up*: Look to the Twins, the starry twins above!
Losing his balance he falls on his back:
Who hath the gutter to his bed is king of welkin high.
Will: Get up, Ned! Greedy bladder, stand!
Ned, *supported*: Behold, whence I command the Milky Way, 50
    the heavenly orbs, and all the deep therein.
    'Twas lodging thus, at the sign o' th' moon,
    that I descried the ostent: Castor without Pollux doth protend
    a misadventur'd journey. When one impedes the tother's power,
    he speaks the most unlucky hour.
Will: Woot thou divine the stars? Ha!
    Thou art so steep'd in piss and ale
    a lanthorn would not glimpse before thy nose.
Kate: Suchlike stars thou canst discern
    are lofted in the hollow orbit of thy head. 60
Ned: Sweet Kate, sweet Lady Kate, how dost thou *move* my blood.
Kate: Roarer, get up!
Ned: Never I laid a better whore adown.
Kate: 'Sdeath, Sir Dogs'-meat, I said not rise, but raise!

---

[326] 3.5.41. *tell it in Gath*: 'let them tell it here, to us, the enemy'. This plays on a once popular expression, after 2 Samuel 20: 'Tell it not in Gath, publish it not in the streets of Askelon/Ashkelon'. In other words, keep your mouth shut behind enemy lines (lest your accent betray you).

[327] 3.5.43. *chy*: is the nominative pronoun for the first person singular, namely 'I'. See 3.6.106–153, a scene largely written in 'Mummerset'.

[328] 3.5.52. *at the sign o' th' moon*: in the open.

[329] 3.5.53. *ostent*: omen. § *Caster without Pollux*: In mythology, the twin gods could never both be in heaven or hell at the same time. In medieval astrology, to see one of the stars and not the other did not bode well for travellers. It was advisable to postpone one's journey pending a better omen. Perhaps the superstition was based on the ship of that sign in which Paul continued his journey to Rome after being shipwrecked (Acts 28.11).

[330] 3.5.60. *lofted*: stored (in the loft).

Ned: Though every pike in London quarter in my Lady Kate,
yet I rise up to thee.
Kate: Thy staff is pickerel than a pike,
more fallen off than fell,
and flappy as a slip o' shotten herring.
Ned grapples; **Kate** *defends;* **Will** *tries to part them.*
Howard, *to* **Hastings**: These shit-rags is but fools. 70
Hastings: For all they're witless,
we shall take their intelligence in worth.
Howard: What can they but twice-sodden coleworts?
London seethes — but 'tis stew'd news.
Hastings: The common voice was ever folly and his whore.
However, in this time we were best hark to virgin dirt.
Come in, Howard.
We shall contest against the measure of this ale-votary.
Howard *and* **Hastings** *approach the others.*
What scum are these dare waste God's peace of night?
Will: Alack, your honours, we come on this great knave
cast here for shame. 80
Ned: Nor 'twas for shame; cast hither through mishap!
Kate: Aye, round man, fie, for shame.
Howard, *regarding* **Ned**: The sturdy lubber stops the ditch!
Ned: A ditch is a flux is a posset a-run through the course.
All's mix'd in corruption, without as within.
This life is a wasteful cock; whereupon I do commend
to your worships your unexampl'd humble servant's
rueful paradox: When I tip up the brim to sip escape,
the selfsame nectar raiseth high my spirit to the stars
doth raze my body, e'en this full so sorry temple, 90
to base earth.

---

³³¹ 3.5.67. *than*: rather than, more than. The fifth word in this line, *than* is sufficient to suggest a word which we would listen for in modern English, *more*. The line in full reads: 'Thy staff is [more a] pickerel than a pike'.
³³² *fell*: potent, useful.
³³³ *shotten*: fish that has spawned, and therefore limp, dying.
³³⁴ 3.5.73. *twice-sodden coleworts*: Literally, twice cooked cabbage. Figurative: 'old news'.
³³⁵ *Wasteful cock*: ditch, drain.

> When I would liefest lightly 'scape this mort'lest flesh,
> he lights most heavily on ground, to mortify.
>
> **Howard**: 'Sblood! I am fain to stick this fellow for a hog.
>
> **Ned**: The world has caught you tardy, sir. Pray spare your blade.
> My master, Marquis Dorset, runs up and down,
> swearing by his Christendom we shall be spitted upon a boar's tooth
> before the moon is new. Duke Richard has usurp'd the crown.
>
> **Hastings**: Edward the Fift is our king!
> To claim otherways were treason.
>
> **Ned**: Your honours may arrest me and you will.
> Myself rests from his provéd case — *Habeo corpus!*
> By these too fleshly presents you may see,
> that first and foremost am I prisoner for me.
>
> **Will**: Chi'll warrant ye, 'tis this self king his service
> doth venture us by night.
>
> **Howard**: How so, sirrah, do you serve the king?
>
> **Will**: The Marquis bid us fetch in troops.
>
> **Ned**: To take his groats …
>
> **Kate**: Old groats, great sterling groats.
>
> **Ned**: … and fight against his foes.
>
> **Will**: Dorset musters his soldiers at Westminster.
>
> **Ned**: Pah! Great Caesar had despair'd to find stray curs enow
> to summon up a ragged cohort in this watch of nightingales.
> *He lies down.*
>
> **Kate**: Each bush is a house divided.
> Who be in her majesty's service proclaim the queen.
>
> **Will**: The lump doth shout out "Gloucester, Buckingham
> and doughty Hastings", swearing God's each oath
> this work was justly done.

---

[336] 3.5.95. *The world has caught you tardy*: You're late. The world got to me first.
[337] 3.5.110. Metal in the new groat coin (worth fourpence) was officially debased in 1483.
[338] 3.5.114. *watch of nightingales*: Ironic. Suggested wakefulness in Middle English.
[339] 3.5.115. *bush*: tavern.
[340] 3.5.117. *The lump*: The majority.

Kate: They deem Duke Richard may of right sunder the prince   120
    from his mam. What a cry of heroes! March mad they be,
    that gird them up and goad them on
    wi' flagons o' martial valour, drunk at a draught.
    Each, louder than his fellows, boasts it, bragging war,
    until he's smote wi' heats and silly fits.
Ned, *rousing*: Strong drink greases the gullet of a man
    until his wits slide, slipping down,
    to take up lodging in his arse.
Howard: The pig has found his judgment seat!
Ned: Sloth tardy common sense hangs back, chary of caco-zeal.   130
Kate: Who have a favour to the queen hie it to Westminster.
Will: Who cry up Gloucester hence towards London,
    claiming for the bloody colour of their deeds
    the shadow of Lord Hastings.
Howard, *to **Hastings***: Whether you will or no, my lord,
    you are appointed enemy to such as these,
    General to the other half of rabble.
Hastings: War reeks from every breath.
Howard: This trash spends them words
    for much ado and little help.   140
    In truth, there should most words be spent
    where 's hope to breed of both sides remedy.
    Shall you, like Janus, open doors to war?
    or garner up the peace? 'Tis of your gift,
    to brew a storm of arms, or slake their fear.
Ned, *standing*: Fig me if you will, here is the case.
    Great lords and mighty,
    being possess'd of greatly bigger snouts than mine,
    slop up surpassing greater riches
    from the greatest golden hogs' trough   150
    England may them gift. Beshrew me for a hog?

---

[341] 3.5.130. *caco-zeal*: misplaced enthusiasm, zealotry. (Cf. cack-handed, clumsy.)

[342] 3.5.140. *much ado and little help*: much noise and fuss to no effect.

[343] 3.5.146. *Fig me*: Give me the finger, Curse me.

No ring of gold adorneth this swine's snout!
As to those nobles, I let not a fart, mind not a fig;
pox take them off; Hob and the devil make sport at their games!
*He goes, assisted by **Kate** and **Will**.*

Hastings: Come away, Howard. Hie we to Westminster.
I am fain to put the queen in comfort. 157
They go.

ACT 3, SCENE 6

*"Cheynygates", the Abbot of Westminster's apartment.
After midnight, April 30/May 1, 1483. A moonless night.* 344

*Enter **Monks** in file, chanting "Miserere mei" (Ps. 50/A.V. Ps. 51).
They cross the stage and go, chanting sotto voce in the wings.*

Sfx: *Three loud knocks on a great door.*

Enter the abbot, **Father John Esteney**, *dishevelled.* 345

Abbot: Three knocks he knocks.
What's he that raps the number of the Holy Ghost?
and signifieth family? But conflict also comes of three.
Calls: Who knocks?

---

[344] I am grateful to P.K. Seidelmann, Director, Nautical Almanac Office, U.S. Naval Observatory, for supplying the lunar cycle during the time covered by *Dark Sovereign*.

[345] 3.6. *Note*: The abbot of Westminster from 1474 until his death on 24th May, 1498, was John Esteney. Before being elected abbot, Brother Esteney had held many lesser offices since 1442. I am grateful to N.H. MacMichael, Keeper of the Muniments at Westminster Abbey, who sent me photocopies of pp.148–9 from E.H. Pierce's *Monks of Westminster* (Cambridge, 1916). MacMichael wrote: 'At the baptism of the future Edward V in 1470 the Abbot (Millyng) and the Prior (Esteney) were godfathers to the prince and Lady Scrope was godmother'. MacMichael is the author of *Westminster Abbey, Official Guide* (Jarrold & Sons, 1977, Norwich).

Sfx: Three more knocks.
Two threes is six: He speaks the ancient star.   346
Male he signifies, and female, conjoin'd, and yet oppos'd.
Sfx: Three more knocks.
Ever thrice he knocks, and three times three is nine.
The wheel is turn'd, a circle done,
the old is out, and new renew'd anew.
But here beneath, whoso would whelm his devil   10
needs must learn his name; for sure no Christian soul,
only but Satan's, keep this hour.
Crosses himself, calls: What's he that knocks without?
Servant, *voice off*: Open, sirrah! Watchman, ope your door!
Abbot: No watchman I, saving for Jesus' holy name.
He is the abbot whom you tumble from his bed.
Servant, *voice off*: I mind not whether y'are watchman,
abbot, or Saint Peter, only do you open up this door!
Abbot: No honest man, no, nobbut rascals,
prowl so deep o' stealthy night. What make you up?   20   347
Servant, *voice off*: W'are of the queen's part.
Sir abbot, open, for Elizabeth, your queen.
Abbot: Whate'er you be will I should be a fool to thee.
Did Michael's host beat at this gate i' silent o' th' night
I shall demand a sign.   348
Q. Elizabeth, *voice off*: Father John,
know me by my voice, if you'll not know my name.

---

346 3.6.5. *the ancient star*: The six-pointed Star of David originates in pagan art. The symbol combines the dual forces recognized in many religions. The equilateral triangle pointing upward represents fire, the sky and the male force; the triangle pointing down represents water, the earth and the female force. They combine to represent the whole. Celtic culture had evolved the same symbolism independently. Cf. *Vita Merlini* and the *Mabinogion*.

347 3.6.20. *stealthy night*: It is not night which is stealthy but the act of prowling. This figure, hypallage, is characteristic of English literature through much of its history, and common in the Period.

348 3.6.24. *I shall demand a sign*: In this usage *shall* was soon replaced by *should*. The transition was under way during the Period. Compare, in the KJV, the use of *shall* in Matthew 20.32 and Luke 18.41, with *should* in Mark 10.51. And yet all four Gospels were translated by the Oxford group of scholars working to create the KJV.

Abbot: Your highness!
   Aside: Now, what grief is toward?
Q. Elizabeth: Prithee, ghostly father, grant me sanctuary anon.   30
   Abbot, *aside*: Did not the screech-owl mock my prayers at complin?
   I thought he was siníster.
Q. Elizabeth: A dozen zodiacs agone,
   when Warwick strove to give my lord the overthrow,
   I was deliver'd of your king, your godson Edward,
   in this self sanctuary. And has the abbot's bed
   a piebald lozeng'd tapestry above it still?
   and martlets on the written coffer at the feet?
Abbot, *aside*: And not a scruple since I lay on it!
   Calls: Aye, madam, you are she.   40
   Aside: Ay me, that venter out of Christ's blessing
   into the warm sun. God wot which trouble comes in apace.
   This queen were bet yclep'd Pandora to be true,
   but "Knock and it shall be opened ... " *He opens the door.*

Enter a chaos of **Q. Elizabeth**, *the* **Duke of York** *(10), the queen's eldest daughter,* **Elizabeth of York** *(17), with others of the queen's five* **Daughters** *by King Edward; the royal family jostled by a stream of* **Servants** *bringing the household's valuables and furnishings to the abbey for safekeeping.*

Abbot, *calling across confusion*: God send you, madam.
   Aside: And pray dispose, for of a sudden I am abbot of misrule!
   To heaven: Father, wherefore dost thou visit upon thy servants
   women in the night? Was this a jest?
   Or dost thou scourge us throughly of our sin?

---

349 3.6.29. *toward*: afoot, taking place.
350 3.6.30. *ghostly father*: spiritual advisor § *anon*: once more, again.
351 3.6.32. *siníster*: Cf.1.3.39.
352 3.6.38. *written coffer*: a carved or illustrated chest.
353 3.6.42. *venter out of Christ's blessing into the warm sun*: To pass from a better to a worse situation. A standard expression of the time.
354 3.6.44. St. Matthew's Gospel, 7.7.
355 3.6.46. *abbot of misrule*: This character, the abbot of *unreason* in Scotland, presided over revels and festival mayhem on holidays.

Whatever it be, lead us not into temptation. 50
Q. Elizabeth: Father John, this holy place
is destinied to be of me alway a part.
Abbot: Though from Mother Church we put ourselves asunder, madam,
yet she never puts us away. 356
What trouble brings you to so a dreadful pass?
Q. Elizabeth: Lost! My life, my children's life, all lost!
Abbot: What woe the realm's
to bring his queen 'pon such distress?
Q. Elizabeth: The king is foully ta'en by Gloucester.
All life, all honour is slung out and lost. 60
I am black, father. 357
Abbot: As toward the hurt of England's daughter I am hurt.
Q. Elizabeth: Astonishment hath taken hold on me.
Abbot, *aside*: Her front doth look t'have forfeited her soul.
O, to find some comfortable word,
ere melancholy draw black flight at frenzy.
To the Queen: Is it deep or no, my child,
meseems thy wounding is not grievous.
Q. Elizabeth: That I have done should cry against me!
Abbot: True repentance is the hasty path from sin. 70
Q. Elizabeth: Mine was but the error! Gloucester hath the sin!
The Abbot *beckons off.*

Enter a monk, Brother Godfrey.

Abbot: Again, Godfrey!
Bid Eric ring the tocsin bell.
Exit Brother Godfrey.
Q. Elizabeth: Hastings told so lithe and subtle words to Council,
— words, mark me, would put the deaf in comfort —
as I constrain'd the earl forgo sufficient army
to defend the king.

---

356 3.6.54. *never puts us away*: never dismisses us, never ignores us.
357 3.6.61. *I am black, father*: In keeping with the Jeremiad nature of the scene, lines 61 and 63 are taken from Jeremiah 8.21.

In meanwhile, Gloucester, forth of the accursèd North,
dispatch'd epistles soft as Sappho, grave as Aeschylus,
setting down self-pining love and loss
as if it were the inescutcheon in th'escutcheon of his loyalty 80 358
he swears doth bind him to his king.
I little wist he penn'd his words in *aqua regis*. 359

Brother Godfrey *returns.*

Promises din to the loudest in the throat of hollow friends.
And more than this, his every action sweateth out
the untamed noisome tang of treason.
My devils rise against me of an evil pact.
   Abbot and **Monk** *cross themselves.*
   Sfx: A great bell begins to toll.
   Off: Monks stop chanting.
   The bell. How signifies the bell?
Abbot: The brothers are rous'd up withal to serve their queen.
Q. Elizabeth: It soundeth all a mort, as if the world were done.
   She busies herself with her tears and her **Children**.

Enter **Monks**, *who assist the stream of* **Servants**
with the royal household's baggage.

B. Godfrey: I never thought to see a queen so smote with woe. 90
Abbot: Her fond conceit shall never out
   the whilst her hope dependeth of relief.
   From Mammon springs the cure she seeks,
   whence only bootless comfort finds.
B. Godfrey: 'Tis as it were the world had chang'd.
Abbot: Her world is, at an instant, chang'd;
   wherewith her lately-stamp'd adversity
   doth tell too well her inmost nature's sooth.

---

[358] 3.6.80. *inescutcheon*: one coat of arms that has been superimposed or incorporated into another.
   Escutcheon here suggests Gloucester's motto *Loyauté me lie*, Loyalty binds me. Cf. 4.6.178.
[359] 3.6.82. *aqua regis*: a mixture of nitric and hydrochloric acids able to dissolve the 'noble' metals.

B. Godfrey: The nature of those things exceeds my reach of mind.
Abbot: My son, that which is real abides.
B. Godfrey: As you put it on me, father, I cannot understand.
Abbot: Abjure thy wits; abide the Rule.
   That passeth here was anciently set down,
      — I put you to Jeremiah!
   But present lend a hand to bring her worldly treasure in.
      Bowing, **Brother Godfrey** *joins the other* **Monks**.
      The **Abbot** *attends the* **Queen**.
      Sfx: *The bell stops.*

Enter two ragged **Servants**. **Servant One** *carries a basket of silver plate;*
Servant Two *pushes a barrow of clothing and curtains.*
Servant 1: Holla!
Servant 2: Who stops my way?
S 1: Other of the poverty — unless a one that full intends
   to turn his back upon misfortune; howbeit, in turning,
   finds he beareth burden of another's chattels
   a' must take upon advantages perforce,
   before he set his face to Fortune.
S 2: For all thou'dst force a riddle through a sieve,
   I scent thy tune.

---

360 3.6.104. I *put you to*: I put you to *study* Jeremiah.

361 3.6.106. The two servants' parts are written in 'Mummerset', the name given to the dialect used in Tudor theatre to convey low, rustic or loutish qualities. 'Mummerset' contained many elements from West Country dialects, particularly South Somerset and Dorset.

The most notable feature is the retention of the German *ich* for I, which lasted into the seventeenth century. In combination with verbs, *ich* eventually dropped the initial *i*, giving aphetic forms such as *cham* = I am, *chave* = I have, *chil* = I will/shall, *chud* = I would/should. Sometimes in nonce use, or for the sake of metre, the initial *i* is retained, giving *icham, et cetera*.

The servant's passage is based on the written style of a low farce, *Gammer Gurton's Nedle*, which may have been written in the early 1550s, though not published in Quarto till 1575. The earlier date would disqualify the play as a source for the language of *Dark Sovereign*, except that Shakespeare takes a brief stab at writing Mummerset in *King Lear*, 4.6, thereby supplying a valid precedent.

On the subject of the queen's servants, Hanham believes (p.165) that the looting of Elizabeth's goods was a tale invented by More. However, it was a moonless night, and they may have reached the abbot's apartment along Thieving Lane! Given the circumstances, it's hard to believe that nothing went astray.

362 3.6.108. *the poverty*: the poor, as a class. Cf. the clergy, the laity, the wealthy, *et cetera*.

363 3.6.113. *riddle*: A play on words. A riddle is a coarse sieve.

S 1: Percase he's fellow wi' thine own.
S 2: Thou'd filch a silver spoon!
S 1: Gog's bones, be not so low!
    'Chould trick thee up in riches tha not dream'st on,
    an' chad thik girt bushel of her chapel plate.
S 2: Thou dar'st not do't for hanging!   120
S 1: Thy cart, my basket, and away.
S 2: Thou'd shop us up t' gibbet's carrion.
S 1: What, noddy, ise show thee wealth!   364
S 2: She'd make away our life to fetch a farthing.
S 1: Then were a body as good peck'd by crows
    for the argent as the rust, as for the thought.
    The fretful hour runs mad,
    each minute madder than the next before:
    The queen's at Turks an' Christians wi' the dukes
    to steal away the very king.   130
    If two poor men steal away her plate, 'twere just.
S 2: Truth, they steal from us besides.
S 1: Be patient, chil be plain wi' thee,
    how Woodville ha' bin about to defame the crown.
    'Tis none o' hers! Beest'ou accoutr'd like these?   365
S 2: Nay, coz, tha know'st it.
    Nor can ich smell thy stench beyond my own;
    but, chil tell thee, their lavender
    and stinking court-odours offend my nose.
S 1: Deck we then our mistresses in three-pile   366
    from the queen ...   140
S 2: ... and greet them in her gracious name ...

---

364 3.6.123. *ise*: Might be described as the subjunctive of promise or threat, equivalent to shall. For example: 'Stand to it, thou dastard, for thine eares; ise teche thee a sluttish toye!' (*Gammer Gurton's Nedle*, III. iii.645; W. Tydeman, ed., Penguin, 1984). Whence *King Lear*, 4.6.245: 'Nay, come not near th'old man; keep out, che vor ye, or ise try whether your costard or my ballow be the harder'. Cambr. gives the spelling in *Lear* as *ice*.

365 3.6.135. *Beest'ou*: Be you...? *Beest* was usually a subjunctive, but it was used as an indicative in Southern and Western dialects.

366 3.6.139. *three-pile*: heavy velvet of three-fold thickness.

S 1: ... and sup off meats in silver bowls,
   like worthies do.
S 2: W'are well deserving for our pains.
S 1: Chil take wealth as my due
   to scrape away the dirt of service.
S 2: Mark her, sitting on the rushes,
   wailing she be heir to Midas' woes.
S 1: Fate smites her low.
S 2: 'Pon us the other face of Fortune smile!   150
S 1: Make shift to set my box
   under the curtain on your barrow. So.
S 2: Dame Fortune, smile on us. We go.
   They go.
   The stream of ***Monks*** *and* ***Servants*** *dwindles away.*
   Monks *escort the* ***Children*** *off.*
   Off: ***Monks*** *resume chanting "Miserere mei".*

Enter ***Dorset****.*

Dorset: Mother, a word.
Q. Elizabeth: What news? What head the dukes'?   367
   How the numbers of the force we raise against them?
Dorset: The night is sad.
Q. Elizabeth: What should this mean?
Dorset: It means I have exhorted many to our part;
   whom never a friend so leaden sober   160
   but his voidance was not instant silvern;   368
   his brain as suddenly beblest of more excuses
   than his shirt have fleas.
   Some, whose forward voice contemn the dukes,
   do more condemn themselves of cowardice;
   some mean us ill nor well; and some be of opinion
   this were useful for the realm ...

---

367 3.6.155. *head*: Suggests a rebellious or mutinous force.
368 3.6.161. *voidance*: verbal evasion (Bacon). *OED* does not find this sense.

Q. Elizabeth: Out, alas, we are undone!
Dorset: ... opining it were better Gloucester
    Edward's ward should rather keep   170
    than that his mother shall.
Q. Elizabeth: Their friends do multiply, and ours do fail.
    We stand alone.
Abbot: Your grace is not alone,
    but in this holy place makes much to God.
    To Dorset: Shall you keep sanctuary, my lord?
Dorset: I'll stay till I take ship for France,
    whence I shall back again repair with force enough
    the shock of war will break these on their treason.
    Fly, mother. Fly we to France.   180
Q. Elizabeth: Go, Thomas, fetch an army. I were best stay.
Dorset: Westminster allows but colour of sanctuary.
    Beware, lest your here-being construe a sullen trap:
    You are their prize. The purpos'd end of these
    is war against our blood.
Q. Elizabeth: My die to fortune's cast;
    my hope to parlous chance is play'd.
Dorset: This is the periloust chance, if it be chance at all.
    They'll surely go beyond us that already cog the die.   369
    The abbey is mainprize at the best   370
    until the dukes dispatch their boist'rous ferrets in.   190
Q. Elizabeth: We shall keep safe.
Dorset: A pretty thought, as soon gainsayed.
    Mind your late lord, who, with his brother,
    this self Gloucester, proud Somerset whilom did slay;   371
    whom, fleeing Tewkesbury's vanquish'd field
    with ten of Lancaster — moreover, with the prior
    of Clerkenwell, a holy knight —

---

[369] 3.6.188. *go beyond*: circumvent § *cog the die*: stack the deck, fix the odds.
[370] 3.6.189. *mainprize*: Loosely, comfortable house-arrest pending trial.
[371] 3.6.194. *whilom*: a while ago, formerly, some time back. The word was already antique, which is why Spenser used it frequently in *The Faerie Queene*.

false Gloucester did tear bloody out of Tewkesbury abbey,
putting all below the axe to die. 372
And doth not rumour yet redound 200
how these destroy'd Prince Edward when the fight was done? 373
Ravening beasts they be, that ready them
against their appetites come to blood. 374
Q. Elizabeth: Son, thou shalt not pluck back my resolve.
To brook our royal name and all our fates, I stay.

Enter **Rotherham**.

Rotherham: God bless your highness still.
Q. Elizabeth: How? Lord Chancellor!
Dorset: Mother, till anon.
   Dorset and the **Abbot** *withdraw.*
Rotherham: I come to hear the only pleasure of my queen:
The times is counterfeit and strange. 210   375
Q. Elizabeth: My pleasure is that we endure,
an't needs like squirrels in a hutch,
but such a hutch as keeps our Nemesis at a bay.
Rotherham: The common voice do have a mind to raise a head
against the dukes and take the king.

---

372   3.6.199. Neither faction was innocent. Gloucester's own father, Richard duke of York, had violated the sanctuary of Westminster Abbey in 1454 to seize the duke of Exeter.

373   3.6.201. *destroyed Prince Edward*: Edward of Lancaster, the only son of King Henry VI and Margaret of Anjou. It is said that Yorkists, including Gloucester, murdered Edward *after* the battle. See note 4.5.92.

374   3.6.203. *against*: in anticipation of the time when…

375   3.6.210. *The times is…* : *Is* may introduce a plural when its subject is a noun (Cf. Ind.1.29). On the other hand, some words with a plural ending — i.e. pains, means — have often been considered singular. News, which is now singular, was once a plural: 'What newes are now currant?' (Lyly). But *the times* has generally taken a plural verb: 'The times are wild' (*Henry IV, Pt 2*, 1.1.9). However, early editions of *Macbeth* give III. iv.79 as: 'The times has bene, That when the Braines were out, the man would die, And there an end'.

   But that's not the end at all, just the beginning of editorial confusion so far as that example is concerned. Craig changed the verb to fit the plural noun: 'The times have been, that…' Globe and Cambridge editions took the other route, changing the noun to fit the singular verb: 'The time has been, that…'

   Which matters not a whit, but it does convey some idea of the confusion and difficulty inherent in trying to resuscitate the demotic language of a by-gone age.

Q. Elizabeth: The notion's to your only mind, my lord.
  Certs it is not to theirs.
  Dorset left not to say the many raise t'oppose our part. 376
Rotherham: Then I can offer nothing, save this:
  I render England's Great Seal to your careful charge. 220
  Gives the seal to the **Queen**.
Q. Elizabeth, *toying with it*: Nineteen years ago
  — the anniversary's today! — King Edward wifed me.
  Before dawn. The same, the very selfsame hour of day.
  The trunk is not so constant to the tree as he to me;
  he pleasur'd me in everything.
  Lo, for long I sway'd England with this seal.
  Till now. Sans son, sans king, it's but a bauble,
  's base a trinket as a galley-ha'penny to my hand. 377
  Putatis ulla dona carere dolis? 378
Rotherham: Madam, wherefore do you charge me thus? 230
Q. Elizabeth: You forsake me, Rotherham.
Rotherham: Hastings sends your highness word, by me,
  bidding me to take busy pains t'assure your grace:
  All will be well.
Q. Elizabeth: Woe-worth him! Woe, and well-away!
  for he is one this many years hath labour'd me to hell.
  Rotherham, you wash your hands from me!
  Think you by renunciation to curry favour with the dukes?
  Besides thy cowardship, Lord Chancellor,
  thy bishop's gown defends thee from the axe. 240
Rotherham: I cannot counsel that I cannot find.
  Madam, I take leave and hope to come safe out.

---

376 3.6.218. *left not to say*: made a point of saying § *the many*: the majority.

377 3.6.228. *galley-ha'penny*: (Brit.: *hayp-nee*) A small silver coin introduced to English commerce by sailors on Genoese galleys trading in English ports. The galley-halfpenny was banned as legal tender in 1410 by an Act of Henry IV. Hence, a worthless coin.

378 3.6.229. *Putatis ... dolis?*: Do you think any gift is free from guile? After the translation of *Aeneid* II 44 by F.H. Dewey (New York, 1917). This sentence precedes Virgil's better-known line, 'Beware of Greeks bearing gifts', a wordplay in Latin.

> The day is sprung, the Thames already stopp'd with boats
> rowed everywhither by the duke of Gloucester's men. 244

Exit **Rotherham**.

> *The* **Queen** *sinks, crying.*
> *Off:* **Monks** *conclude "Miserere mei".*

ACT 3, SCENE 7

London, Thursday, May 1, 1483.

Hastings, *to an ill-armed* **Crowd**, *the* **Audience**, *or both.*

Hastings: My lords and commons, Londoners,
all you which have great heart to this affair,
I urge you eschew bitterness, to seek forth truth.
By that I honour, trow I Gloucester sure,
and fastly faithful to his prince. 379
King Edward's house are under an arrest
to keep the dukes from jeopardy;
'tis not to jeopardy the king.
Some: Aha! No. No.
Hastings: There stick they, only but until the thing be judged, 10
indifferently, by the Council: We shall appease all griefs. 380
Know ye, of a surety th'authority remaineth to that side where is the king.
Some: Aha!
Hastings: Countrymen, I treat you — nay, herefor I chide —
put not the times to bloody judgment till ye do know truth!
Nor turn your private grudges into common hurt,
unless th'unsteady hour come so far out of joint

---

379 3.7.5. The line is Sir Thomas More's. Much of Hastings' address to the lords is adapted after More, altered by me for the benefit of metre and 'modernized' into Period English.
380 3.7.11. *indifferently*: impartially.

it never should be brought in frame again.
    Heat but engenders ire, the which, consuming up,   20
doth render good with ill, nobility of soul with base,
and so an end. Deny t'incline to baseness; pluck it out.
In likewise put off arms; come not abroad by warring companies.
And look how far you are the body of the weal,
so far the common weal is you.
If, therefore, that you love your land, your king,
your lives, your loves, your self, begone!
That hearth you have, betake you home!
    *The **Crowd** breaks up, revealing **Truth**.*
    ***Hastings** makes to go.*
Truth: Thus noble Hastings, boldly,
keeping London from commotion;   30
bedulling the hot edge of war to whispering churlish peace.
Hastings, *aside*: God grant I said truth.
But if I went beyond the moon I pray they look not through me.   [381]
I wot not which of that I spoke were false or true.
*He goes. Exit the **Crowd**.*
Truth: Meantime, Duke Richard wrote comfortably
to the lord mayor, eke to the Council,
telling he not held the king under an arrest;
he rescued England rather from the house of Woodvilles
and perdition; uttering these was such as would not spare the child,
that wasted the worship and the life of his father.   40
    Whereupon, Gloucester caus'd Rivers with his company
be guarded towards York. Himself came up to London
with King Edward, Buckingham withal,
and not above five hundred men.
They brought carts on, fraught wi' arms
emblazon'd with devices of Woodville.
Beside the waggons criers cried those evidenc'd the complot
these had laid to lay an ambush for the dukes.   [382]

---

[381] 3.7.33. *went beyond the moon*: exaggerated.
[382] 3.7.48. *those ... these*: the former ... the latter.

*Enter **Rumour**.*

Rumour: Aha, dost speak afrights? cry panic terrors?
   inflict dread? How now, Verity? 50
Truth: How? Not now! Sister, thou com'st too soon.
   Thy part is not yet.
Rumour: I spied the waggons in London road.
Truth: What part dost thou play?
Rumour: Why, of ev'ry each one a little, save only thine.
Truth: Come on your ways: This part is mine.
Rumour: Saving that thou wottest not is mine.
Truth: What's mine to know is mine to say.
Rumour: Unless, of this affair, thou canst not truly say.
Truth: I' name of our father, Chronos, 60 [383]
   by thee am I so astonied, I am from use of myself!
   How well I wist, I well wot nothing any more! [384]
Rumour: Nay, ne canst thou, nor not I.
   But it makes no matter for this matter:
   Verity, as thou affects, say on.
Truth, *to the **Audience**, distressed*: It seems to me
   each latter age doth stand upon a rising tower of former time,
   and to look down to old affrays. Yet everywhere is fog;
   nothing is clear. Then needs we stumble at each cobble-stone.
   *Turns on **Rumour***: Thou *know'st* I cannot that I cannot know! 70
Rumour: Then I'll relate the clamour doth attend on Edward
   as he rides in progress.
   ***Rumour** upstages **Truth**.*
   Ignoble ignorance, th'immortal slip of mortal men,
   from immemorial descent transcendeth every age.

---

[383] 3.7.60. *our father, Chronos*: 'Truth is the daughter of time'. Thus the proverb, after Seneca's 'Time discovers truth'. The old adage is better known now from the title of a novel, *The Daughter of Time* (1951), by Josephine Tey (a pen name for Elizabeth Mackintosh). Tey's novel has become a favored source for Richard III's defenders.

   Saturn, or Kronos, is also identified with time, the result of a late-medieval muddle between Kronos and Chronos.

[384] 3.7.62. *How well ... any more*: However well I used to know, I don't know anything any more.

'Twas thus in this. Whifflers 'fore the dukes did so move the rabble
it gan bay at the queen and her family,
threating them to hang them. The wise wist wiselier,
weening that th'aforetold arms were put in readiness
to war against the Scots. The same perceiv'd 80
that Gloucester's hope ran over-high, vaunting secretly   385
the straining, purblind steed of fierce Ambition.
Truth *upstages* **Rumour**: But Gloucester caus'd the aldermen
and nobles swear allegiance to their king,
whereon breasts of all hearts were lighten'd and rejoic'd.   386
    Edward his father's councillors,
to whom most part remain'd their offices,
appointed Gloucester protector of the king.
Their voices fresh in resolution,
Duke Richard dismiss'd Rotherham of office, 90
trusting the Broad Seal to Russell in his stead.
Rumour: Yet notwithstanding, Gloucester in 's fear nigh swelt,
lest some should raise parts.   387
Truth: Endow'd he Buckingham with such power
as few in England own'd before, nor never after,
wishing thereby to buy his strength to steadfast friend.
Rumour: But Harry's mind was maz'd through vanity,
his purpose mostwhat nothing steadfast, not for e'en himself.
Truth: Hastings, he that kept the peace and smoothed his way
to serve the king, gain'd no reward of it. 100
    Therefrom springs up future trouble …
Rumour: … certs as harvest sprouts from grain …
Truth: … as weeds spring after rain.
    Whence troublous May drew on to June …

---

385 3.7.81. *vaunting*: extolling, boasting, bragging.

386 3.7.85. *breasts of all hearts*: In this figure, where a heart is taken to be a mind or a soul, the analogy is extended by according it bodily organs. Thus: 'The kneis of my hart sall I bowe' (Gude & Godlie, 1567); 'I … in Thy feare, knees of my heart will fold' (Sidney, Psalm 5.3, 1580); 'Upon the knees of our hearts' (Act I, King James, 1604); and 'Behold the ears of my heart' (Matthews, 1620). § *and rejoic'd*: Without a preceding comma, *rejoic'd* continues the passive represented by were *lighten'd*, thus: 'Breasts of all hearts … were rejoic'd', a usage consistent with the Period.

387 3.7.93. *raise parts*: stir up and recruit opposing factions (Bacon).

Rumour: ... and ay a score of rumours cropp'd for each gainsayed.
Truth: Each breathing draws a whisper in ...
Rumour: ... which, changing ...
Truth: ... breathes a susurration to the air ...
Rumour: ... to other ears ...
Truth: ... but for their head not a ones are wiser. 110
 I warrant the lord protector did not bear a fasten'd mind
 through May.
Rumour, *backing towards one wing*: Truth, come away!
Truth *backs towards the other*: Time's only ruttier 388
 must seek the kingdom's way. *Running, she goes.*
Rumour: Whither Truth, Rumour must follow.
 Calls after: Though thou command each instance, sister,
 that follows is not so constrain'd. **Rumour** *pursues* **Truth**. 116

ACT 4, SCENE 1

"Crosby's Place", the Protector's residence, c. June 5, 1483.

Enter **Catesby** *and* **Buckingham**, *meeting*.

Buckingham: Ho, Catesby!
Catesby: God save your grace.
Buckingham: Where is the protector?
Catesby: I saw him even just a wink ago,
 pale-cold, as marble as the walls.
 I never saw a dial that was not less contráry, 389

---

[388] 3.7.113. *ruttier*: chart, map. A ruttier conveyed more than directions to reach a destination; hard-won personal knowledge and experience went into crafting one. The earliest maritime ruttiers were confidential documents, build up through a career by individual mariners trading along commercial trade routes. A ruttier might be a cornucopia of commercial value, to be seen by an owner's or ship-master's eyes only.

[389] 4.1.6. *never ... not less contráry*: Cf. 2.1.15. Given this construction, the sentence reads: 'I never saw a sundial that told the time as precisely as his face betrays his mood'.

nor did confirm his sun so well as his physnomy doth.
He manifests each perturbation, biting the nether lip,
snatching his dagger as he imagin'd each hand were Cassius.
Buckingham: Husht! Lo, where he comes. 10

Enter **Gloucester**, *pensive.*

Catesby: Beware, your grace, from one possess'd,
whose own familiar scourgeth him with fear.
This is the veriest homily of Virgil's Gnat,
where dread with anger blend so much his sense,
unreason may bite near. 390
Buckingham: Can he be seeking aught that seeth naught?
Catesby: Whatever he looketh after,
he seems he were loath to find. His step wants purpos'd pace.
Buckingham: He may not stumble!
One too many fortunes hangs of his resolve. 20
Catesby: Which quality I judge him wanting of.
Needs your grace must light a lamp
will drive his storm of thoughts forth of their matrix.
Do, do, we must examine them.
Buckingham: Leave us, Catesby. I shall sound his mind alone.
Catesby withdraws.
Why, how now, your grace!
Gloucester: Welcome, Harry.
Buckingham: The grim demean belieth the good word.
Gloucester: The substance of our act is troubles.
Buckingham: The substance of our act is power, 30
pluck'd from lucky accident.
Gloucester: The substance is doing with accidents again. 391
Fate's a play oft goes afore unseen, until 's felt afterwards.
Enemies that ranged them before me of old,
of late rise large in hating at my back.

---

390 4.1.15. *unreason*: ill-considered or rash actions. Cf. Spenser, *Virgil's Gnat*, 310.
391 4.1.32. *is doing with*: is getting involved with.

Buckingham: Thresh your enemies: tares always sprout with corn.
Gloucester: Which the tares, and which the corn?
    I know not those and these asunder. 392
Buckingham: The weeds are gather'd; whilst the queen
    with her boist'rous whelp languish in "Cheynygate". 40
    They are put out. But those are curiosities. 393
    Gird greatness to you, an't become your proper self. 394
    Ah, greatness, felicity and physic to the gods;
    as balm to nobleness; a lash to frailty.
    None element as fitly turns all stings.
Gloucester: Than mine, no greater greatness is,
    besides the king's.
Buckingham: A thought, your grace, is such a slender thing
    as doth not shake the trembling air.
    But if it have ingenerate virtue, 50
    then is it seemly that it grow.
Gloucester: What mean you, Buckingham?

Enter **Thomas**.

Thomas: My lady your wife is come to London.
Gloucester: How?
Buckingham: I yield your grace's ear and favour
    to the beauty of my lady Anne.
    Exit **Buckingham** *with* **Thomas**.

Enter the **Duchess Anne**, *attended by a* **Lady in Waiting**.
The **Duchess** *makes much ado of removing a cloak, gloves, et cetera.*

---

392   4.1.38. *those and these asunder*: I can't tell the former from the latter (apart).

393   4.1.4. *curiosities*: trifles, trivia, distractions.

394   4.1.42. *an't*: The sense of this simple conjunction is as carefully ambiguous as Buckingham is slippery. On paper the printed words can only mean *if it*, followed by a subjunctive, and therefore hypothetical, verb. However, if *an't* is heard as *and*, the verb becomes an imperative. If Buckingham is about to suggest treason, he is approaching the subject very cautiously.

Anne: What, no greeting?
   Spouse mine, art thou moody?
   Smooth thy creas'd front: I find thee melancholy, chang'd.
   And, distress of weather speaks a storm. 60
Gloucester: Thou wert better stay at Middleham!
Anne: Here's sour welcome home!
Gloucester: 'Fore God, I would the power lay at York!
   Anne gives over her cloak.
   *The **Lady in Waiting** goes.*
Anne: What is thee? Art sick o' th' sullens
   that thou call'st me to an account for England's history?
Gloucester: Southren honour's little lack of dead. 395
Anne: Regard me! *She looks into his eyes.*
   Hast thou the jaundice? Nay.
Gloucester: Dost glass thyself? 396
Anne: Then thy feckless melancholy should proceed of atrabile. 70 397
Gloucester: London is a midding-pit.
   Flatterers spring up like doubtful agaric. 398
Anne: It's said black bile doth make for cunning. 399
   Richard, art thou wiser?
Gloucester: Slanderers, like flies on dung, abound.
Anne: The unaccustom'd weight of state makes thee to stoop.
   Is power, like astringents, of that nature
   that it purse thee so?
Gloucester: Woman, I am not thy butt to scold.

---

395 4.1.66. *Southren*: Cf. 'Contention between the Northren and Southren students at Oxford' (Holland, 1610).
396 4.1.69. *Dost glass thyself?* Are you looking at your own reflection (as reflected from my eyes)? A not uncommon expression in the Period. Sidney uses it at least twice in *Arcadia*. More obscure is, 'Dost look babies?' An expression used exclusively within the Period, babies also refers to the tiny reflections one sees in another's eyes.
397 4.1.70. *atrabile*: black bile, or the bile of melancholy, one of the four 'cardinal humours' of classical Greek medicine.
398 4.1.72. *agaric*: 'Several species of fungi of the genus Polyporus with significant medical properties' (*OED*). Gerard's *Herball* describes it thus: 'There groweth also upon the Larch tree a kind of Mushrum ... good for medicine, which beareth the name of *Agaricus*, or *Agaricke*'.
399 4.1.73. *black bile doth make for cunning*: This assertion rests upon a line in Carew's 1594 translation of Huarte's *Examination of men's wits*: '*Atrabile*, of which Aristotle said, That it made men exceedingly wise'.

Anne: No blood is shed. All's safely done.
 The comfort of thy new found office succour thee!
Gloucester: How bitter the taste of others' joy.
 My succours came of Edward; he, my only duty and my right.
 A man may far, that wears his greater's charge upon his coat.
 No right reposeth in't; no wrong. Whose duty is his certain,
 treadeth out a so-mark'd way the blind
 — and the blind-hearted — may venter in.
 Amazéd-I am just amongst an alien wood,
 his marches pathless, and his paths untried.
   There was a day — does it remember thee? —
 since once in younger, foolish-witty years, we ventur'd out
 on the River Youre to stand on the ice, hearing it so crack
 whose strength had soon yielded to hurl us down.
 How thin the ice; how deep, how swift the torrent runs below.
   Shall he be resolute, that is so unresolv'd?
Anne: From unease beware, lest like a spawnling
 it should engender in thee, devouring the sanctity of reason.
Gloucester: Unease is not equivocal!
 It springs from still experience, that very quality
 wherewith a man absorbs his nurture out of others' minds.
 The I *per se* must need descry his own environry
 through windows that he graveth in his brain.
 If sugar sit at the heart as gall,
 'tis what experience did teach.
 The species of this iron world
 is not the sprite of mine invention.
Anne: The mind doth make the fact, or good or ill.

---

[400] 4.1.92. *River Youre*: The river Ure. The spelling is from John Speede's map, *The North and East Ridins* [sic] *of Yorkshire*, 1610.

[401] 4.1.96. *spawnling*: OED does not recognize *spawnling* before 1698. However, the quotation it gives for that year is very similar to one published by Shelton in 1612: 'God ... doth not abandon the little flies of the air, nor the wormelings of the earth, nor the spawnlings of the water'.

[402] 4.1.99. *still experience*: long experience.

[403] 4.1.105. *the species*: the appearance, outward forms. The sense is that of *species expressa* of medieval scholastic philosophy.

Gloucester: If I fear of murder in a dream,
   though the murderers be phantom,
   yet the dream is made on them is real.
   What bug doth so beguile my sleepings, that,
   in wakings, I wi' sweat reek 's humour out?
   taxing the dark of lurking shades.
   I can not otherwise but that my dreams are schoolmasters,
   the which, by night, instil the tenor of my days.
   Note how they steal on.
Anne: The shapes of things?
Gloucester: The days! After Edward's coronation,
   if he might, he'll make us drink as we have brew'd.
   When the sun shall end his pavin thrice,
   that little bull will go beyond the check.
Anne: Not treat with imps! They are in the nature of fearfulness.
   Long living with thee thought t'have made me know thee.
   Suddenly it seems I know thee not.
Gloucester: Whoever would know me throughly,
   let him stand upon my self same place,
   and to study God's invention in the glass.
Anne: Our enemies are put away. No harm assaileth thee.
Gloucester: I owe too brief a span,
   beyond which date a father's son of perfect age
   shall take his vengeance on my head.

---

[404] 4.1.113. *taxing the dark of*: rebuking the dark for.
[405] 4.1.117. *The shapes of things?* From Studley, 1574: 'They stirred up … divers terrible ghosts and shapes of things'.
[406] 4.1.120. *pavin*: pavan, a stately dance, used figuratively to represent a year, three years in this context. OED does not find a figurative use for *pavin*. However Davies, 1594, thus: 'The moon … ends her pavin thirteen times as soon as doth her brother'.
[407] 4.1.121. *the check*: restraint, in this case legal restraint. There was no telling when the young King Edward might be crowned in his own right. Gloucester's office of Protector would then cease. At that point, he and other members of the 'Old Nobility' faction might be brought down and destroyed by the queen and her Woodville faction.
[408] 4.1.122. *imps*: In addition to evil spirits suggested by Gloucester's nightmares, the word was commonly used in reference to the offspring of a noble house. Perhaps even the duchess is not certain what meaning she attaches to the word here.
[409] 4.1.123. *thought t'have made me know thee*: brought me close to knowing you.
[410] 4.1.129. *owe*: own, v. The sense here is, 'I don't have much time'. See note 1.2.86

Anne: Thou alone hast right to bear a rein upon the king.
Gloucester: Small rein bear I upon the Council,
 which is moulded overmuch of Woodville clay.
 And Hastings! that to Edward is the most loyalst.
Anne: If nothing lets to make thee safe else,
 then — thou sayest thou must be king.
Gloucester: Dost thou not do obedience, Anne?
Anne: To you alone, my lord.
 A woman makes no homage but devotion.
Gloucester: Were I the Almighty Arbiter of earthly government,
 I should root up thy tongue, pluck out thy brains;
 thy heart, each vicious office of thy treason quosh.
 However, by that love wherewith we were incorporated one,
 no less than by my proper thought, my mind intendeth unto thee. 411
Anne: 'Tis lots to blanks that thou canst well succeed.
Gloucester, *aside*: There be that are suited with ill tasks.
 I'll by and by fetch Catesby. His better doth not breathe
 that can discover Hastings' mind,
 as who is Hastings' best belovéd agent, 412
 and an inward of Buckingham's to boot.
Anne: Thou hast too far progress'd, my lord,
 than that thou canst go back,
 for then th'event goes backward too. 413
Gloucester, *aside*: He was no serpent spake to Eve in Eden;
 he was a lawyer. Catesby is such another, 414
 whose subtile nature disreputes the rest.
 Moreover, Catesby can the sleight of womankind.
 Speaks: Woot thou be queen?
Anne: I, my lord?
Gloucester: Aye, madam. Thee.
Anne: If so be …

---

411 4.1.145. *my mind intendeth unto thee*: I find myself tending to agree with you.
412 4.1.150. *as who*: than one who. Cf. Ind.1.30.
413 4.1.154. *th'event goes backward*: the outcome changes for the worse, the thing goes all to hell.
414 4.1.156. The adage about the lawyer in the Garden of Eden was a favourite with my father-in-law, Will Burtin, late of New York. As a young man he heard it often in Cologne.

Gloucester: I read thee, Anne. Ambition thee unmasks.
   Thou wolt be queen; I am well will'd to live.
   If that I live, why, then I must be king,
   else shall I surely die.   166
      Exeunt.

ACT 4, SCENE 2

Lord Hastings' apartment, perhaps June 12, 1483.

Enter **Catesby**.

Catesby: Did he not speak freely of his hope?
   Then 'tis no rumour — no, nor muse-monging
   of sland'rous tales: great Gloucester would be king!
   His weary duty is pluck'd down of a hydra-headed longing:
   jealousy, couchéd in stern righteousness, remains.
   (Forfend righteousness! Nothing so much as that ill humour
   doth so soon excite a guilty conscience, or so mad the brain.)
   Ho, Gloucester would unhorse Edward, dub himself majesty!
   It's a marvellous offence, a hideous handy-dandy
   to change one's station with a king.   10
      Then, at one breath he came to a full point:
   I am to sound out Hastings, yet turning the cat in the pan   415
   for to conceal him did sire the bastard thought.
   Hastings! that so truly temper'd is.
   Gloucester will I should put out his fire with gunpowder.

---

[415] 4.2.12. *turning the cat in the pan*: Francis Bacon explains this expression best: 'There is a cunning, which we in England call the turning of the cat in the pan, which is, when that which a man says to another, he lays it as if another had said it to him. And to say truth, it is not easy, when such a matter passed between two, to make it appear from which of them it first moved and began' (*The Essays*, J. Pitcher, ed., Penguin, 1985). Pitcher's footnote gives *cate* or *cake* for Bacon's cat. However, *OED* states: '[Origin unknown: the suggestion that cat was originally CATE does not agree with the history of that word.]'

I must distil out elixir someway
from double draughts of vitriols,
else shall I forfeit either of both mighty friends.
    Hastings was fair Fortune's angel to me.
Of his bounty sprang my wealths and present fame.
I little lack, indeed, than that I were his son.
But Fortune shifts, ev'ry her quick strokes
translating every one. Liefer me were emulate hoary Plato,
and to partake of Fortune's game. I'll pack the cards,
and importune my lot with her again. There is no other way.
How shall I weigh Lord Hastings in these balance
with the favours Gloucester will afford me
if I serve the time, the better to assure this new-made king?

Enter **Hastings**.

Hastings: God save you, Catesby.
Catesby, *startled*: No less unto you, my lord.
Hastings: How! my solemn advocate springs like a filly foal.
Catesby: We live in the treacheroust times.
Hastings: 'Twas never but ever this. Though not so yet,
    but that we cannot still avert unsafety i' th' state.
    Calls off: Piers, a bowl of claret!
    To Catesby: You'll drink a draught or two.
Catesby: I must about affairs, my lord.
Hastings: Hardly come; chary in staying; you'd sooner away!
    Tarry, except you be the tide. Mass, good William,
    y'are a shuttlecock today! Are you your wonted well?
Catesby: Well, my lord. In health.
Hastings: I permit you none other state. You are my ears,
    my every sense of the protector's mind. What news today?

---

416 4.2.24. *pack the cards*: stack the deck.
417 4.2.28. *serve the time*: follow the path of least resistance, go along with whatever is expedient.

*Enter a **Servant** ...*

> *... who gives **Hastings** a bowl of claret, and goes.*
> ***Hastings** drinks first, as custom demanded.*
> *The bowl then passes between the two men.*

Catesby: None of the worst. Gloucester, with his inwards,
contrive a glorious coronation for a king.
Hastings: I eschew the protector's sunder'd no-councils.
He commends false-guiding favourites to his closet.
Betters, that had best have underpropp'd his state,
he doth exclude as we were trash. He winnows us
that long time served King Edward — and that right loyally. 50
We are not chaff he can out-spurn so lightly.

*Enter **Elizabeth "Jane" Shore**.*

Jane Shore *kisses **Hastings**, acknowledges **Catesby**:*
Master Catesby.
Catesby: Good time of day unto you, Mistress Shore.
*Exit **Mistress Shore**.*
Hastings: Have I not given you copious favours, William ... ?
Catesby: Yes, just, my lord.
Hastings: ... that any he, at friend, can gift another?
Catesby: Indeed, it's so. I greatly stand in your debt.
Hastings: Then return it now in my particular!
Elsewhat of duty I forgive. The dukes set me on side,
even in soft words despite. Report them truly to me: 60
each time they take their course by destinies; each motive; [418]
évéry complót and each propose. [419]
You are my only true intelligencer at "Crosby's Place".

---

[418] 4.2.61. *take their course by destinies*: predict their next move. *By destinies* hints at the soothsayer's art.
[419] 4.2.62. *évéry complót*: If *évéry* is sounded as a trisyllable, the ictus falls naturally on the second syllable of *complót* and the line scans in iambs. The stress on *complót* varies among Period authors.

    Do you look to intercept the commerce of their minds!
    In nothing else but only this I charge you: Do not fail!
Catesby: Whatever I shall hear, I solemnly vouchsafe
    to tell every whit. You know me not else.
Hastings: Drink to 't, William. Red wine doth red the blood.
    Catesby drinks, without enthusiasm.
    I re-tell 't again: I seem you are not well.
Catesby: It took effect of rumour's sting, my lord,   70
    and that's the tittle-est-amen of it.
Hastings: Tattle too much stirr'd translates to truth.
    Proclaim it, scotch it, and have done!
Catesby: Whispers hath how Gloucester takes his course
    to the crown.
Hastings: England would in no case hear of it!
    I am not innocent of it, but I deem it a vicious charge,
    not to be named on the same day with Gloucester.
    Is not his motto *loyaute me lie*?
    Nor doth the word want strict example of his life,
    but the rather doth confirm the measure of it.   80
    Natheless, untruth, from welling springs of discontent,

---

420 4.2.67. *You know me not else*: You don't know me if you think otherwise.
421 4.2.70. *It took effect of*: It's the result of. *OED* does not recognize the modern sense of *to take effect* before 1771. It is used here in an earlier sense, meaning *originates from*, or *derives from*.
422 4.2.71. *that's the tittle-est-amen of it*: That's all there is to say, That's the end of the matter, And that's that Cf. 2.5.10.
423 4.2.73. *scotch it*: *OED* cites 'Theobald's generally accepted conjectural reading of *Macbeth*, 3.2.13, "We have scotch'd the snake, not kill'd it" and defines the verb as meaning 'to inflict such hurt upon (something dangerous) that it is rendered harmless for the time'. The verb is preserved in the Globe ed., and Craig, but apart from the *Macbeth* example, further usage dates from the late eighteenth century. Possibly that is why Cambridge gives the verb as *scorched*, meaning to be slashed with a sharp weapon.
424 4.2.77. *to be named on the same day with*: named in the same breath, tarred with the same brush, found guilty by association.
425 4.2.78. *Loyauté me lie*: 'Loyalty Binds Me'. Gloucester's earlier motto was '*Tant le desiere*'.

full oft weaves seeming truth. Gloucester's dark ways 426
still still bring grist to foemen's mills, 427
displeasure to his friends.
    Mark, William, it is not *truth* fears me,
but the gather'd voices of the rabble,
casting counsel stern as 'twere Star Chamber. 428
When all comes to all, the Council shall resist,
unless the king. 429
Catesby: Do you utter in good authority, my lord? 90
Hastings: In best authority, as Stanley, Morton, Rotherham.
Myself, though my step-daughter wed Dorset,
yet did I oppose the Woodville pact.
Nor other shall rise to give semblant of their tyranny.
If Gloucester will play Antony, and Buckingham
the part of Catiline, my Cicero should face them.

---

[426] 4.2.82. *dark ways*: secretive ways. Compare the note about the title at the first entry of the Glossary. Gloucester's 'dark ways' were not untypical of his time. Francis Bacon gives an account of Philippe de Commynes' description of King Edward IV's and King Richard III's brother-in-law, Charles, duke of Burgundy:

    'It is not to be forgotten what Commineus observeth of his first master, Duke Charles the Hardy; namely, that he would communicate his secrets with none, and least of all, those secrets which troubled him most. Whereupon he goeth on and saith that towards his latter time that closeness did impair and a little perish his understanding. Surely Commineus mought have made the same judgement also, if it had pleased him, of his second master, Lewis the Eleventh, whose closeness was indeed his tormentor. The parable of Pythagoras is dark, but true: *Cor ne edito*, Eat not the heart. Certainly, if a man would give it a hard phrase, those that want [lack] friends to open themselves unto are cannibals of their own hearts'.

Ross, describing portraits of King Richard, remarks: 'The more flattering of the two early portraits, that in the Royal Collection, shows a not uncomely man, despite the obvious lines of anxiety on his brow. The Antiquaries' painting, on the other hand, shows a gaunt, bony, tight-lipped face, again with a suggestion of anxiety. It is noticeable that in both he is shown as being older than his true age' (Ross, *Richard III*, p.140).

[427] 4.2.83. *still still*: all the time, on every possible occasion.

[428] 4.2.87. *Star Chamber*: A court of conciliar jurisdiction which, evolving under Henry VII, was refined under Henry VIII by Wolsey. Star Chamber as a court was functioning by about 1530, making it a reference with which a Period author and his audience would identify. Not so Lord Hastings, who supposedly voices this line in 1483. *Dark Sovereign*, then, like other plays of the Period, reflects the precepts dictated by the time in which it was written as much as the older period it presents. Shakespeare, after all, wrote into *King John*, 'Our cannon shall be bent Against the brows of this resisting town', although his setting precedes Crecy, the first European battle to use cannon.

[429] 4.2.89. *unless*: except.

The Council shall carry the stroke i' th' realm.

*Enter the **Servant**.*

Servant: Please your lordship,
  Lord Stanley's man desires urgent conference with you.
Hastings: He'll come to the matter soon enough. 100
Catesby: By your leave, my lord, I'll go.
Hastings: Till the next morrow, William, at the Tower.
  ***Catesby** goes. The **Servant** takes the bowl*
  *and ushers in Thomas Lord Stanley's **Agent**.*
Hastings: Shall you speak the urgency your heels advertise?
Agent: Despite the times are swart,
  my master will have them darker yet.
  He is dispos'd to quit London.
Hastings: Show me his reason for 't.
Agent: He is extremely in fear of Gloucester,
  regarding him as a sad-natur'd man, suddenly advanc'd,
  whose reason of state is to be from fearfulness. 110
  And therefore his ascent doth, as it were,
  breed an unquiet policy; which, by course,
  doth goad him on to jealousy, whence ire, whence tyranny.
Hastings: Of whence comes Stanley's anguish'd news?
Agent: I know not. An' but his lordship had withstood
  full many a storm ere this, you would not believe them.

4.2.97 *carry the stroke*: have the clout, wield the power.

4.2.105. *will have them*: imagines them (the times) to be even darker than they are.

4.2.110 *reason of state*: Suggests personal motivation for (political) action, departing from high moral standards with regard to justice or fairness. Self-protection. Unmitigated self interest. Cf. note 4.3.7

4.2.112. *by course*: in the natural course of events.

> For all that, my message is: He never tofore did see the like
> to this strange quiet time. A wanion waits nigh. [434]
>
> **Hastings**: That cannot be!
>
> **Agent**: The dukes is in a mind to overthrow the Council. 120
> Gloucester goes near t'exalt himself more than the king. [435]
>
> **Hastings**: 'Twere a naughty scope; he'd never the near! [436]
>
> **Agent**: My master's quite put out of countenance.
>
> **Hastings**: An't be so, the dukes shall answer our *Quo warranto*! [437]
>
> **Agent**: Needs perforce I must repeat my master o'er again,
> who entreats your lordship: renounce your prejudice
> on natural predictions! Look forth thereof. [438]
>
> **Hastings**: Stanley looketh thereof clean beyond!
> I am stiffnecked of nothing, save only it touch honour.
> As touching this … 130
> *Aside*: If it were in measure so, Catesby had brought me word.
> No man hath greater love for me than Catesby has,
> and he most inward wi' the dukes. But not a hint at all.
> Does truth with love or seeming madness lie?
> *Speaks*: Say on!

---

[434] 4.2.118. *wanion*: In its earliest, literal sense, *wanion* referred to the fourteen day waning period of the moon, which was held to be less than propitious. There was indeed a full moon on the night of Thursday, June 12th and Friday, June 13th, in the year 1483. Even before the Period, *wanion* had taken a figurative meaning as a time of crisis or bad luck.

[435] 4.2.121. *goes near to*: is on the point of.

[436] 4.2.122. *scope*: intention, aim, goal, ambition.

[437] 4.2.124. *Quo warranto*: A 'writ formerly in use, by which a person or persons were called upon to show by what warrant [*quo warranto*] he or they held, claimed, or exercised an office or franchise'. *OED*.

[438] 4.2.127. *prejudice on natural predictions*: premature judgments based only upon (a few) known facts (Bacon, *Of Prophecies*).

Agent: My lord?
Hastings: Nor deed nor thought but has his wherefore. Tell it!
Agent: Moreover than my master's ear-intelligence,
    he had a fearful dream … 140
Hastings: A dream, quotha!
Agent: … wherein a violent boar his tusks did scorch your heads 439
    until the living blood ran out about your shoulders, both.
Hastings: That heedeth foolish dreams, feeds folly.
    We have nothing done but our devóyer; which nothing less 440
    should bring pain of peril on our heads.
Agent: Such is the imprint of his dream o'ershades his heart,
    he determines not to tarry more. Lord Stanley waits upon you;
    bids you ride with him tonight. You'll be from danger
    before day. 150
Hastings: How the moon now?
Agent: The moon, my lord?
Hastings: The moon!
Agent: O aye, she's full. 441

---

439 4.2.142. *scorch*: slash. Cf. note in 4.2.73. Sir Thomas More uses the verb *rase* here, taking it from the *Great Chronicle*, according to Hanham (p.l65), prompting her to dismiss the boar-in-the-dream story as a figment of More's imagination-by-association, because '*rase* was a word very commonly used in connection with wild animals'. Indeed, More was not the first to apply *rase* to the actions of Gloucester's totem animal, the boar. Compare More: 'Him thought that a boar with his tusks so rased them both by the heads, that the blood ran about their shoulders', with Malory: '[Sir Lancelot and Beaumains] rasshed to gyders lyke borys tracynge rasynge and foynynge' (*Le Morte d'Arthur*, VII. iv, Caxton ed., 1485). More may well have been influenced by Malory or another author in his formative years, retaining the word association, casting it later into a dream-tale of his own devising.

    The great majority of instances — there are dozens — in *Le Morte d'Arthur*, use rase, (or *race*, *raise*, *raze*, *rash*) in a human context. Thus: 'Sir Lancelot … pulled down knights and raced off their helms' (X. xli); or, 'Sir Palomides raced off his helm, and smote off his head' (X. xliii) (J.M. Dent ed., 1893). If More intends the verb *rase* in this context, then his usage may owe nothing to a symbolic source.

    But he may still be writing fiction. If there ever was such a dream, it was surely dreamed up later, perhaps by Stanley, in the relief and exaggeration of hindsight. It is hard to believe that a man of Stanley's ilk would confide such nonsense to the Lord Chamberlain of England, let alone through a servant, no matter how 'trustie'.

440 4.2.145. *nothing less*: least of all.
441 4.2.154. I am grateful to P.K. Seidelmann, Director, Nautical Almanac Office, U.S. Naval Observatory, for supplying the lunar cycle during the interval covered by *Dark Sovereign*.

When clouds not stand between, she's great enough to ride …
Hastings, *aside*: I never heard Thomas Stanley commended
  to be lunatic.
Agent: … only, beware your horse have not moon-eyes.
Hastings, *aside*: So!
Agent: Please it your lordship, melt in mind;
  take the urgent hour. Lord Stanley waits.   160
Hastings: If we come in with danger,
  I had liefer have men see it false,
  than to think we wore faint heart and fled.
  Commend me to your master.
  Let him hold nothing in fearing. Pray him stay.
  Gloucester shall remain as sure to me as my hand does.
Agent: Send you well, my lord.
Hastings: Until the morrow light.
  I look for Stanley to the Tower betimes.
    Exit the **Agent**.
Jane Shore, *voice off, calling*: William, O William.   170
Hastings: Expect me, love.

Enter Jane Shore.

Jane Shore: Sweet William, hurry to bed.
Hastings: Sweeter-Jane-in-bed. *He pinches her.*
Jane Shore: La you, my lord!
Hastings: To bed, my dove, to bed.   175
    They go.

ACT 4, SCENE 3

The Tower of London, possibly, Friday, June 13, 1483.

Hastings, Thomas Stanley, Morton, Howard, *the three perpetual* **Councillors, Rotherham, Buckingham,** *with* **Attendants** *as may be, await the arrival of* **Gloucester.** 442

Stanley: Do it, Hastings. Heed my urging.
   Off wi' us, while 's yet we may.
Hastings: We durst in wretched times before.
Stanley: Each minute's instance that we tarry
   draws to a too late Now. Make haste, Hastings. Away!
Hastings: It may be the state of times is dangerous,
   but larger danger stalks this matter of estate. 443
Stanley: If a man but do himself to ware,
   the signs are ominous.
Hastings: I grant you, Stanley. 10
   Mought the day prove fairer in the blossom than the bud:
   My horse did this morning stumble thrice in the way.
   Howbeit, an atomy of reason weigheth up a peck of omens.

---

442 4.3. *Note:* The majority of informed opinion holds that this meeting took place on Friday, June 13th. The minority believes that the meeting was held one week later, on Friday, June 20th. From a tactical point of view it would seem more sensible to delay moving against Hastings until after the duke of York had been taken from sanctuary in the abbey (Monday, June 16th). It is hard to believe that the queen would have relinquished her son under any circumstance short of direct force, given the example of Hastings' assassination just four days before.

   The structure of *Dark Sovereign* reflects the earlier date, though for unconventional reasons. Lunar charts covering the period from Gloucester's *putsch* to his death seemed to suggest, at first glance, that the king was subject to bouts of action consistent with the full and the dark phases of the moon; in short, that the king was, in the most literal, medieval sense of the word, a lunatic. Friday, June 13th coincided with a full moon. There is insufficient evidence to support this theory. Cf. note 5.1.32.

443 4.3.7. *matter of estate:* 'I call matter of estate, not only the parts of sovereignty, but whatsoever introduceth any great alteration or dangerous precedent...' Bacon, *Of Judicature.* Cf. note 4.2.110.

Stanley: Where interest rules it is not reason,
 but unreason, fears me.

Hastings: Attend me, Stanley. Reason be your physic,
 your alone antipathy with adverse signs.
 Our duty falls out a plain matter:
 we must helm this bus'ness upon honourable ways.

*Enter **Gloucester**, cheerful.*

> *As conversation ensues, the lords take places at a long table:*
> ***Hastings** at one end, then **Stanley, Morton, Howard,**
> **Rotherham** and **Buckingham**.*
> ***Gloucester** sits at the other end, apart from the others.*
> *The three **Councillors** remain standing.*

Gloucester: Good morrow, noble souls.
Lords: As much unto your grace.
 God save your grace.
Gloucester: Good words, the goodest hearts, a thanks requite.
 Excuse the lateness of the hour. I was ta'en tardy by the day.
 But now, fair greeting, one and all. Is't not a glorious thing?
 We convént to set an adamantine seal upon the king.
Buckingham: As adamant, so steel, so our resolve.
 Never was pleasinger cause advanc'd.
Morton: The gather'd voice of all subscribes your grace.
Gloucester: And yet your favours are enstamp'd
 of too too solemn joy. Be glad!
 I crave a further moment, lords; I would to breakfast, too.
 I am gave to understand you have good strawberries

---

444 4.3.15. *unreason*: rash or hasty actions. Cf. 4.1.15.
445 4.3.26. *convént*: As a verb, convént takes the stress on the second syllable.
446 4.3.29. *subscribes*: agrees with.
447 4.3.30. *favours*: features, facial expressions.

at your garden, Morton. Prithee, let us have a mess of them. 448

Morton: Strawberries? And gladly.

But I would I had some better thing

as ready to your grace's pleasure as my strawberries.

*Signals an **Attendant**, who goes.*

Gloucester, *rising*: Do you confer a while.

To you I shall entrust the order and the ordering

of everything. In especial, look you be resolv'd of this: 40

The celebration will not have sufficient moment,

but that ye do pomp enough

beseeming best King Edward's coronation day.

Render me that you prick when I return. 449

Exit.

---

448 4.3.34. Thomas More's account thus: 'The protecteur ... sayd unto the bishop of Elye: My lord you have very good strawberies at your gardayne in Holberne, I require you let us have a mess of them' (Cambridge, 1883).

    Gloucester's alleged request for strawberries may say more about Thomas More than about Richard Gloucester. In an attempt to prove or disprove this tale, efforts have been made to determine whether strawberries grown in Holborn could have been ripe by mid-June. Less attention has been given to the symbolism of ripe fruit in the world of More and his contemporaries.

    More wrote *Richard III* by 1513. Across the Channel, Hieronymous Bosch, a man of equally conservative religious and moral views, painted his *Garden of Earthly Delights* between 1510 and 1515. Its central panel depicts nakedness and untrammeled lust, the motif being aided and abetted over and over again by that hieratical symbol of licentiousness and greed, ripe strawberries. Given More's times, and his mind-set, he could not have popped a better symbol into Gloucester's mouth than that with which he chose to set this scene.

    It is not surprising that More's reference to strawberries set historians on a false trail for a literal explanation. The symbolism of Bosch — and More — was soon lost as the Renaissance swept over Europe: it was elucidated again in the 1970s by the Dutch scholar Dirk Bax.

    In 1983, Jack Leslau suggested that Hans Holbein's portrait of Sir Thomas More and his family contained many rebuses or visual clues, suggesting that the two little princes had survived the reign of *Richard III*. (See Geraldine Norman, *The Times*, Friday, March 25, 1983, p.12.) Without entering that debate, it does seem clear that More's commission (1527) put Holbein to work devising rebuses or clues on several levels, including symbols of royalty. A dangerous business, that: Henry Howard, earl of Surrey, would die some years later for nothing more than marshalling his coat of arms with that of his ancestor, Edward the Confessor. If More's reference to strawberries is symbolic, it may be regarded as an early stage in his evolution from speaking in overt rebuses, or obvious symbols, to the covert or cryptic rebus, the only way in which dangerous knowledge could be presented in a perilous age.

    One may speculate that Sir Thomas, who did more than any other early writer to stamp 'wicked' on Richard Gloucester's reputation, was himself bound to descend into a symbolism every bit as devious and dark as the qualities he attributes to King Richard's personality. Cf. note 4.3.92.

449 4.3.44. *Render me that you prick*: Give me an account of what you select (from the agenda).

Hastings: Methinks your fear too much, your hope too small. 450
Stanley: Never as yet saw I his secret mien
   educe this sprite of frolic May-day.
Morton: Please you it prove not an ill. 451
Howard: A jovial disposition's hardliest express'd 452
   of one that is in reputation of his saturnal soul. 50
Morton: And a lunar impression withal. 453
Howard: He falls betwixt these twain.
Morton: Wherefore he is endow'd with both's natural sympathies.
Stanley: Whose shadow falls unsurely between signs
   can nowise cast a steady part.
Morton: He is none of these that shrink from lies:
   That disposition ran contráry with his own.
Stanley: If Gloucester's present temper be not feign'd,
   then he had mined the three souls deep 454
   to broach such measure of 't. 60
Hastings: Glad yourself, Stanley.
   As joy exceeds all other jewels, rejoice.
Rotherham, *to Buckingham*: The duke of late was never
   so greatly put in heart. What shall this signify?
Buckingham: I doubt not but that soon he will discover it.

Re-enter **Gloucester**, *moody. He sits.*

Gloucester: What are they worthy, that imagine to destroy me,
   being I am protector of the king?
      Silence.

---

450 4.3.45. *hope*: trust, confidence.
451 4.3.48. *ill*: is here an adjective, implying its noun from the reference to *frolic May-day* in the previous line. The expression *ill May-day* entered the language after rioting in London on that day in 1517. Ben Jonson uses it figuratively in *Epicœne, or The silent woman*, 1609.
452 4.3.49. *hardliest express'd*: expressed with the greatest difficulty.
453 4.3.51. *impression*: A strong influence brought to bear on the intellect or the emotions. § *impression*: see also the 'wax' figure at 3.3.130.
454 4.3.59. *the three souls*: The combined essential vital forces, said to be: vegetative (physical growth); the sensitive or sensible (life and awareness through the senses in 'brute beasts'); and the reasoning quality (said by some to be exclusive to humans). Cf. 5.3.16.

Hastings: Those are surely punishworthy,
whose soever treason it may be.
Some Lords: Aye. 70
It's so, indeed.
Gloucester: She is that witch, my brother's wife,
that formerly was clepéd queen;
and other, which be about to do such things with her.
Now shall ye see how that sorceress conspir'd with this,
the hot whore Mistress Shore, whose affinity hath wasted
and forpin'd me with their witchcraft.
They work their goëty upon me with yet staining sin.
I am spiteblasted.
> *Sir Thomas More described Richard's action at this point: He pulled up*
> *"hys doublet sleve to his elbow upon his lefte arme, where he shewed a*
> *withered arme and small…"*

Look where they act their will; how by still practice 80
of their seven filthy arts the quick flesh cankers.
Meanwhile …
Councillor 1, *aside*: Meseems Elizabeth were wiser
than to work such mischief.
Councillor 2, *aside*: The queen would nothing less
than cleave to the despites of Mistress She
that play'd a stewes with Hastings, Dorset — and her king!
Councillor 3, *aside*: The doxy's like a ready hearth.
Councillor 1, *aside*: Where never wants a readier poker.

---

455 4.3.74. *which be about to do*: This does not mean 'on the point of doing'. Rather, it should be read as: 'who go around doing'.

456 4.3.77. *witchcraft*: was the easiest charge to lay, and impossible to defend against. Witchcraft had reached epidemic proportions in the collective mind of the day, and society's response was often hysterical, brutal and swift. Five years after Gloucester addressed this Council, Pope Innocent VIII issued a bull calling on Christian nations to rescue the Church from the black arts of Satan. Similar bulls were issued by Popes Alexander VI (1494), Leo XI (1521), and Adrian VI (1522), launching Christian Europe on an orgy of hangings, burnings and drownings which would last nearly two centuries. The thrust of Gloucester's alleged reasoning and the nature of the supposed plot are given by Desmond Seward on page 100 of *England's Black Legend*. Seward's book is hostile to the king.

457 4.3.78. *goety*: A form of invocation to the spirits, that was practised in graveyards.

458 4.3.80. *still practice*: constant practice.

459 4.3.84–85. *nothing less than*: do anything rather than.

Councillor 2, *aside*: This matter but serves to pick a quarrel.
    The duke lets as though his wound had been fresh.   90
    Not a one is here but knows the lord protector's arm
    was wearish from a child.   460
Gloucester: How may they best be serv'd
    which hath gone about to break me thus?
    Silence.
Hastings: God'santy, if these so heinously have done,
    they well merit of punishment …
Gloucester: How saidst thou, sir? Thou giv'st me "if"!
    I tell thee, hit be so that they have done.   461
    And their treason I shall make good on thy body. Traitor!
    He strikes the table as a signal.

    *Armed **Men** rush in, "as many as the chambre might hold".*
    *They seize **Hastings**, **Rotherham** and **Morton**.*
    *One **Man** cuts at **Stanley**, who ducks to avoid the blow.*
    He is dragged from beneath the table, bleeding from a head-wound.
    *Meanwhile, other **Men** bring in a **Priest**.*

Gloucester: I arrest thee of thy treason.
Hastings: What, me, my lord?   100
Gloucester: Yes, thee. Shrive thyself, and make an end apace.
    Soon shalt thou lay down thy head to treason's block.
Hastings: I claim the right by Magna Carta!
Gloucester: The Charter, much! None hath right of treason.

---

460 4.3.92. *wearish*: disfigured, shrunken, spastic. *Wearish* is more frequent in the Period than 'withered'. In the matter of Richard Gloucester's supposed disfigurement, Ross (p.139) concludes that 'There is no reliable evidence for the popular Tudor idea that he was hunchbacked'. And again (p.140), 'It took the reputation and literary ability of Sir Thomas More to stamp upon the Tudor imagination the idea that Richard was "little of stature, ill-favoured of limbs, crook backed, his left shoulder much higher than his right, hard-favoured of visage"'. Hanham (p.165, note 3) notes: '…Rous states … that Richard's right shoulder was higher than his left, and More reverses this. Was his [More's] memory at fault, or was he wryly aware that he too walked with the right shoulder higher, as Erasmus tells us?'

461 4.3.97. *hit*: it. This is the Northern emphatic form. *Hit* migrated south, finding a niche in the letters of Queen Elizabeth I before retreating north again in the seventeenth century.

Hastings: The article holds well:
"No free man will we seize, ne yet destroy;
nor will we go upon him but by lawful judgment
of his equals ... "
Gloucester: There is no way but one with thee.
The article thou tastest on is death! 110
To **Guards**: Hence ye with him. Hence!
Hastings: "We will deny none's right, nor justice!"
Gloucester: By Paul, I'll not away until I see thy head off.
Housel thee! Away!

Most **Armed Men** *leave with* **Stanley**, **Rotherham**,
and **Morton**. **Hastings** *is taken off last.*
The **Priest** *is seen to give him absolution.*

Hastings: *Confitior deo omnipotenti ...*
  Other **Armed Men** *remove* **Hastings** *and the* **Priest**.
Hastings, *voice off*: *... tibi pater quia peccavi nimis
cogitatione verbo et opere, mea culpa, mea culpa,
mea maxima culpa.*
Priest, *voice off*: *Misereator tui omnipotens deus
et dimissis peccatis tuis ducat te ad vitam eternam.* 120
Hastings, *voice off*: Amen.
Priest, *voice off*: *Ego te absolvo a peccatis tuis ...*
  Off: *Sounds of confusion.*

Enter a **Servant Girl**, *running, holding a basket covered with a red-stained cloth,
which she brings to* **Gloucester**.

Gloucester, *recoiling*: Wouldst have me Herod to a traitor's head?

---

[462] 4.3.108. *'No free man ... equals'*: Magna Carta, clause 39.
[463] 4.3.109. *no way but one*: The phrase suggests that death or ruin is certain.
[464] 4.3.110. *The article ... death*: Puns on the article of death, which implies being on the point of death.
[465] 4.3.112. *'We will deny none's right, nor justice!'*: Magna Carta, clause 40.
[466] 4.3.114. *Housel thee! Loosely*: Confess your sins! Get to confession!

Servant: Cham bidden bring yr. grace a mess o' strawb'ries! 467
Removing the cloth, she reveals strawberries.
Priest, *voice off*: In nomine patris, et filii, et spiritus sancti.
Hastings, *voice off*: Amen! 126
  Gloucester reaches toward the sound.
  Sfx: An axe strikes a block; and a head strikes the floor.
  Fast curtain.

ACT 4, SCENE 4

Enter a Crier, with a long document.

Crier: Oyez, oyez, all manner men,
  your ears for news is my exchange.
  I make a proclamation in King Edward the Fifth's name.

  A Crowd gathers, including Kate, Ned and Will,
  several Persons and a Scribe, with others as may be.

  We do hereby publish and give knowledge that my lord Hastings
  did this morning imagine and contrive a reach with other 468
  that were in purpose to have slain our best-belovéd uncle,
  our protector, Richard duke of Gloucester, and our
  best-esteeméd uncle, Henry duke of Buckingham, with him.
  It was these traitors' mind to rule our person,
  and our reign afterwards, as our realm were suited 10 469
  with their only will;
  wherefor my said Lord Hastings died the death two hours since.

---

[467] 4.3.123. *Cham*: I am. See notes on Mummerset at 3.6.106.
[468] 4.4.5. *a reach*: a scheme.
[469] 4.4.10. *as*: as if.

　　　　Moreover than this, take note, how the traitorous Hastings
　　did formerly entice the king our father
　　with overmuch that made to the disesteeming of his honour.
　　This, that erstwhile was our father's and our chamberlain,
　　did greatly hurt the peace of England:
　　as by evil company; by his sinister procuring;
　　by th'ungraciousness of his ensample; and by 's vicious living,
　　and in especially with Elizabeth, called Jane,
　　the wife of William Shore.　　　　　　　　　　　　　　　　20
　　　*Exit the **Crier**.*
Will: He winded such a heavy instrument again such simple sin!
Ned: *Verba ventosa*. Hastings was worse accounted of　　　　470
　　than Mephistopheles. If wenching was a matter for the axe
　　I had been lopp'd long sin.
Kate: He toll'd a harder instrument than thine,
　　for hardly canst thou sin. Wast ever man?　　　　　　　471
　　or winter-wither'd stalk always?
Ned: Saist 'ou me so, thou gaping fricatrice?
　　To the heavens: Cruelty, thou art a tripe too much desir'd!
Kate: As little loved!　　　　　　　　　　　　　　　　　30
Will, *to **Person 1***: This other matter met a sorry stop.
Person 1: 'Tis pity. Hastings was a full man, and a wise,
　　and of great reach.　　　　　　　　　　　　　　　　472
Will: Yond herald's script did tear the cat too much.　　　473
Scribe: Believe it, coz!
　　Besides, this crier's masters would put another trick upon us.
　　To snatch words from dukes' brains — which commonly
　　be not of one language, but speak out of faction —

470　4.4.22. *Verba ventosa*: Windy words. After Vulgate, Job 16.3. (KJV: *vain* words).

471　4.4.26. *Wast*: is grammatically correct, though Shakespeare and subsequent writers used *wert*. The phonetic value of *wast* is preferred here.

472　4.4.33. *reach*: intellectual grasp. The line was originally written as an epitaph on Rivers, to whom it more accurately applies. However, it does not fit into the simplicity of Act 4.9 without adding complication. So let it represent Hastings; it's not so far from the mark. It seems to me there was always a certain symmetry between these arch-rivals of the time.

473　4.4.34. *tear the cat*: bluster, exaggerate, 'protest too much'.

composing them, dictating them, sometimes spelling, ⁴⁷⁴
some slitting goose-quills, now blotting out 40 ⁴⁷⁵
to change signification, now compiling all again ...

    Hastings' bloody gorge still bleeds like a freshet,
whereat his deaded humours smoke like a pinch'd candle.
And therefore, their report lies loudly.
Yond herald's scribe needsly had the better part
of dawn to dark to frame that roll of sins.
I well wot that I speak. I am recorder of the rolls at Pauls.
My best endeavour to write such court-hand faulteth
in some little time — and who can write so swift
as he outruns time? No. If this indictment were written 50
after they cut his head, or fiends or fairies wrate it.

Person 2: Well then, murder faced the lie.
From the very first he was fordone:
It was the law of Lidford. ⁴⁷⁶

Person 3: To lay this crime on Hastings' charge
was such a grindstone as the dukes might whet their axe.

Ned: It smells of the candle.

Kate: The ink-horn to boot.

Person 1: Aye, a' tastes all o' th' lamp. ⁴⁷⁷

Scribe: The stench of learning in Ambition's thrall. 60

Person 2: Bishop Morton!

Scribe: Nay. A' speaks in lawyers' pretty turns
and slippery tricks.

Person 2: Catesby!

Several: Catesby, aye!

Person 3: Thilk proclamation pricketh near his mark.

*The **Crier** returns.*

---

[474] 4.4.39. *spelling*: proof-reading, spelling.
[475] 4.4.40. *some*: Often used where *sometimes* would otherwise have to be repeated. Cf. note Ind.2.68.
[476] 4.4.54. *law of Lidford*: lynch law.
[477] 4.4.57/59. These three lines are variations on a theme, implying labour expended by candle-light on a document that rings hollow, contrived or just badly written. Only when applied to a sermon were such comments considered complimentary. A sermon, after all, should be a labour of pastoral love.

Crier: At our dread liege's command — which power
of the kingdom is confirm'd in the hand of his true,
well-belovéd and faithful Council — the said Hastings
(whose name the same that traitor shall so much resound) 478
taken openly at treason, was done to peremptory dispatch, 70
unless delay embolden mischievous and naughty persons
which might purpose to deliver him from us.
Now, by that traitor's well deserving end, our realm shall,
by the grace of God, rest in good quiet and in peace.
   *The **Crier** goes.*

Ned: The white boar did slash off his head
ere the black ox might tread on his toes. 479

Person 1: Thus is taken off a pretty humanician 480
in 's consistent age. 481

Person 3: But how of this can Gloucester avail?

Person 2: Marry, but he showeth himself marble to pity.
From henceforth the Council will well take the wind of him. 80 482

Person 3: It seems to me, how well all lesser natures bleed 483
t'avail a higher nature's end, herein the bigger nature's end
was bled t'avail the less.

Person 1: 'Twere almost just and it were so.

Person 2: As how?

Person 1: 'Twere bet that Hastings' end avail'd some end,
all be, to show that others' ends with mischief run afoot, 484
he bleeds afresh. Else what a wasteful end of such were this: 485
To end, and in his ending, make a useless end at all. 88 486
   Exeunt omnes.

---

478   4.4.69. *the same that: the same as.* A construction not infrequent after *same.*

479   4.4.76. *the black ox*: old age, adversity. *OED* does not find this until Addison, in 1711. However, Mulcaster uses it in *Positions*, xxxvi, 139 (1581).

480   4.4.77. *humanician*: student of the humanities. Absent from *OED*. Cf. Holinshed, *Chron*. II, 44/1.

481   4.4.77. *consistent age*: the interval of full maturity before the onset of old age.

482   4.4.80. *Take the wind of*: to do [one's] bidding.

483   4.4.81. *how well*: although. Usually used in a concessive sense, in the form 'how well ... yet/but well...'. Cf. note 1.1.81.

484   4.4.86. *all be*: albeit. Also given as *albe, allbe*.

ACT 4, SCENE 5

"Crosby's Place" in Bishopsgate.

Enter **Gloucester**.

Gloucester: Why so, it's done. His death is done,
th'acerbity whereof hath suck'd the courages
out of the Council. But, however the intent [487]
by Hastings' death achievéd is, his shade,
no less eternal than the act,
still and anon doth dwell i' th' head.
O, if I could, I should reach clysters in to pluck it out.
How long ere it abate, quitting the unquiet mind?
Or doth th'infection of impulsive death persist,
to grow apace, his cause contagious, cankering the brain? 10 [488]

---

[485] 4.4.87. *bleeds afresh*: A corpse was believed to start bleeding again when its murderer was made to approach it. In time, therefore, *bleed* came to imply revelation, as in: *This crime will bleed*, This crime will be exposed. Hence, as here, to serve as a continuing example. See *Richard III*, 1.2.56; *Julius Caesar*, 2.1.171. D.D.R. Owen finds this notion first in French, in Chrétien de Troyes' *Yvain*, c. 1177.

[486] 4.4.88. *a useless end at all*: a wholly useless end.

[487] 4.5.3. *however*: however much.

[488] 4.5.10. *contagious*: Refers to contamination of the soul by the sins of the body. The notion goes back at least to Boethius (d. 525).

The reverse logic may account for More's fixation upon Gloucester's alleged 'deformity'. See Leviticus 21:17–24 and Psalm 51:5. The latter is relevant here: "Behold, I was shapen in iniquity; and in sin did my mother conceive me." (I sang this often as a chorister, mostly in Latin.) Setting aside modern counter-arguments, it is clear that the late medieval mind considered 'shapen' as involving physical deformity. Apart from Thomas More, here is the vicar John Skelton (a 'celibate' Catholic priest as well as poet, and a tutor to the future Henry VIII). Skelton presented his newborn bastard son to his congregation, thus: "How say you, neighbors all? Is not this child as fair as the best of all yours? It hath nose, eyes, hands, and feet, as well as any of yours. It is not like a pig, nor a calf, nor like no foul nor no monstrous beast. If I had brought forth this child without arms or legs, or that it were deformed being a monstrous thing, I would never have blamed you to have complained to the Bishop of me..." [for being a priest fathering a child 'in iniquity']. (I am grateful to Carol Thoma, Ph.D., for quoting Skelton from the *Norton Anthology of English Literature*.)

Cf. physical deformity caused by the full moon, at 5.1.31.

   Forget th'unhappy hour; forget the day;
the very fact forget! Nor ancient blood-wite
nor weregeld can Hastings' death assuage
— albeit these too enfeebling thoughts may be th'exacted they.
   Enough! I can no more take ruth,
nor, being sensible of grief, dare not to grieve.
Let weep who will; let weep who wont to weep.
Mine eyes, as parch'd as Africk sand,
retir'd my mood from thence too soon a day.
What cost compassion? Death. His ever presence   20
needsly is the goad must set me on. *Makes to go.*

Enter **Incubus**, *a boisterous dwarf, dressed like Gloucester, who proceeds to play the traditional King Richard of Tudor imagination.*

Incubus: Richard, we would a word in time.
Gloucester *reacts, as if to his own thought,*
 never perceiving the other as a physical being:
 It seems that I am stay'd,
 — and that upon the leisure of an inkling. Which?
Incubus: An inkling, pah! Here Incubus, thine Incubus.
 Come tarry, tarry Richard. Come.
Gloucester: My foolish brain to entertain dark thinkings thus!
 Again he offers to depart.
Incubus: Is not Incubus our proper familiar?
Gloucester: How, this sudden inward voice?   30
Incubus: Why, I am thee, and thou art me,
 so thee and me be indivisible. Hold, Richard. Stay!
Gloucester: Then speak!
 And if this fiend-like notion should be me, I should cry hold,
 hold friends with it, and hold his inkling true.

---

489 4.5.13. *blood-wite, weregeld*: forms of blood-money (O.E. Law).
490 4.5.15. *take ruth*: take pity.
491 4.5.21. *must set me on*: urge me on.
492 4.5.34. *cry hold*: surrender (to it).

If else, I would be rid of thee.
Incubus: We are well rid of Hastings. The princes remain still.
Gloucester: How often do I think upon my brother's pretty sons.
Incubus: Those nephews put Incubus in great jeopardy.
Remember, since some sixteen years agone, the earl of Desmond   40
chid at Edward for the ignobility of her he brided.
Gloucester: By fatal consequence, the Woodvilles
made him shorter by the head, and slew his sons.   493
Incubus: What saist thou to the deaths of babes?
Gloucester: To waste a life were sin ...
Incubus: ... but that it were politic.
Gloucester: These shall be bastards, both.
Incubus: Bastards?
Gloucester: Bastards!
Incubus: Were he sired of rape by devils,   50
yet a bastard may destroy a man of Christian birth.
Let them be dead! To claim them bastards
shall invoke a grievous load of law,
and to lay weight upon the Parliament how they'll adhere.   494
Gloucester: Law's quarrels blunt 'gainst greatness.
If, peradventure, one carry to the mark, his edge is turn'd.
Incubus: Doth the lion weep (quoth Buckingham) to raze the lamb,
whom very Nature sets just in his way?
What ailest thou, my 'nother I?
Gloucester: I am not in the vein for murder.   60
These shall bastard infants by their bastard father be.
Incubus: Thou, thou mak'st thy proper father to wear the horn!   495
clep'st our mother of rare piety — adulteress!
Our rudeness will be call'd in question.
Gloucester: None will credit to it.

---

493 4.5.43. Seward (p.42), and Ross (p.33, note 37) described Desmond's fatal slip.
494 4.5.54. *to lay weight ... adhere*: force ... to take sides.
495 4.5.62. *wear the horn*: be a cuckold. Frequent in Period drama.

    Though, when Edward wed his chamberer, our mother,
    in abhorrency and self-will, did him threat
    to clepe his kingly body fitz and bastard.
    But now's a time, as power gets power,
    and got, doth still increasing power attain,   70
    so others' silence doth connive the suasion of a lie
    no man dare mock.
    Moreover, bastardy is such a state none may deny.
    I shall infer that very no-treason
    why Clarence quaffed his end in Malmsey:
    Our brother Edward was the bastard offspring
    of a bowman, Blayborgne.
Incubus: A French to boot, whose bolt found forth his mark!
Gloucester: Great Warwick purpos'd it;
    Charles Burgundy call'd Edward by the Blayborgne name;
    and Clarence — th' ever child of folly —
    did applaud it to the echo, and his end.   80
    Therefore, by this figure of dry mock,
    this echoed instrument of irony,
    let Clarence' death avengéd be,
    and Edward's issues dispossess'd.
Incubus: The matter must his precedent ere it prevail.
Gloucester: Precedents from earthly quivers spring
    as thick as heaven hath stars. The second Richard
    was conceiv'd a bastard slip of a French priest.
Incubus: How lusty, covetous these Frenchmen are
    to stick their prick in English virtue.   90

---

496 4.5.66. *chamberer*: Queen Elizabeth had once been a lady-in-waiting in Queen Margaret's household. Thomas More thus: 'In service with Queen Margaret'.

497 4.5.77. *purpos'd it*: suggested it, started it in circulation. Cf. *cat in the pan*, at 4.2.12.

498 4.5.81. *dry mock*: irony.

499 4.5.86. *quivers*: wombs. The word is used in that sense in Ecclesiasticus 26.12. By extension, in a patriarchal society, it implies progeny.

500 4.5.88. *conceiv'd*: OED notes that conception was often considered a male function, the female womb being but the vehicle in which the father's foetus came to term. This usage is most frequent 'in expressions originating in the Eng. version of the Creed'. Thus, *Paternoster*, 1509: 'Jesu Christ his only son ... the which is conceived of the holy ghost, borne of Mary the maid'.

Gloucester: No man but has his fault.
   'Twas Somerset sir'd Henry Sixtus' son.
   But, to a point: Am I not the perfect man my father was?
Incubus: Yes, verily we are. And more.
Gloucester: Am I not the perfectest mirror of his frame?
Incubus: Yes. The likeness is well mark'd.
Gloucester: Do I resemble him more than my brothers did?
Incubus: Yea, indeed, 'tis such.
Gloucester: Then it was not I,
   but Edward's seed, and Edward's humour-brethren
   sprang from contradictious paradox.
   We shall convey the duke of York straightways unto the Tower,
   to the king, and after cry them down for bastards.
Incubus: We must procure the offices of priests.
Gloucester: We'll cloak the princes' bastardy
   with reverend purple. This race,
   by view of Holy Mother Church, shall be bebless'd.
   Exeunt.

---

[501] 4.5.92. *King Henry VI* was afflicted with both piety and madness, the former to such an extent that he is said to have shunned Queen Margaret's bed for long periods, in consequence failing to produce an heir. Rumour had it that the duke of Somerset performed the king's duty for him, fathering Henry's only heir, Edward of Lancaster. King Henry, in more lucid moments, ascribed his son Edward's paternity to the Holy Ghost. This same Edward of Lancaster was later betrothed to Lady Anne Neville, whom we meet in 1.1 mourning his loss.

[502] 4.5.93. *the perfect man*: a copy of the man. Gloucester seeks reassurance that he bears a family resemblance to his late father.

[503] 4.5.96. *mark'd*: noticed and remarked upon. Indeed, this resemblance was remarked upon.

[504] 4.5.98. Note the use of *Yes* and *Yea* in Incubus's responses. In its purest form, *yes* was reserved for an affirmative answer to a negative question. *Yea* was the affirmative reply to a positive question. Cf. French, *si* and *oui*. Early editions of the KJV preserve this distinction, but it was lost in the revision of 1881, when *yeses* were antiqued into *yeas*. *No* and *nay* have a similar history.

[505] 4.5.100. *humour-brethren*: Personality, temperament or general disposition, as determined by the relative proportions of the body's four main fluids, or humours. This sense was sometimes mocked by Shakespeare and Ben Jonson. See *Love's Labour's Lost*, III.i.24; *Every Man in His Humor*, III iv.

[506] 4.5.10. *contradictious paradox*: That which runs contrary to accepted belief.

[507] 4.5.106. *race*: course of action, course of events.

[508] 4.5.107. *by view of*: under the supervision of. Loosely, with the (tacit) approval of.

ACT 4, SCENE 6

"Cheynygates", Monday, June 16, 1483.

Queen Elizabeth *and some of her five* **Daughters** *busy themselves with needlework.* **Richard Duke of York** *rushes around in a hobby-horse.*

Sfx: *The din of armed men, off.*

Enter **Elizabeth of York**.

Elizabeth of York: Men in harness keep stations all about, mamma!
Q. Elizabeth: Then now is as it ever was, Elizabeth.
Elizabeth of York: Me seems they are many the more and harder men
    than ever they were before.
Q. Elizabeth: Westminster is not Jericho-walls
    to fall before their din.
Elizabeth of York: It's noised that eight boats came on the tide
    from London!
Q. Elizabeth: If they imagine of their clamouring
    to drive us hence, misprision on their heads!

---

509 *Stage Direction 4.6*: Although it is difficult to determine whether Thomas More writes fact or fiction, his eighteen page account of the Council's debate about sanctuary, followed by Canterbury's (Bourchier's) confrontation with the queen, seems to ring true. Certainly other sources leave no doubt as to the episode's conclusion. Hence, this scene follows More's account.
    Seward states that the party, led by Gloucester, included Buckingham, Howard, Canterbury (Bourchier, in my first printed edition) and Russell. Howard's domestic accounts paid for the eight boats (line 7). More was reluctant to name names. He gives Bourchier's escort as 'divers other lordes'.
    Russell's presence may be inferred from the Croyland Chronicle account, which is brief and peculiar. Written thirty-four months later, it reads like an obvious *non mea culpa*, designed to rid the shadow of guilt by association.
    Seward suggests that Howard was responsible for the comment given in lines 135–6. It seems likely, given the short list of participants, but More mentions only 'another Lorde'.

510 *The hobby-horse* was no stranger to the Period stage. Stephen Gosson (c. 1579) speaks of 'dauncing of gigges, galiardes, and moriscoes, with hobbi-horses' in stage performances. Shakespeare and Ben Jonson thought the hobby-horse worthy of mention; and William Sampson played with the motif in *The Vow-breaker; or, the Fair Maid of Clifton* as late as 1636.

511 4.6.9. *misprision*: scorn, contempt.

Elizabeth of York: Dost think they mean to take the marquis? 10
Q. Elizabeth: We shall return their writ *Non est inventus*,
God be thanked. Dorset is fled; he makes for Brittany.
Aside: Blow fair, ye winds. For once be not proud,
but carry sweet Thomas amaine.
Elizabeth of York: Mamma, think'st thou these men for ill?
Q. Elizabeth: Hush, child! *Privately*: I know it.
Their arméd manners speak for violence of thought.
Natheless their ambassy is curs'd,
and bless'd be this day 'tis so.
Elizabeth of York, *looking off*: Great persons are coming this ways! 20
Q. Elizabeth: Act the woman, Elizabeth! Prick on thy clout!
Elizabeth of York: Yea, mamma.
Maybe these would do thee suit and services.
Q. Elizabeth: Do they whatever service,
it were conceiv'd from spleen.
Elizabeth of York, *looking off*: They speak to Father John,
and he ... now bowing ... suffers some of them passing.
Cardinal Bourchier is come, mamma. Look else!
Q. Elizabeth, *aside*: What means this by that ancient
and vertiginous prelate? Canterbury is more dead than quick. 30
Elizabeth of York, *looking off*: Aye, quickly. They come on apace,
the cardinal twixt Lord Howard and Harry Buckingham.
Q. Elizabeth: As quickly come, sirs! Come, come all away!
*The **Queen** removes herself and her **Children**.*
The duke's hobby-horse remains centre-stage.

---

[512] 4.6.11. *Non est inventus*: Originally a legal term, used by a sheriff returning a writ to indicate that a defendant, being absent, could not be brought to trial. By the Period, the term was largely allusive, but preserves a literal sense here.
[513] 4.6.21. *Prick on thy clout*: Do your needlework (on your embroidery frame).
[514] 4.6.28. *Look else!* See for yourself. Literally: See if it be otherwise.
[515] 4.6.30. *vertiginous*: dizzy-minded, senile.

Enter **Thomas Bourchier**, *cardinal archbishop of* **Canterbury**,
supported by **Howard** *and* **Buckingham**,
attended by **Bishop Russell** *(mute), with others as may be.*

Bourchier / Canterbury: Lords, if you demand of me
    to breathe out vehemence to the queen ... 516
    I must crave pause ... to breathe myself
    ... to fetch my breath ... The skein of things knits too fast.
Howard: Time flies, your grace,
    while Reason scuds behind, catch that catch may.
Bourchier: Instruct me, Buckingham: I'll know again your reason.
Buckingham: The hour to ruminate from company,
    lord cardinal, is past and gone. 40
Bourchier: This busi-ness is hard to be understood.
Buckingham: The voice of Holy Church,
    conjoinéd to the temp'ralty, doth in sum beseech you
    (worthy shepherd of Christ's flock) amend the present pass.
Bourchier: You would solicit, then ...
Buckingham: I solicit nothing. No vantage doth resort
    to my account. I am but humble advocate
    for our prince's highness' hest.
Howard: We are that league, your grace, 50
    whose duty's for the nonce to represent before the queen
    the moot and substance altogether
    of our stern-brow'd cast of thought.
    — The like that the Council was this morning resolv'd of.
Buckingham: The queen guards in the duke of York with her,
    in the sanctuary, distant from 's brother the king,
    whose special pleasure were to keep his brother by him,
    at the Tower.
Bourchier: The little boy hath surely done no wrong!

---

516 4.6.34. *breathe out*: speak with conviction.

Buckingham: She wills this of her woman fear and frowardness, 60
    to bring in obloquy against the lords,
    and courage the commons to murmuring upon the Church.
Bourchier: Can you Euripides, my lords? [517]
Buckingham, to *Howard*: He falls in age to wander.
Howard, to *Buckingham*: Do you set up our rest [518]
    upon this ancient hag? He's twice a child! [519]
Buckingham, to *Howard*: Informal though he be, [520]
    we have not a more better Troyan Horse.
Howard, *to Buckingham*: So, so,
    the notion holds the mirror up to common sense; 70
    holdeth, as 'twere, measure with his wooden wits. [521]
    The emperor Caligula install'd a horse high priest!
Buckingham, *to Bourchier*: By your grace's solemn intervention,
    we must obtain York his deliverance out of Westminster.
    For so we shall convey him to the presence, to the Tower.
Bourchier: But Nature will the mother keep her child.
Buckingham: This tiny boy hath neither wisdom to crave sanctuary,
    nor, of's tender years, has he accrued the malice
    to deserve it. Nor life, nor yet his liberty,
    may not by lawful process be abridg'd. 80
    To immure this boy, an innocent, from brotherhood, doth,
    of a surety, besmirch the honour of his highness' Council,
    and to profane the glorious favour of the Church.
Bourchier: Our Lord protect the sanctities of Church!

---

[517] 4.6.63. *Can you Euripides?* Do you know (the plays of) Euripedes? Euripedes was a playwright remarkable for vicious female characters.

[518] 4.6.65. *Do you set up our rest ...?* Did you set this up so that everything depends upon ...?

[519] 4.6.66. *twice a child*: An old man is twice a child. *Senex bis puer* (Old proverb).

[520] 4.6.67. *Informal*: Deranged, Stupid. Falling down daft. A usage peculiar to Shakespeare in *Measure for Measure* V.i.233. I support this interpretation by citing the Bard's balanced use of *formal* to describe good health in *Comedy of Errors*, V.i.105.

[521] 4.6.71. *the notion ... wooden wits*: To hold a mirror up to something reflects it, makes a nonsense of it, or, in fifteenth century terms, mocks it. Hieronymous Bosch gives mirror writing to the skating monster-messenger in his Saint Anthony Triptych. Cf. *Hamlet*, 3.2.23.

Buckingham: This sullen state redoundeth greatly
    to the king's dishonour, and by name as well to the clergy
    as the lords that be about his grace. As we to you,
    do you implore the queen in right of Council,
    — and is more, in right of Church — that she entrust her son
    unto your grace's office and high name.   90
Bourchier: A woman doeth as women are.
    So as Xanthippe with Socrates,
    this queen is proud, and obdurate to boot.
Buckingham: Then we shall, by th'authority royall,
    hence Richard from this abbey jail,
    and fetch him up to the Tower ...
Bourchier: ... My lords!
Buckingham: ... where he so cherishéd shall be,
    the queen will stand reveal'd in malice, frowardness
    and folly, which names the shackles she immures him here.   100
Bourchier: To try which ill adventure
    you would violate the Church!
Buckingham: Then ferret the duke by dent of word
    ere we do so in deed. All could we thus,
    we are no men to war with women and the Church.
    Face th'event, and brace, your grace!
    Methinks the queen comes. I'll go. *He goes.*
Bourchier, *aside*: O sorry day!
    How sore the cost of office, when needs it costs the pains.

Enter **Queen Elizabeth**.

Q. Elizabeth: God save you, lords.
    Canterbury, what news i' th' world?   110
Bourchier: Peace be to your highness' house.

---

[522] 4.6.86. *and by name ... to*: and especially to ...
[523] 4.6.92. *Xanthippe*: The reputedly shrewish wife of Socrates.
[524] 4.6.104. *All could we thus*: Although we could [threatening].

Q. Elizabeth: May it be long part and parcel
  of King Edward's peace. How be it, your severe aspéct
  looks like to sound a jarring note of discord.
Bourchier: The lords resolve the duke of York were the better
  for being to his brother, at the Tower.
Q. Elizabeth: Between high-minded voice
  and express'd thought indeed's disharmony.
Bourchier: That is so pleasing to the Council
  will as surely boot the realm.
Q. Elizabeth: How! Here's wilful knavery.   120
Bourchier: If it pleasure the king to keep with York,
  shall not York be pleasur'd too?
Q. Elizabeth, *aside*: How each lie protests their truth!   525
Bourchier: King Edward's every nature doth approve,   526
  that he shall better have his brother with him
  for his comfort and disport,
  than the company of wise and ancient men.
Q. Elizabeth: Richard is sick, wherefore I marvel
  that the lord protector is desirous he should keep him.
  If death impeach his natural years,
  nor Gloucester's blood-dipp'd might,   130
  nor all the wastes of unused time his memory will allay.
  Nothing doubt: A mother's nature is best nurture.
  And sith that I, like other of my house, may not come hence
  for jeopardy, the duke rests here by me.
Howard: Why, madam,
  do you know why those should stand in jeopardy?
Q. Elizabeth: Nay, and nor I wis why my brother, nor my son,   527
  nor other of my house should be in prison neither!
Bourchier *restrains* **Howard**: Let my entreaty satisfy.

---

525 4.6.123. *their*: Before the general adoption of *its*, *their* might be employed as the possessive pronoun following a singular noun qualified by *each* or *every*. OED notes drily: 'Not favoured by grammarians'.
526 4.6.124. *approve*: prove, show, demonstrate.
527 4.6.137. *I wis*: This form is incorrect here. It was used near the end of its range instead of *I know* or *I wot* (from *wist*, v.). *Iwis*, written as one word, is properly an adverb meaning certainly, assuredly.

Asphestus shall be burn'd with fire 140
before your highness come in jeopardy.
Q. Elizabeth: Whereby may I have trust in you?
The dukes mete brimstone upon other heads
to have their spite at me.
Bourchier: As you do think t'embrace your son,
e'en so they will not suffer you to coop him in the abbey,
indenting with your baseless fear, 528
lest you will away with him secretly.
If you will not bring Richard out,
meseemeth those account it as no breach of sanctuary 150
to fetch him forth. Which I do verily believe they will.
Q. Elizabeth: Hath Gloucester so great zeal toward him,
he feareth nothing but he should escape him? 529
Bourchier: Good madam, for hatred of the dukes
you look beyond them quite. 530
Q. Elizabeth: One asp another not more hates.
How doeth the Church as touching this affair?
Bourchier: As touching sanctuary, this privilege
the lords hath not agreed to be needful unto York, which,
being green of age and innocent, neither his no-sin,
nor malice, can no wise deserve it. 160
Q. Elizabeth: *Ecce* evil's echo, as I deem! 531
By this impetuous visitation, making summons,
you would tire me, find me feeble in the sudden time,
a woman sole, her rampart fall'n, her mind unmanned,
her breast brent up in ire. But for all, I am the stronger, 532
knowing he lays extremity indeed that sendeth this
so high good grace to effect so low pass.
How holds the shepherd, that this holy place,

---

528 4.6.147. *indenting*: being caught up with (part of the queen's own covenant with her fear). The line suggests that Queen Elizabeth is making the young duke of York a victim of her own terrors.

529 4.6.153. *He feareth nothing but*: He feareth most of all that, His greatest fear is that.

530 4.6.154. *look beyond them quite*: completely misunderstand them.

531 4.6.161. *Ecce*: Behold, Hark to, Listen to.

532 4.6.165. *breast*: Suggests breastwork, after the figurative use of rampart in the previous line.

which may defend a thief, cannot preserve a lamb?
Bourchier: I'll warrant your fear is fear'd 170
    at groundless, causeless sand.
Q. Elizabeth: Lord cardinal, your words dishonour you!
Bourchier: Know, madam, how great grief I feel ...
Q. Elizabeth: Wouldst seethe a kid in it own mother's milk? [533]
    Fourscore years have you endur'd England's wars
    and England's strifes. To marshal innocence, in chief
    above the powder of experience, doth little credit you.
    It maketh to a passing strange device. [534]
Bourchier: Good lady, think you that you be
    so very far beyond our care?
Q. Elizabeth: Yea, verily, if God's proper agent 180
    will cast out an innocent to succour the ungodly.
    Ye may not take my horse from me, nor yet a penny
    from my purse whiles I bide here. But you will steal my son! [535]
        How we by a circle go! You will I should bring out Richard,
    — I, who fleeing hither with quick child thirteen years past,
    brought forth your king, enwombéd in these walls,
    the same that now. Though each hot and bloody prodigy of war
    whelm'd England in destroy, King Edward's foes,
    yea, even Warwick, did but honour to my sanctuary. [536]
Bourchier: Pray your highness be not taken with distemper ... 190
Q. Elizabeth: Why art thou so *sudden*
    that thou shouldest be overseen? [537]
    An idiot may ween I shrink to yield my son

---

[533] 4.6.174. *Wouldst ... milk?* The queen is reminding the prelate of the biblical injunction in Exodus 23.19. Wyclif thus: '... in the mylk of his moder'. § To use *it* for the possessive pronoun echoes the only similar usage to find its way into the first edition of the KJV (See note on 1.1.154). That example in Leviticus was altered in 1660.

[534] 4.6.178. For the second time (Cf. 3.6.80) the queen draws an analogy from heraldry.

[535] N.H. MacMichael discusses sanctuary in *Westminster Abbey Occasional Paper* no. 27, *Sanctuary at Westminster* (1971), 9–14. (Cf. MacMichael at 3.6.Note.)

[536] 4.6.189. *even Warwick did but honour* ...: Warwick honoured ..., Warwick did no more and no less than honour ...

[537] 4.6.192. *sudden*: prone to act rashly, foolishly. Sometimes applied to the elderly, as in 'His Grace is old and sudden' (Tourneur, *The Revenger's Tragedy*, 4.1.93). § *overseen*: deluded, mistaken; deceived.

into those monsters' power, which have his brother
to their hand. If both shall fail, (whom God preserve!)
Gloucester — whose curséd microcosm bodies évéry each cause
of heaven's tears — Gloucester would be heir to all
what my sons' inheritance compounds. By the space of
eight and twenty years have we experienc'd how th'attachment
of this realm consid'reth nothing kindreds-tree,
nor neither bonds of blood nor fealty! 200

Bourchier *makes to go*: We had liefer go,
than that our here-remain discomfit you.

Q. Elizabeth: The all-perceiving law, though it be indifferent
and blind, is far-unwilling any should have the ward of one
whose death will vantage him.
Be as little as a doit so holden of another, thus the law.
By how much the more it should the dukes constrain,
who have good lust t'attach the whole dominions!

Bourchier: Prithee, madam, deny your frenzical fear,
unless it usurp upon your sense. 210
This burden sorteth with us not. 538
But withal we are not men without our troth.
Are we so dull the certain future looks not out?
Or were we born in Little Witham, 539
that we nothing see what Gloucester wills?

Q. Elizabeth: Canterbury, that you hold faith I not doubt,
nor of some other that are here.
I fear, in case your proper senses be deceiv'd;
for fright doth seel the eyes as interesses blind the soul. 540

---

538 4.6.211. *sorteth with us not*: doesn't suit us, is not appropriate or agreable to us.

539 4.6.214. At a time when the primary meaning of wit was mental intelligence, the East Anglian village of Little Witham achieved mild notoriety for its name. In the sixteenth century, 'to be born in Little Witham' meant to be born stupid.

540 *seel the eyes*: Seel as distinct from *to seal*. Cf. *night-seel'd, at* Ind.1.56. This verb was peculiar to the sense of sight, or the (deliberate) deprivation of it. Hawks had their eyes sewn shut (seeled) during training. The usage here is akin to William Wilberforce's comment to Parliament regarding supporters of slavery: "There are none so blind as those who will not see.".

Bourchier: Be he curs'd a dismal curse
   as did deliver up an innocent, if he perceiv'd
   the least hint of a Stygian sin at end!
Q. Elizabeth: I can no more!
   She goes, seeming to flee.
      Confused, **Bourchier** *offers to depart. Then ...*

Re-enter the **Queen**, *with* **Richard Duke of York**.
Q. Elizabeth: Lord cardinal, I put you in trust with my son.
   Convey him to the king; look no harms befall him,
   otherwise 'twill auspicate a heavy hurt to England's state
   which shall occasion you, of all untrue, the heaviest shame.
   Keep Richard safe, and Edward is sure; the safety of tone
   is vested in the life and quickness of the tother.
   Take him: I deliver him with all his brother's life in him.
      Lords, I charge you herewithal:
   Keep him which I commit into your trust;
   else, as surely as I live, I'll ask requital before God,
   and to demand of you a reckoning before the world.
   I beseech you, for the trust his father put with you,
   as far as ye do think I fear too much,
   be you well ware unless you fear too small.
      The **Queen** *embraces the* **Duke of York**.
   Farewell, my own sweet son: God send thee good keeping.
   Let me kiss thee once before thou goest out.
   God alone knows when we'll kiss together once again.
   God bless thee, Richard.
   God bless my son.
      The **Queen** *relinquishes* **York** *to* **Bourchier**.
      She goes, crying, and does not look back.
      The **Duke of York** *cries, "weeping as fast".*
      Bourchier's *party goes.*
      The hobby-horse remains.

---

[541] *Stage Direction. The hobby-horse remains*: A Period audience would have empathy with the symbolic value of an abandoned hobby-horse. Shakespeare and Ben Jonson made use of a now-apocryphal line from a lost English ballad, 'The hobby-horse soon is forgot'.

ACT 4, SCENE 7

Mid June, 1483.

Enter **Gloucester** *and* **Ratcliffe**.

Gloucester: Keep your way to Pontefract! 542
    Rid Rivers, Richard Grey, Sir Richard Haute
    and Thomas Vaughan. Do them die.
    Look every dread be rooted out,
    that they'll never fetch treasons again.
Ratcliffe: They'll not draw breath past my arrive.
    He makes to go.
Gloucester *calls after*:
    Switch and spurs, Ratcliffe! Ride on the spurs.
    Their death not yet the fear from my breast clears.
Ratcliffe: I will away toward York with quick dispatch. 9
    Exeunt singuli.

---

542 4.7.1 *Keep your way*: Don't stop. Go without interruption.

ACT 4, SCENE 8

The Guildhall, Tuesday, June 24, 1483.
*The **Lord Mayor** and **Aldermen** await **Buckingham**.*
*A crowd conceals **Truth** and **Rumour**.*

*Enter **Buckingham**, with **Percival**, **Nesfield** and others as may be.*

Buckingham: Friends, by your favour, I shall break my mind
    to you upon a weighty matter subject, and a great.
    Through two and twenty years King Edward took
    our substance off; his reign produc'd an evil age,
    upon which he died, leaving false shadows for the state.   543
    Thievery sans law is theft;
    and theft, all have it benefit of law, is tyranny.   544
    Such taxes Edward poll'd, such imposts pill'd,
    makes England to groan still. Did we, his subjects,
    bear his queen one minim of the love we bear to York,   10
    the court would not so soon be profligate.   545
    Friends, remember since th'afflictions that proceeded   546
    from his government — if government may so
    from harlots and Elizabeth! I'll tell you,
    Mistress Shore of late bore the greater sway, and more is,
    by her access unto Edward lay at him to do her bidding   547
    more than all the lords in England.
Alderman 1, *aside*: Men say he speaks
    the eloquences of three Greeks.

---

543   4.8.5. *upon which*: in consequence of which, as the result of which.
544   4.8.7. *all have it*: although it may have.
545   4.8.11. *profligate*: overthrown, brought down.
546   4.8.12. *remember since*: think back, recollect.
547   4.8.16. *lay at him*: This might seem like a crude reference to the lady's function in the king's bed, and Buckingham might certainly intend a *double entendre*, but *lay at* means to urge, to seek to convince, to importune.

Alderman 2, *aside*: A' was ever noted with eloquence.
'Tis a wind he has; a' playeth sweet, then blows to foul. 20
Buckingham: "Woe to thee, O land, when thy king is a child".
Nor shall a bastard sit in throne except he have right.
Scarce one is here but did not hear the reverend clerk,
good Doctor Shaa, defend which cause at Paul's.
The little boy, which we call king, was trod out
by bigamy twixt Edward and the Woodville wench
that was Queen Margaret's chambermaid whilere;
— this form, in despite of the contract of marriage
with Princess Bona, wherethrough Warwick espous'd the king
at his express'd command. 30
Moreover, that he troth-plight was, he plighted troth
to Eleanor, the earl of Shrewsbury's daughter.
We may go further and find worse:
'Twas very Nature affianc'd him Mistress Lucy,
by reason that she loathly bore their son.
Those examples precedent us in the issue:
From Edward's lechery no woman ventur'd safe,
lest, well-looking on his bitch-fewterer's eye,
she look'd rather to despairs.
Alderman 1, *aside*: He takes pains to move us. 40
Alderman 2, *aside*: I think rather 'twas a smooth-fac'd speech,
which, though it were fat to the ear,
yet did cloak every gloze unless itself.

---

548 4.8.21. Ecclesiastes 10.16 (KJV). Edward Hall, in *Chronicle (The union of the two noble and illustre famelies of Lancastre and Yorke)*, 1548, thus: 'I remembred an olde proverbe ... that "often ruithe the realme, where chyldren rule, and woman governe" '.

549 4.8.30. Princess Bona of Savoy was King Louis XI's sister-in-law.

550 4.8.35. Edward IV's putative match with Dame Elizabeth Lucy emerges for the first time in Sir Thomas More's account, written thirty years after the king's death and fifty years after the supposed betrothal. 'She was almost certainly the mother' of Edward's natural son, Arthur Plantagenet, according to St. Aubyn, who describes this betrothal in *The Year of Three Kings*.

551 4.8.38. *bitch-fewterer*: A fewterer tended dogs or game-animals. *Bitch* has been used opprobriously of women since c. 1400.

552 4.8.43. *gloze*: a sham, pretence, deception.

Buckingham: Be afeard no more! I am to set us free,
   to lift at that self yoke doth burthen ye,
   proferring one whose blameless manners, being wieldy,
   stay our very prop of honourable government.
   My honest motive bids me ask: Will you Richard Gloucester
   to your king? Or, to henceforth fortune Woodville,
   will you let benevolences whether?   50
   Did Gloucester wear one crown, the threefold diadem
   — peace, order, and propriety — should be attain'd unto by all.
Alderman 1, *aside*: Here's neither barrel better herring!
Alderman 2, *aside*: He'd have us to like of Barábbas!
Buckingham: "Blessed art thou", quoth the Preacher,
   "when thy king is the son of nobles".
   Whereof we thank God, that one sole heir of York
   hath title of the crown.
   Gloucester may do us this good turn, but …
   There is not a poor petition, but his grace will overmatch it   60
   on a modesty, except we can his own humility outface.
   Good ye, that to England bear your loves, proclaim your mind.
   Let your mouths offer how ye will,
   whereby I may persuade Gloucester to accept the throne.
      Aldermen whisper among themselves like "a swarm of bees".
Alderman 2, *aside*: How doth the redditive air jar for lyings!
Alderman 1, *aside*: Challenge his too earnest brow of power.
   Give him the lie, do!

---

553 4.8.44. *I am to*: It is my duty to (*the future tense of obligation*).

554 4.8.50. *let benevolences*: continue to be bled for the benefit of the royal treasury. A 'benevolence' was a 'loan' or contribution levied without legal sanction. Edward IV first imposed it, c. 1473. He required subjects to contribute to his treasury as a goodwill gesture to his rule. § The verb *let* in the sense of *lease* is appropriate, since benevolences were supposedly loans. § *whether*: Placed at the end of a sentence when required to emphasize choice. Shakespeare: 'Was this a lover or a letcher whether?'

555 4.8.51. *Did Gloucester wear…*: If Gloucester wore…

556 4.8.52. *propriety*: Loosely, the right to hold onto one's own property.

557 4.8.53. *Here's … herring*: This expression takes many forms, including 'Six of one, half a dozen of the other'.

558 4.8.55–56. Ecclesiastes 10.17 (KJV).

559 4.8.65. *redditive*: Responsive air: giving an answer, an echo. Usually used of specific statements.

Alderman 2, *aside*: I esteem the earnester value to my head.
Buckingham: The lord protector would more graciously incline
   to us, if our petition have favour of the aldermen of London.   70
   I fear else he'll refuse so grievous great a load.
      Aldermen continue to buzz.
Alderman 1, *aside*: How is dissimulation woven of fair words!
Alderman 2, *aside*: Of rhubarb words! Too fair, and very free.   560
Buckingham, *to Percival*: These company plays mum as hatters' blocks!
Alderman 1, *aside*: He bids us London knows not where.
Alderman 2, *aside*: Or knoweth pretty well!
Buckingham, *to Percival*: They are strucken dumb!
   How can I do them speak? *Speaks*: Lord mayor!
Lord Mayor: Ha?
Buckingham: Why are these so marvellously hush and mum?   80
Lord Mayor: Hum, perhaps they have mistook your grace's favour.
Buckingham, *to Percival*: A sleeveless tale!
   To Nesfield: To, Nesfield, to!
     Nesfield moves to stand among the Aldermen.
   I'll speak it o'er again. By that ye bear to England
   — which love surely sorteth to your fortunes' fates —   561
   will ye take Richard Gloucester as your king?
Nesfield: Hollo, hollo, King Richard, ho!
Buckingham: I thank you.
   Nor shall I let to name your heart-dear salutation,   562
   whereto I'll add petition of the loves ye bear   90
   the lord protector's name.
     Exit Buckingham, furious, trailed by Attendants.
     The Aldermen disperse,
     revealing Truth and Rumour in their place.
Truth: *Qui tacet consentire videtur.*
Rumour: She says that ancient Wyclif said:
   Silence doth consent.

---

560 4.8.73. *rhubarb words*: bitter words (Sidney).

561 4.8.85. *sorteth to*: results in. The sentence might be read: 'Your loyalty will surely result in your (good) fortune'. Or, with the hint of implied threat: 'Stay on side if you know what's good for you'.

562 4.8.89. *let to name*: neglect to mention, make a point of mentioning.

Truth: Thus, from coward silence of the many,
  some few do lay hold on the crown. 96
  *Exeunt **Truth** and **Rumour**.*

ACT 4, SCENE 9

Pontefract Castle, Wednesday, June 25, 1483.
The last day of King Edward V's reign.

*Enter **Grey** and **Vaughan**, in chains,*
*followed by **Guards** and **Ratcliffe**.*

Vaughan: I see the old adage will be fulfill'd:
  Edward's issues shall be shamefully betray'd.
  But I attest the witness of the living God
  t'expound my innocence.
Ratcliffe: You have well appeal'd.
  Lay down your head and die.
Vaughan: Indeed, I die in right. To greaten one
  by blameless nephews' loss and others' death
  is escheat vile. Well look you, Ratcliffe, 563
  unless you die not in wrong. *All go.* 10 564

*Enter **Rivers**, with **Guards** and the **Executioner**,*
*the axe with the edge towards **Rivers**.* 565

---

563 4.9.9. *To greaten one ... escheat vile*: The line is based on *The Faerie Queene* I.v.25. *Escheat* was originally a legal term referring to the reversion (or seizure) of an estate when a tenant died without leaving an heir. The effect was the same if a defendant was convicted and attainted. *Vile* follows its noun here, not only for the benefit of meter, but because native Welsh speakers occasionally invert noun and adjective when speaking English. Cf. 5.4.73 & 82.

564 4.9.10. *not*: is redundant. Sometimes used in threats or warnings for emphasis.

565 *Stage Direction: the axe with the edge towards* comes from a similar scene in *Henry VIII*, II.i.

Rivers: How swift doth goodwife Fortune wheel away,
    wends haughty-hearted on,
    capricious as the sun, that of a day
    hurls spiteful fire on desert plains,
    and smiles benignly upon Eden.
    Have to thee, tidy wife, perhaps unwitting,
    that with besom makes a many little lives away.

    Mutability! Humility should be thy other name.
    Glory! Thou art neighbour'd by the Gordian knot
    we humains labour ceaselessly t'unloose,
    to find in fine thy kernel mortified as stone.

    Would heaven might rest me, take me in.
    Thine own account was ever cast for man to see:
    When quickened things below is done away,
    the glory is most thine, and thine alone.
    Henceforth my mortal portion is th'unceasing dust of bones.

    On, on! Sithence my ended life must end,
    let it be speedly done.
        Exeunt.

---

[566] 4.9.11. Rivers did write a ballad during his final imprisonment. Originally recorded in Rous's account, it was published in Gairdner's *Richard III*, and more recently in Hanham (p.119–20). The style is not such that it could be adapted for *Dark Sovereign*, hence my shorter verse.

[567] 4.9.16. *tidy*: timely, or, as an epithet of admiration. The modern sense dates from 1706.

[568] 4.9.17. *besom*: a twig-broom similar to a witch's broom.

[569] 4.9.27. *Sithence*: Seeing that, In view of the fact that, Given that.

ACT 5, SCENE 1

***Sfx**: A flourish.*

*Enter **King Richard III (Gloucester)**, bearing the crown.*
He sits, sets down the crown, and seems to contemplate it

King Richard III: Diadem, rare manna,
   highest, fondest, ficklest gift to glad in!
   Trinket, without sense to feel or mind to wit,
   thou arbitratest all,
   and foundest sovereign policies of realm.
   Still mute, unto thy speech the great take mindful heed.
   Thou paltry cap, how cam'st to gull
   who see thee 'ray thyself with spiritual force?
   Thy little heft of gold with baser stuff
   doth peise less than piepowders' weights   10   570
   to turn the scale against a pennyworth of pease.
      But, for all, as men compare t'unfashion'd earth,   571
   so dost thou lift us over those the very heav'ns until;
   which, pierc'd withal, do their affection let, who,
   being to fall, distilléd is, till that to us
   each heart works out his crescive love.

---

570   5.1.10. *peise*: weigh, v. § *piepowders' weights*: A piepowder was an itinerant merchant, 'called pied-puloreux, or dustifute' Scots. (*OED* quotes Skene, 1609). Richard III's major reform involved overhauling 'courts of piepowder' which arbitrated market trading disputes. 'To every of the same fayres is of right perteynyng a court of Pepowders to mynystre to theim due justice' (1483, Act I Richard III, c. 6 para. 1).

571   5.1.12. This passage began as an experiment in playing with language:

In Renaissance English:	*In modern English:*
...as men compare t'unfashioned earth,	To the degree that men are above common dirt,
so dost thou lift us over those †	so you (the crown) raise kings above them
the very heav'ns until;	almost to heaven. ††
which, pierc'd withal, do their affection let,	Heaven, impressed by majesty, releases affection, †††
which, being to fall, distilléd is, till that to us	which, having to fall, condenses, bringing about
each heart works out his crescive love.	the growth of love in his subjects to their king. ††††

   † *those*, the former | †† the 'Divine Right' of kings | ††† divine love
   †††† the medieval 'Dew makes grass grow' analogy

The Philosophers' Stone nor his magics convey not more power
to the sage than thou. So sole a crest surpasses all:
How art thou mell'd together in the sacred glory of the crown?
*The **King** falls to brooding.*

*Enter **Truth**.*

Truth: How glorious soever the crown, 20
King Richard cannot choose but he must let advantage slip.

*Enter **Rumour**.*

Rumour: A tub must need fill before it overflow.
This new-anointed king may not reap love,
who nothing can requite.
Truth: King Richard hath invested in high office
such which were his familiars before.
He appointeth not but few he only loves,
and knows least cause to fear of.
Rumour: Other he thinks may overbear him,
and to conspire treasons. 30
*To the **King***: Moon-calf, art thou moody? 572
Truth: He is no moon-calf, Rumour, but a moon's-man. 573
A' first drew breath near the full moon's tide.
Wotst thou not? A moon-calf is a whetstone born deform'd. 574

---

572 5.1.31. *Moon-calf*: A congenitally deformed or retarded offspring, presumed born under the adverse influence of the moon. See the quotation in the note below.

573 5.1.32. *moon's-man*: Truth is trying to explain Richard's cold, lunar personality in terms that contemporaries would understand. 'Yf a man or a woman be born on sqwyche [such] a day off the mone, ye schal conceyue that he ys, or sche ys, dysposyed so as to have wurchyp [honour], or ellys trouble' (Metham, 1460). King Richard was born two days after the full moon, on October 2, 1452 (Ross).

574 5.1.34. *A moon-calf is a whetstone born deform'd*: Though Truth delivers this line, it is not precise. *Whetstone* was slang for a stillborn fetus. Newton (1580) combines three terms: 'A mole in a woman's body, otherwise called a whetstone, or a moon-calfe'. Newton notwithstanding, moon-calf was applied to the living (Cf. Drayton's *The Moon-calfe*, c. 1627), while mole, mola and whetstone were applied to the miscarried or stillborn.

> Here, saving for his arm falls out of flesh, 575
> is not a man deform'd — unless of the fearing he has.

Enter **Incubus**, *running. He whispers to the* **King**,
who remains apparently unaware of him.

Rumour, *speaking of the* **King**: Poor *mola*! 576
Truth: Pooh! A' was not cast! Thy mental man discerneth *mola*, 577
    fast'ning that thy brain cannot explain;
    wherewith thou wouldest define thy dark suspicion, 40
    affixing reason on dread.
Rumour: His nurse ought rather have wean'd him
    when the lesser light adorn'd a sign in the extremities. 578
Truth: Richard is not out of tone with far stars!
    He differeth from his kingdom'd here,
    where he is domified! 579
        Exit **Incubus**, *running.*

---

575 5.1.35. *arm falls out of flesh*: arm is withered. Cf. Note Gloucester's putative disfigurement, 4.3.92.
576 5.1.37. *mola*: See 5.1.34, above.
577 5.1.38. *cast*: miscarried.
578 5.1.43. *lesser light ... extremities*: There is a time, Ecclesiastes tells us, for everything. In the late medieval mind, suiting an action to the time — that's to say, auspiciousness — was often determined by the alignment of planets or the phases of the moon. Belief in the moon's presumed influence can be simply stated: 'From the new moon, to the full, all humours do increase, and from the full to the new moon, decrease again' (W. Fulke, 1563). Similarly, 'The moone intendeth or remitteth her influence at one time more than an other' (Heydon, 1603). That being the case: 'The Moon, in her approach and coming toward, filleth bodies ful; and in her retire and going away, emptieth them again' (Holland, trans. Pliny, 1601). Agricultural lore, which survives in pockets in the West of England as well as the Appalachian States, still holds it wise 'to grasse and sowe in growing of the moone, And kitte [cut] or mowe in wenyng is to done' (Anon. c. 1440).
    Furthermore, in the course of each lunar month, the moon — the lesser light — rises for two or three nights in each zodiacal sign, each sign being assigned governance over some organ or part of the body. Common lore dictated that the time for weaning children, like planting and harvesting crops, demanded compliance with celestial signs, the most propitious moment for weaning being when the moon rose in a zodiacal house representing one of the limbs, rather than a vital part of the body.
579 5.1.46. *domified*: A verb used exclusively in astrology, meaning to recognize the divisions of the heavens into the twelve constellations; hence to be able to apportion the planets into their respective 'houses' (Latin, *domus*). Truth uses the verb in its literal sense, but with irony, mocking Rumour's astrological digression.

Rumour: Methinks his lady mother lay too long
   with mandrakes at her breast.
   See, he groans for fellow-feeling;
   seems to sigh forth sympathy thereof. 50
   *Truth and **Rumour** spring away when the **King** speaks.*
King Richard III: Why am I heart-sick still?
   God he knows, how I do inly rage:
   The inward tempest may I quiet, nor ever wholly quit.
   What art thou, that thou should'st suborn me this?
   How art thou limn'd? How flesh'd?
   Whether art thou witch's potion? warlock's curse?
   or beest thou but creature of my head?
   I am let to know none other name than evil
   for this nameless dread, that with a trice
   wins of my noblest will. 60
   Never afore was king so thoroughly bemired.
   Again he falls to brooding.
Truth: It seems to me he catcheth every buzz to greaten it.
Rumour: 'Tis Até speaks. Besides, thy part is mine.

---

580 5.1.50. *Methinks ... sympathy thereof:* Rumour is suggesting:
   a/ that Richard was malformed by his mother's use of mandrakes as a fertility potion. Gerard's *Herball* comments that mandrakes aid still births, but says nothing about congenital malformations. Gerard goes on to say that 'great and strange effects are supposed to be in mandrakes, to cause women to be fruitful and bear children, if they shall but carry the same near unto their bodies'. See the story of Rachel in Genesis 30, an account with which Gerard takes issue;
   b/ that the use of mandrakes may result in 'molas and false conceptions' (Sir Thomas Browne, 1646). Hence Rumour's assessment of Richard;
   c/ that, just as mandrakes were said to groan when they were dug from the earth, so Richard's moods and sighs might be a sympathetic reaction, akin to the trauma of being plucked from the womb. The second book of Pliny the Elder deals with this doctrine of sympathy, a notion owing its longevity to the great respect in which the Middle Ages held Pliny;
   d/ that Richard's character might have been imprinted by mandrakes at birth. Cf. note 2.3.94.
   We should remember that King Richard III was the eighth child of a mother who surely had neither need nor time for mandrakes. Piety was the Rose of Raby's vice.
581 5.1.54. *this:* like this, thus.
582 5.1.55. *How art thou limn'd?* How are you to be described? / captured as an image?
583 5.1.60. *wins of:* triumphs over, wins out over.
584 5.1.63. *Até:* impulse. Até was the Greek goddess of rash deeds. *The Dictionary of Classical Antiquities* defines Até: 'She personifies infatuation; the infatuation being generally held to imply guilt as its cause and evil as its consequence'. Cf. *King John*, II.i.63.

Truth: Nay. A' comes over himself with his past,
 which commands him dark notions
 neither the wit of Rumour nor Truth shall illumine.
Rumour: Prithee pardon. Say on.
Truth: Each calumny and inward voice doth entoil him
 with phantoms of disloyalty.
Rumour: Sometime real, sometime imaginary. 70
 At sometimes it's himself appointeth each
 to every these invented treasons.
Truth: As now we'll let the summer go by.
 Twice a moon has pass'd: Libra, this king his sign,
 comes fast upon, his pair of weights in hand.
Rumour: Wherewith conflict comes fast on.
Truth: Viler matter grows to mistful shadows,
 spews incensive flesh.
 There are that think to free the princes from the Tower:
 When these are seen no more ... 80
Rumour: ... they think t'avenge them upon Richard,
 an' if they were dead.
Truth: The shrilly clamour of rebellion rose
 the South throughout, from Kent to Cornwall.
Rumour: And Buckingham, to boot. But sister, soft! Who comes?

*Enter **Ratcliffe**.*

Ratcliffe: Damned Southern traitors rise
 upon your highness's throne!
King Richard III, *reviving*: The taste of bloody action
 likes me better than the musing on 't. 90

---

585 5.1.71. *At sometimes*: On occasion, occasionally.
586 5.1.74. *this king his sign*: This is the old possessive form, which I use in the play a few times with masculine and neuter nouns in *Dark Sovereign*. In time the *his* degenerated to an aphetic form, merging with the noun, in this case as kinges, before becoming the modern *king's*.
587 5.1.76. *conflict comes fast on*: The weights in Libra's scales were said to offset each other, as balance and conflict.
588 5.1.77. *grows to*: becomes an integral part of ... Cf. 1.3.97.
589 5.1.78. *incensive*: angry.

At arms! At arms! Attend me, Ratcliffe;
do you provide our going! Look't be done,
and in no drowsy-headed manner
we'll unhorse these traitrous rebels at a blow.
*The **King** and **Ratcliffe** go.*
Truth: He'll to discover bigger enemies than he thinks for.
For all King Richard too much requited Buckingham his aids,
that noble's self, that three months since
holp Richard to the throne, calls on rebellion too.
Rumour: Harry is compounded of a labyrinth of 's fury
far much greater than the king's.   100
So Buckingham possess the earth entire,
he'd scale an eagle's creance to attach the stars besides.
Riddle me, riddle, a still swine that squealeth,
unfathom'd though shallow, pray who may he be?
Truth: Natheless, we must make doubt to give him wrong'd.
The buzzing contrives, that Harry would redeem himself.
Rumour: Truth, that duke's a vicious whelp
that lusteth for each little pretty thing,
the which attain'd, still is he not content.
Truth: To a having mind, all is too small.   110
Let's talk in private more. Rumour, come away!   111
They go.

---

590 5.1.102. *creance*: In falconry, the long, thin cord used to restrain untrained birds in flight.

591 5.1.103. *a still swine that squealeth*: Rumour is playing with a proverb which she does not trouble to complete; a Period audience would have understood it. John Heywood's *Proverbes* (1546) gives: 'A still sowe eats up all the draffe', meaning that the cleverest pig is too busy eating the swill to waste time squealing.'

592 5.1.105. *make doubt*: hesitate.

593 5.1.110. *having mind*: The original reads, 'To a having mind, all is too little' (Mabbe, 1622). The text of *Dark Sovereign* drew on perhaps tens of thousands of references in Period literature. Some sources contributed single words, others phrases, an idea, or syntactical constructions. Almost all are clearly noted in some 4,000 unpublished working pages of notes. Others inevitably lived for a time in mental space, assimilated but unattributed, only to surface later, virtually intact, in the text. This line is one such. Let it stand, as my thanks to many Period authors for their unattributed contributions to *Dark Sovereign*. Written into an early draft as if it were my own (July 29, 1985), I 'discovered' it and its source again in December, 1986.

ACT 5, SCENE 2

October, 1483.

*Enter **Russell**, followed by **Bede**, a slovenly scribe-cum-cleric, labouring under a writing tablet, quill, and ink-horn slung at the belt of a stained cassock.*

Russell *dictates*: As we seek pardon of God,
    owe we the like to men.
    For are not these His gifts and creatures too?
Bede, *aside*: Yes, verily.
Russell: Wherefore, to the end that boundless time
    address our good repute, we pen this brief,
    deferring hope the future will excuse us ...
Bede, *aside: Te exculpatio, cancellari.*
Russell: ... aparting us, holding us more precious
    in esteem than this, our present spiteful age.   10
Bede *writes*: ... present ... spiteful ... age ...
Russell: Bede, how doeth our narrative?
Bede *reads*: The Southren shires rose ...
Russell: I'll venture on observation without book,   594
    how these marvels came to pass.
    Dictates: That people thought, by hot incenséd anger
    or to set the princes free, might they still live,
    or if that their last end were pass'd ...
    Russell *crosses himself.*
      Bede, *encumbered, tries to follow suit.*
    ... to venge their childish life.
Bede *writes*: ... hot ... incenséd ... passions ...   20
Russell: It seems to me our brother, John of Ely,   595
    unclasp'd at the last that book which is the mind
    of Buckingham, whose high noblesse

---

594 5.2.14. *without book*: from memory.
595 5.2.21. *John of Ely*: Bishop John Morton (later, of 'Morton's fork' fame).

the errors of his youthly taken-on conceit sum up.
'Twas Morton persuaded Harry, perchance by moral arguments,
to set his face against the king.
Bede *writes*: ... John Morton ... bishop ... Ely ...
Russell: Intelligences speak, how my Lady Margaret,
   which erstwhile was countess of Richmond,
with Elizabeth, that once was queen,   30
should devise a cautelous plot,
whereby the Lady Margaret's obscure son, one Henry Tudor,
earl of Richmond, coming on with force from Brittany,
would wive King Edward's eldest daughter,
and t'ascend his throne.
Bede *writes*: Margaret Beaufort ... with ... Elizabeth ...
Aside: No animal is more revengeful than a woman.
Russell: Expunge their names.
Bede: How!
Russell: Write down *Quidam*.   40
Bede: *Quisquam?*   41
Russell, *rising anger*: Nay, *nec quisquam. Quidam!*   42
Bede: *Quippini?* But *quisnam?*   43
Russell: *Quidam!*   44
Bede: Verily, my lord, *sed quinam iam?*   45
   Whether would you liefer either of these three:
Any body? Somebody? Or no body at all?
Russell: We strain courtesy. Strike out the ladies' names.
Bede *writes*: ... prick ... out ... the ... ladies' ...
Russell: *Quod libet!*   50
   Bede: ... curtsies.
Russell: However, these things came to pass:
   At the urgence of Buckingham, Harry Tudor did embark,

---

596 5.2.24. *whose high noblesse ... sum up*: whose nobility consists of the sum total of his errors during a spoiled youth.

597 5.2.30. Lady Margaret and the queen consulted the same Welsh physician, one Dr. Lewis. He carried their private notes to each other into and out of the abbey.

598 5.2.3. *should devise*: perhaps did devise, (subjunctive of imputation).

599 5.2.37. The line is Cicero's.

> — and fell was his force — for England,
> to claim his princess, the inheritrix,
> and eke her father's crown.

Bede: King Edward's ... eldest ... daughter ...

Russell: But some, for eagerness, rose too soon, whereon,
> as if the elements did hurl their treasons at their heads,
> the other world conspir'd with Richard's cause   60
> with such a rack of wind and rain
> as thought to stop the Washes with Welsh hills.

Bede: The ... every ... seldom ... weathercock ...
> that ... stay'd ... his ... steeple ... drown'd.

Russell: The tempest for a ten day gave such buffets
> in that sort as whelm'd the continent, o'erturn'd the deeps,
> and threated to pluck stars from off their far-off frames.

Bede: ... Edward's ... eldest ... daughter ...

Russell: Were it not the storm did vanquish them,
> they had rather warr'd with Richard.   70
> But Tudor's fleet, being broken, was driven away;
> which caus'd Buckingham from forth of Wales not but in chains.

Bede: Your chronicle, Lord Chancellor,
> runneth faster than my feather flies.

Russell: We'll breathe awhiles:
> There needs a little time to dry up ink.

---

600 5.2.40–45. From the audience's point of view, the Latin passage must carry on the players' evident phonetic confusion. However, it does make sense in Latin, along the lines of Abbott and Costello's baseball sketch, 'Who's on First, What's on Second'.

Quidam means *someone*, but from classical times to medieval law-Latin it implied 'A certain person or thing (known but not named)' (Cassell's). *Quidam* was used as a modern journalist employs 'A usually reliable source' or 'A source close to ...'. However, Bede fails to grasp the subtlety of the larger meaning (or the importance of confidentiality), so the passage continues:

40. Write down *Quidam*.	Write 'Someone'.
41. *Quisquam?*	Anyone at all?
42. Nay, *nec quisquam. Quidam!*	Not just anyone / Not nobody. Somebody!
43. *Quippini?* But *quisnam?*	Why not? But who in particular?
44. *Quidam!*	Somebody!
45. Verily, my lord, *Sed quinam iam?*	Verily, my lord. But what now?

601 5.2.50. *Quod libet!* Do as you please!

602 5.2.51. *curtsies*: The more frequent spelling of courtesies in the sixteenth century. The missing syllable returned in the seventeenth.

Bede: And as to speak of ink, my goose-quill's dry.
Russell: As well the well of my resolve.
   Go thy ways, Bede, till anon.
   I'll walk a small while abroad. Then,   80
   (fair Clio be my help!), we shall tell history anew.   81
     Exeunt singuli.

ACT 5, SCENE 3

Salisbury. All Souls' Day, Sunday, November 2, 1483.

Enter **Buckingham** *from his trial, with* **Guards**, *"tipstaves before him; the axe with the edge towards him; halberds on each side".*

Enter **King Richard**, *following, alone.*

King Richard III: Keep him from my sight, do!
Buckingham, *restrained by* **Guards**: Highness, permit me speak!
King Richard III: Untruest creature that hath life!
   Content thee with thy doom.
Buckingham: Please your majesty, a word!
King Richard III: Let be to rail.
   Treason may no uttering saving blood.
Buckingham: A word. An' if my life
   hang of your potent ear, grant me a word!
King Richard III: Shall my ears be easy?   10
   Nay, they shall not gull resolve.

---

603 5.2.81. *fair Clio*: History, personified as one of the nine Muses. Clio represented epic poetry and history, and is usually portrayed holding a scroll or book. The name in Greek suggests 'She who celebrates or extols'. My precedent here is Chaucer, who invokes Clio in *Troylus* II. See also Spenser, *The Teares of the Muses*, lines 55–114.

604 5.3. *Stage Direction.* See *King Henry VIII*, II.i. Shakespeare (or an editor) gives this direction around line 55.

"Compassion's Nature's fools' cloth".
Today is All Souls' Day.
Why then, the dead shall keep you goodly company.
To **Guards**: Come, guard this to Salisbury market-place.
The axe divorce his souls.
   All go, the **King** *alone.*

ACT 5, SCENE 4

Before the cathedral, Rennes, Brittany. Christmas Day, 1483.

__Jasper Tudor__, __Dorset__, and __Lords__ of Henry Tudor's 'court' in exile await his arrival.

Enter **Christopher Urswick**.

Jasper Tudor: You are, I ween, Master Urswick.
Urswick: The same, my lord.
Jasper Tudor: Come you from John Morton, out of Flanders?
   or is't you serve our prince's mam?
Urswick: Those offices, both, Lord Tudor, is my parts.
   Myself comes from Morton;
   my service of my Lady Margaret.
Jasper Tudor: One body but one body's end may singly serve.
Urswick: I am their common voice,
   t'impart their bold design to you.
Jasper Tudor: *Dux femina facti*, so!

---

605 5.3.12. Gloucester turns against Buckingham the phrase that Buckingham earlier threw at him. (Cf. 3.4.132.)
606 5.3.16. *souls*: The plural alludes to the 'three souls' concept put to dramatic use by Jonson and Shakespeare, in *Poetaster* and *Twelfth Night* respectively. See 4.3.59.
607 5.4.8. *singly*: honestly, honorably, without conflict.
608 5.4.11. *Dux femina facti*: So, the leader of this exploit (is) a woman! Virgil, *Aeneid* I, 364.

Our Harry Tudor was a young-year'd lad, when I,
preserving him from York, took ship for Brittany;
whose every watch, when their turn-keeping came,
saw me to stand, a sort of ragged christopher
which did invoke the hissing seas to be not sluggishly at help;
roaring to the worlds' twice-roaring currents of the deeps,
had they have been contráry.
Each breath, indeed, who bellied not our sails,
each seeming spiteful wave would beat us back   20
nor failéd I to curse, till all the whale-path boil'd
as if Leviathan himself haul'd forward our swift bark.
Urswick: Until your havening-place, my lord?
Jasper Tudor: Look you, though the shipmen thought me mad,
not yet stay'd I from hurling imprecations
against elemental and celestial till we gain'd Brittany.
Methinks, indeed, the master had like t'have thrown me
after Jonah, into the sea.

*Enter **Henry Tudor**, earl of Richmond.*

Henry Tudor: Welcome merry Christmas, lords.
Lords: Keep merry Christmas, lord.   30
  God save you, Richmond.
Henry Tudor: Why then, we'll to it apace.
First and foremost, muster we affairs.
'Fore God and my fellows, which were toss'd wi' th' edge
o' th' tyrant's sword upon these exil'd shores, this swear I,
as I shall be king: If heaven make warrantise,

---

[609] 5.4.12. Jasper Tudor's part is written for a Welsh cadence.
[610] 5.4.15. *christopher*: An effigy of the saint, nailed to a mast or carried as a talisman.
[611] 5.4.17. *the worlds'*: The worlds are the heaven and the earth, hence the *twice-roaring currents*, of wind and waters. *Deeps* may be taken as a true, rather than a poetic, plural, referring to the sky's deep as well as the sea's. Cf. 5.4.26.
[612] 5.4.18. *have* is redundant. See 1.1.62.
[613] 5.4.26. *elemental and celestial*: The two worlds mentioned in 5.4.17 could also be regarded as one world divided into concentric spheres, namely the earth and the sky above. 'The world is divided into two regions: Celestial, and Elemental' (Eden, 1561).

I shall wive Elizabeth of York. We shall repay Thy helps
with such a match as we will unify the ancient lines
of Wales and England. York shall marry itself with Lancaster;
Cadwalladers' foredoom in Tudors shall effect, 40
co-mingling in our issues Beaufort and Valoys.
Dorset: English, Welsh, and Brittains all;
ye men as well of Lancaster, as York;
such few belovéd as whose life escap'd the tyrant's clutch,
oppress'd with exile from mad treason, rarely foul:
Where once we joinéd at a strife, join we at unity,
to cross the main, to rid the dread!
General assent.
Henry Tudor: Heaven in righteousness, win with us our cause,
and we will do thee grace. Although, indeed,
sith we have right, we'll conquer in our proper strengths, 50
endue us with thy mightful hand: to wrest the moated isle
from tyranny; with pówer each imbruéd act redress; break chains;
and to supplant th'oppressor's throne. Or die we in th'affray!
Dorset: Long lifetimes hence, let men still distant say:
At Rennes, upon an ancient Christmas morn,
our present polity compacted was;
accustom'd peace, of exiles' travails born.
Henry Tudor: Witness you my farther indentures. If i' th' end
I do survive the fight, but prove my solemn troth a lie,
may God his host smite me to die, 60
unworthy life, and brought to shame!

---

614 5.4.40. *Cadwalladers'... effect*: Cadwalladers' destiny will be manifest in the Tudors. Cf. Warner (1592): 'But that Cadwalladers Fore-doomes in Tuders should effect Was unexpected'.

615 5.4.41. *Valoys*: The French royal house of Valois. Spelling reflects the anglicized pronunciation. Marlowe uses both in *The Massacre at Paris*, Act V, as well as a possessive, *Valoyses*. Note 'Philip de Valoys', 1605.

616 5.4.42. *Brittains*: Bretons. Although Shakespeare uses the modern form, Bretons, in *Richard III*, this form is more usual in the Period.

617 5.4.45. *rarely foul*: foul to an unusual degree.

618 5.4.51. *Although ... mightful hand*: This mixture of sentiments would not have found expression in the fifteenth century, but a post-Reformation author might have combined them. *In our proper* (own) *strengths* is equivalent to 'by ourselves' or 'by us alone' and excludes a request for divine assistance. Later in the sentence Henry Tudor hedges his bet.

Dorset: Unto the cathedral, friends! Give each to other 's hands.
We'll swear an oath that will confederate ourselves
with Henry Tudor, earl of Richmond,
soon our sovereign, alderliefest king.

Henry Tudor: If strength in tribulation lies,
hole us sore deep in suffering. Harder we'll come forth.
On, friends! Seal we this thing, and done.

Exit **Henry Tudor**. *Others follow, except ...*

Jasper Tudor: Look you back wi' the oath we make today.
Urswick: I shall, my lord. 70
Jasper Tudor: This matter mark! Beyond immortal longings
for the crown, the wheels of Tudor's mind keep way
wi' th'ancient British tale, wherein a dragon scarlet
strave against another, which was white as whales' bone.
The scarlet cockatrice at first prevail'd, but faltering,
fell back, whereon the white worm carried it at last.
'Tis since the wizard Merlin prophesied this and what else,
now a thousand years. Our nation's not remain'd to us;
all is distracted still — till Arthur shall return,
who only can let slip the scarlet dragon of the Welsh 80
and Bretons against England. And moreover,
thi' self dragon red that is my nephew's act,
co-meddles in his mind, no less than in his blood,
with Lancaster's red rose. Whenas Harry wins the crown,
the dragon of the Welsh, like Arthur out of Avalon,

---

619 5.4.65. *alderliefest*: dearest, most beloved. This word was already antique when Shakespeare used it in 2 *Henry VI*, I.i.28: 'Mine Alder liefest Soueraigne'.

620 5.4.67. *If strength ... forth*: Bacon's essay *Of Adversity* was developed from a speech by Seneca. And Seneca's aphorism, 'Fire is the test of gold, adversity of strong men', pops up time and again in English literature of the sixteenth and seventeeth centuries: viz. 'The whetstone of adversity' (Wm. Baldwin, 1564); 'Sweet are the uses of adversity' (*As You Like It*, II.i.12). Ben Jonson (1636) writes 'He knows not his own strength that hath not met adversity'; and Milton, in *Paradise Lost*, XI.63, 'Tried in sharp tribulation, and refined By faith and faithful works, to second life...' Older of all is: 'Perseverance is a sign of will power'. Thus Lao Tsu in the *Tao Te Ching*, 33 (Gia Fu Feng, translator.)

621 5.4.69. *Look you back wi'*: Make sure you report back with.

622 5.4.73. *dragon scarlet*: The adjective is in post-position normal to a Welsh speaker. Cf. 4.9.9 and 5.4.82.

623 5.4.79. *distracted*: divided.

624 5.4.82. *act*: vital or ennobling principle. Passion, obsession.

shall rule the English evermore. 625
Derwydon doethur / darogenwch y Arthur! 626
Mark you now, when prophecy gainsayeth right,
what's certain sooth nor man nor wizard can foretell.
But prophecy and right herein is one. 90
Our will, with heaven's blessing, shall be done! 91
   Exeunt, following the others.

ACT 5, SCENE 5

February, 1484–85.

*Enter **Russell**, dictating, as he thinks, to **Bede**.*

Russell: The afterclap of scowling mutiny is this:
   King Richard gives the South t' th' rule of Northern lords,
   which, all and some unsensible,
   not neglect to tramp old customs;
   yea, and they break years of painful fealty
   hard-wrought progenitors had made. 627
   How painfully soever won, the king takes least thought
   how he lets Northern foxes preach among Southern geese,
   whose stiff-necked prides he counts for more less
   than his own close dread. 10

*Enter **Bede**, furtively.*

---

625 5.4.86. For an account of the dragon lore, see Geoffrey Ashe, *The Discovery of King Arthur*, Debrett, London, 1985. Caxton, in *The cronicles of englond*, lxii.40, puts it: 'The whyte dragon strongly fought with the reed dragon and bote him evil and him overcome'. See also *The Faerie Queene*, III.iii.40–44.
626 5.4.87. *derwydon doethur / darogenwch y Arthur.* Druids erudite / Prophesy for Arthur.
627 5.5.6. *break years ... had made*: destroy the close-knit pattern of social inter-relationships built up by the hard work of many generations.

*Unaware of **Bede's** late arrival*: And you, Bede,
look you write my mind in more than measur'd wise!
Bede: Furnish me, Lord Chancellor, with a little time.
I'll pen each syllab, captive without prejudice
each jewel of a wise sentence you unloose.
Writes, aside: Like ... to the ... Assyrian ... host ...
from ... forth of the North ... they ... came.
Russell: Thus, impal'd within the privy fullness of his heart,
Richard leaseth out such love as the South him bears.
    As touching commons, the king lays down little
but what is right and good. Hit notwithstanding,
his partial favour strows confusion in many's mind.
Their will to pleasure King Richard is sometime smitten
with so queer resolve as that it doth stiffen sinews,
commune up the blood, and stir all hearts
to set their breasts against him.
Bede, *aside*: God help the while; the world is woe.
Russell: How I bethink the year's last wither'd age.
In February, King Richard caus'd the lords vow
new and solemn vows — a flock of words
which some unkiss'd, unknown to me, compos'd!
Bede, *aside*: Which naughtiness forfend!
Russell: ... whereby all adher'd to Richard's issue,
Edward of Middleham — frail lad — but that his singularity
was to this king sole heir and only son. O worldly vanity!
Our oath was not so soon put forth,
but April tears portended greater woes.

---

[628] 5.5.21. *Hit*: It (emphatic, Northern).
[629] 5.5.25. *commune up*: After *Henry V*, III.i.7: 'Stiffen the sinews, commune up the blood'. Craig and Globe eds. give *summon* for *commune*, a reasonable interpretation. Cambridge gives *conjure*.
[630] 5.5.31. *unkiss'd, unknown*: After Chaucer's 'unknown and unkissed'. Also in Heywood. Russell is upset because King Richard chose someone 'unknown' even to Russell to write this 'flock of words'. Russell had been a well-regarded ambassador to the deceased King Edward IV. Now it is clear that he has come to believe that Richard is excluding him from the inner circle. Around this time Russell did in fact write two speeches in English intended for what might have been the first parliament of young King Edward V. That was not to be.

The year's-mind for King Edward's death approaching near, ⁶³¹
this boy, which was call'd Edward also, sick'd, and died.
   Both cross themselves.
Bede, *aside*: What auguries lurk here for men to draw?   40
Russell: No one conjectur'd the little boy's soon dying.
That thing, which touch'd the king and queen so nighly,
almost reduc'd them to almost madness
by which sudden cause of their grieves.
Betokenings, what auguries lurk here for men to draw?
Bede, *aside*: Ha?
Russell: And so to Christmas revels ...
Bede: Pish, pish.
Russell: ... which grieves me to speak. Let this suffice:
A many noted how the king presented sumptuous apparels   50
to Queen Anne; the likes to which, the very likes,
gave he also to King Edward's child, Elizabeth of York,
the same this Henry Tudor makes vow to wed.
Bede, *aside*: How folly breeds liking ...
Russell: Either of the ladies like the other wore!
Bede, *aside*: ... and liking breeds lust.
Russell: Men thought ...
Bede: Tut, tut.
Russell: ... his heir deceas'd, his queen so sick
as like to die, men ween she is Elizabeth,   60
— whom King Richard marks to manifest favour —
who in her person bears that bud of 's hope,
intrinsical as her youth and beauty is. So the hum:
That thither Richard's wished-for doom of destiny,
with his affection, flies.
Bede, *aside*: Why ponder men on ever evil?
Russell: You might then see ... ⁶³²

---

[631] 5.5.38. *year's-mind*: first anniversary, the celebration of same.
[632] 5.5.67. *You might then see*: You would then have had the opportunity to see ... The Croyland Chronicler's phrase, usually given in translation as 'You might then have seen', actually applies to Christmas ceremonies held two years earlier, when King Edward IV still presided over a relatively care-free court. See Ross, *Richard III*, footnote 76, p.xliv.

Bede: How?
Russell: Nay. Think what you will. No more I'll say.
Bede *writes*: … little … boy's … soon … death … 70
Russell: This script, Bede, I thee entrust.
   Non facias copiam describendi! 633
Bede: Trust assuredly, my lord.
   I shall describe no copy of our conference. 634
Russell: If I am spared, of due I'll reduce this 635
   into an ancient Latin record, better suited to have his keep. 636
Bede: Shall I write *explicit?*
Russell: *Liber non explicitus est.* 637
   We had rather wait such a catastrophe 638
   as time will bring.
Bede: Then *num quid vis?* 80 639
   Russell: *Pax tibi*, Bede. *Iam volo tibi pax.* 640
Bede *bows: Cancellari, item tibi pax.*
   Both make to go their separate ways.
Bede *writes*: So … the … hum …
Russell, *aside: Non mea culpa, Domine.* 641
Bede *writes*: … with … his … affection … flies … 85
   Exeunt separatim.

---

633 5.5.72. *Non facias copiam describendi!* See that you don't make (or give anyone permission to make) a copy! The line plays on a standard formula, *Facere copiam describendi*, which scribes wrote on documents to give subsequent readers permission to copy them.

634 5.5.74. *conference*: conversation.

635 5.5.75. *of due I'll reduce this*: as a matter of duty I'll translate this.

636 5.5.76. *ancient Latin record*: The Croyland/Crowland Chronicle.

637 5.5.77–78. *explicit*: Literally *unrolled*, indicating that one has reached the end of a rolled document. Bede asks 'Have we reached the end?' To which Russell replies, 'The book is not finished'.

638 5.5.79. *catastrophe*: dénouement, finale. Russell's comment seems to endow him with prophetic ability. However, the meaning of *catastrophe* is not as drastic as in modern English; and the use of the verb *will* does not suggest that Russell has the power of prophecy. Prophecy takes *shall*. The use of *will* merely admits that there is bound to be some resolution to the situation.

639 5.5.80. *num quid vis?* Also given as *num quid me vis?* meaning 'Is there anything else you want (from me)?' or 'Will that be all?' Just as these figures anticipate a negative reply in English, in Latin the initial *num* virtually mandates a negative response.

640 5.5.81. *Iam volo tibi pax*: Indeed, I wish you peace.

641 5.5.84. *Non mea culpa, Domine*: It's not my fault, O Lord.

ACT 5, SCENE 6

Wednesday, March 16, 1485; the day of a total solar eclipse.

*Enter **Queen Anne**, in nightclothes,*
coughing into a bloody handkerchief.

Q. Anne: Although Death touch me ay more nearly,
    in my latter days his mandate fears me less.
    Percase else had I fear'd also to live,
    for death the only pain is(,) due upon mortality.   642
    This sickly form was, in th'event, a pallid intermedium
    whence quiddity flows on. On! Almost on!   643
    To sleep, and sleeping to forsake this earthly pains!
        Hold! Make stay of death a moment still!
    My peace with God is fast.
    Needs now must I until the king, to claim his love,   10
    which then, my essence dying hence, I'll let alone.
        Why keeps he from my fatal-boding bed?
    If so he shuns me, not by reason he would void my life,   644
    but rather knows not how to take my yet-life to the best,   645
    then I shall send, to let the king to know me needs his love.

*Enter **King Richard**, passing through.*

    My lord, come succour me!
King Richard: Madam, hardly do I know you.
Q. Anne: Although we are a queen, more aid crave I of thee
    in this dire hour, than all that hath been before.
    If that the love thy living hath to me   20
    were gather'd to the instance, give it now.

---

[642] 5.6.4. *pain:* penalty. The comma is optional.
[643] 5.6.6. *quiddity:* the real nature or essence of a thing.
[644] 5.6.13. *void:* suggests both *avoid*, and to put away or remove something undesired.
[645] 5.6.14. *take my yet-life to the best:* put the best construction on what remains of my life.

King Richard: The instance to his past slips fleeter than a thought.
To have, to hold th'imperious Now, and lose the future,
is the same that forfeiture. Child Edward pass'd.
Our life already is made up, and lost.
Q. Anne: Good my lord, think on the evening twilight,
how the last and level sun doth stay the rushing night,
to see the traveller safely from the darksome road.
King Richard: How say you, Anne?
Q. Anne: Why look'st thou strange on me?   30
Bestow of me thy love, my right.
And thy affection be the verdict on my life, I am content.
Deliver me over more softly to th'approaching shades.
King Richard: It will not be.   646
Q. Anne: Richard, I wull know the fire at sunset!   647
Lighten me before I die.
King Richard: The world appears foreign from me,
like dark stars that owe but small import.
Q. Anne: Art thou so light of love my end is naught?
Even they whisper: Lo, the king wills she were dead!   40
As thou tendrest me, dehort them from it.
Comfort me. I long after thy embrace.
King Richard: Why there, there, there, a mightier love is,
than obtaineth here. The inwit doth subsist apart,   648
as if all thing and none had been attain'd.
Q. Anne: Deny me not of love; an' if thou must, mask thy disdain.
At least fast echoes from thy passion on me till we part.
King Richard: From this anatomy all passions in sort is fled.
Q. Anne: I fear to con, but say it: Whither fled?
King Richard: Why, they hide themselves   50
against the evil tenor of the times.
Q. Anne: How sayest?

---

[646] 5.6.34. *It will not be*: It's not going to happen. It cannot be accomplished. In seventeenth century terms, the expression is less terse than it appears.

[647] 5.6.35. *wull*: desire to, want to.

[648] 5.6.44. *inwit*: reason, intellect, understanding; wisdom; mind, soul. The standard word in Middle English, by c. 1600 *inwit* had been replaced in many senses by *conscience*.

King Richard: Once I knew them.
    When Edward lov'd me.
    Other wish'd me dead.
Q. Anne, *aside*: Gods me! He falls distracted of his wits.
    Speaks: Escape th'enchanting forces of thy fearful dread!
    Reveal the world the ancients show'd:
    The garden of the mind is harmony.
    Root up the weeds; aspire thy fairest flowers to sow.   60
    May not sometime sweeter memory sometimes prevail?
King Richard: In memory we find ourself.
    Nay, more than brutish beasts,
    the five wits do conjoin to give us conscient to ourself.
    As seed springs out of earth, but is not earth,
    e'en so, on mémbrances our very self consisteth, and is made.
Q. Anne: Or whether heav'n or hell lurk inwardly,
    the sum of senses is not truth!
King Richard: Such senses as I feel, I cannot sum.
    Of passions, anger, love, hate, fear,   70
    — of every wit am I bereft, benumb'd.
    I am become to be as seas ytost:
    great billows run to wrack without;
    the while is emptiness within.
    By that, methinks, I am come on first matter again.
Q. Anne: Cánst not from thy hollow tower descend,
    and instant say thou lovest me?
King Richard: Indeed we loved, my love,
    in sweetest years that seem as rhodomel,
    before death gaped to take my brother in.   80
    If love live on, I find her not, to thee, or me.
Q. Anne: Extend compassion, an' thou canst!

---

[649] 5.6.58. *Reveal*: Display, Exhibit; Find in your heart. § As we found in 2.1.51, 'the Ancients' was sometimes expressed with a seeming singular, '*the Ancient*'.
[650] 5.6.70. *passions*: desires (when used in the plural).
[651] 5.6.75. *first matter*: original chaos; an inchoate child-like state. Cf. note 5.6.100.
[652] 5.6.79. *rhodomel*: honey produced from the nectar of roses.

King Richard: What colour hath Compassion? 653
How is she favour'd? And how clad?
What are her terms of life? 654
Q. Anne, *aside*: What does he hear, that other ears not hear?
What moves him? whom — as an apple being worm'd, dies inly —
I perceive vacuity t'have come upon him. 655
Is not my spouse grown daz'd of real and imagin'd strokes?
King Richard: For that formerly I reach'd to take ruth, 90 656
in submission, so; and for she look'd askance,
and mocking, wills to come upon me from afar;
and for I feel her jesting, privy, close, and all about;
thérefore we declare Compassion to be dead. 657
Q. Anne: How is she bodied forth?
King Richard: As woman. Calm. And still. And mighty to behold.
Q. Anne: Am I not woman, Richard? Come!
King Richard: Though gods may weep, they never bleed.
Thy form is frailty. We may abide no further harms.
Q. Anne *sinks, exhausted*.
King Richard: Send, therefór, to get a potion of narcissus. 100 658
Numb thyself, and dwell beyond.
Q. Anne: No more. No more. God help.
My reason's shot at madded air.

---

653   5.6.83. *colour*: Frequent in Bacon, roughly equivalent to the modern shade, as in 'shade of meaning'. See Bacon's *Coulers Good & Evill*.
654   5.6.85. *terms of life*: physical description, likeness (Marlowe).
655   5.6.88. The pronoun *him* is redundant, having been expressed by *whom* in the previous line. The usage was not infrequent during the reign of Elizabeth, having strayed into Educated English from Hebrew, a language in which the pronoun is repeated in a relative clause (*OED*).
656   5.6.90. *For that formerly I reach'd to take ruth*: Because formerly I made a point of being compassionate.
657   5.6.94. *For that ... and for ... and for ... therefore ...*: Because ... and because ... and because ... therefore ... Cf. *Richard II*, I.iii.125–139.
658   5.6.100. *narcissus*: On the simplest level, the king might be recommending narcissus to the queen for its pharmacological properties: 'The root, by the experiment of Apuleius, stamped and strained, and given in drinke helpeth the cough and collicke ...' Gerard, *Of Daffodils*.
   Or he might be recommending narcissus for its narcotic effects (note the etymological link) described by Pliny the Elder (*Historia Naturalis* II), by Plutarch, and by Ovid (*Metamorphosis* III). Gerard also notes: 'Sophocles nameth them the garland of the infernal gods because they that are departed and dulled with death, should worthily be crowned with a dulling floure'.

King Richard: Rise up, my love. Haste thou to seek
a lasting presence, whither it be repos'd.
*The **King** goes.*
*The **Queen** sinks, coughing, crying, dying.*
***Lights**: Begin to dim.*
Q. Anne: The sun! Where goes the sun? *She dies.*

*Enter a clamour of **Servants' Voices** in darkness.*

Voices: The sun's ta'en off the sky!
He's but eclips'd. The moon dusketh his light.
Strike fire. We'll light th'impertinent night.
Hold! A candle by the day's a sorry omen.
Who's afeard!
Nor never so sorry as thik prodigy above.
How's this?
Queen Anne she lieth dead.
Now here's an osténtǃ
God grant her highness grace.
So be it.
Amen. Say "Amen". The lady hath best need of it.
All: Amen.

In the traditional legend, Aphrodite punished the youth, Narcissus, for rejecting the love of a nymph, Echo, by dooming him to fall in love with his own reflection, seen on the surface of water. The tale has at least two endings: either, that he pined away for love of himself; or, hypnotized by his own beauty, he fell in and drowned. Ovid's version as given by Gerard reads: 'But as for body none remain'd; in stead whereof they found a yellow floure, with milke white leaves ingirting of it round'.

Removing narcissus from pharmacology and myth, and placing it in the realm of psychiatry, one post-Freudian concept of narcissism is not that an individual falls in love with self, but, to escape and overcome the shocks of temporal life, ceases rather to recognize the difference between self and surroundings, thereby undergoing severe narcissistic regression.

That modern hypothesis is, like so much, not modern. Francis Bacon, in *Of Friendship*, paraphrases *Saint James*, 1.23–4: '... as men that look sometimes into a glass, and presently forget their own shape and favour'. That state of severe emotional withdrawal was understood and described by Wyclif and other late fourteenth century writers as 'womb-joy'.

Whatever King Richard had in mind for narcissus must depend upon the reader's interpretation.

[659] 5.6.109. *impertinent*: unsuitable, untimely.
[660] 5.6.117. *So be it*: Amen.

Lights: *come up again.*
Diana goes.
> Their travail's spent. Here's light come again.
> As that porténT of Nature passes, so this lady's nature passeth too.
> This other night will never mend.
> Come, take her up. Bear we her highness to her chamber.
> We will so. 128

All go, bearing the **Queen's** *body.*

ACT 5, SCENE 7

Mill Bay, Milford Haven, Wales, Sunday, August 7, 1485.

Sfx: A martial flourish.

Enter **Henry** *and* **Jasper Tudor**, *with* **Captains** *and* **Lords** *as may be, beneath the banner of Cadwallader's red dragon.*

Henry Tudor: What landing-place is this,
> whither auspicious-boding surges welcome us ashore?

Jasper Tudor: Why, we been hard by Milford Haven, fair nephew.
> Here is our native home.

Henry Tudor: The very air of Wales smells sweet.
> Where lies Abimelech?

---

[661] 5.6.121. *Diana*: The moon.
[662] 5.6.122. *travail*: The usual word for the labour of child-birth applied figuratively to eclipses of the sun and moon. *OED*, under *Travail*, quotes Holland, 1601: 'Seeing these things, and the painful ordinary travels (since that this term is now taken up) of the starres'. Hakewell further defines this figure: 'Eclipses of the sun and moon, in which they are commonly thought to suffer, and to be as it were in travail during that time' (1627). Dryden's *Georgics*, II. 679 (1697), stretches this figure into the eighteenth century.
[663] 5.7.3. *been*: be, are. This antique usage survived into the Period. Cf. *Pericles* II, Prologue 28.
[664] 5.7.6. *Abimelech*: had himself declared king of Shechem about 1150 B.C., slaughtered his seventy 'brothers' and was himself slain three years later. It is Henry Tudor who implies this parallel with King Richard, not Truth.

Jasper Tudor: His court lieth at Nottingham, a town of strength,
   for the nonce to come upon us boldly with his Northern might.
Henry Tudor: Then may our march proceed as towardly towards England
   as that wind that fetch'd us Wales. On, *Y Ddraig Goch!*   10   665
   If we but breathe, we tarry over-long.
   Forward the **Standard-Bearer**.
Jasper Tudor: Captains, take up your companies. We'll night.
   The morrow we'll fly, like King Bladud, to close with the boar.   13   666
   ***All** go, behind the standard.*

ACT 5, SCENE 8

Nottingham Castle, mid-August, 1485.

Enter **Thomas**, *polishing a helmet, with which he begins a 'dialogue'.*

Thomas: Aha, to escape the stew at last!
   Kitcheners! Or harpies, whether.
   What these sweaty, black and rosy hags are.
   There's a tohu and a bohu below   667
   would tap the very spirit of a man to vent his soul.

---

665   5.7.10. *Y Ddraig Goch*: the Red Dragon of Wales. Here, the flag of the Welsh. After Henry Tudor was crowned King Henry VII, he promoted the Red Dragon of Wales (with a beige chest and belly) to be a 'supporter' on the royal coat of arms of England. In the context of *Dark Sovereign*, that deed helped to fulfill Jasper Tudor's prophecy at 5.4.88: 'Whenas Harry wins the crown, the dragon of the Welsh, like Arthur out of Avalon, shall rule the English evermore'.

666   5.7.13. *King Bladud*: An important god/king in British (Celtic/Welsh) mythology. The simile is based upon Bladud's ability to fly. He was associated with the worship of Minerva and the civilizing influence she represents.
    The *boar* symbolizes, first, Richard's totem animal; second, in the Welsh tradition of the Tudors, the force of evil. Cf. the interpretation of King Arthur's dream in Malory's *Le Morte D'Arthur*, V.iv. (1469). Contrasting with the boar, the pig in Celtic tradition is often the benign sign of Bladud and Merlin.

667   5.8.4. *tohu and a bohu*: confusion. After the Hebrew, rendered in Genesis 1.2 as 'without form and void'. *OED* cites Rabelais, whence the expression entered English during the Period. A definition from 1619 gives: 'A chaos, a Tohu and a Bohu, a mere confusion'.

Taps the helmet: Note me, sirrah:
Old women are the prattle of old voices;
old men attest the silence of old dreams.
   He may sit in the king's chair:
Ah me, when youth seems yesterday,
when yesterday's forgot, this then is age.
   He polishes; and listens: Husht, Sir Helmet,
for a second scruple, prithee hark!
Do you hear it, sir? Do you hear it?
Why, the blessèd silence, sirrah! Hark!
There is glory in silence. What's naught is all.
   He polishes.
   Speaking as the **Helmet**: Why then, Thomas,
dost thou banish it with worthless words?
Thomas: Wott'st thou not, Sir Ignorance?
Silence is of darkness kindred, twin and empty tablets
that a body may inscribe with light.
I am to take my chance to give a little fire.
Helmet: What candle, my foolish Thomas,
canst thou throw upon the silence and the dark?
Thomas: Why, a foolish little taper, may it please your majesty.
Helmet: Thou art an often hearer of the counsels of the great.
Would thou, advise me!
Thomas: Were I my king, I'd straightly charge my lords
to keep themselves in our peace. *Pause*: Where's here?
   Taps the helmet: Sir Kettle, we command you speak!
Helmet: Peace, Thomas?
Thomas: Aye. The sullen bloody peace of lords no more.
It is the honest peace of simple men I seek.
Helmet: Thy quest is of the holy grail.
Swift flying scorn shall ever strike thee down.
Thomas: How so, your grace?

---

668 5.8.8. *attest*: call to witness, speak to the truth of.
669 5.8.12. *a second scruple*: a second in time.
670 5.8.26. *Would thou*: If you wish to.

Helmet: Thou couldest not understand,
  for naught tak'st thou of life save life the self.
  War speaks to duty and the right of property.
Thomas: Moreover death.
Helmet: Assuredly of death. 40
Thomas: Spare us of righteousness from governors and priests!
Helmet: Leave it and let pass, my Thomas,
  my poor, and my distraughted fool. 671
Thomas: Verily well said,
  for poverty was ever preach'd as honest virtue by the rich.
Helmet: 'Twere better so.
  Blind-born men are blind; the deaf as adders deaf.
  How shall a base fool discern the wisdom of the great?
Thomas: May not a hoary head sip wisdom yet? 672
  I'faith I am bound to wonder: 50
  Am I the least man among fools?
  or the least fool among men?
  Our family of Plantagenets steeps each one
  throughly in other his own kindred blood.
  But for all they are greatly blooded, 673
  yet seldom come they better;
  and despite their blood is very great,
  meseems they are seldom wise.
  Where been the little princes, lord? 674
Helmet: Resting, Thomas. Resting. 60
Thomas: How deep, my lord? How deep?
Helmet: If thou wouldst save thy head upon thy neck,
  rescide thy tongue. Dost fear me, Thomas? 675
Thomas: Fear I you, lord?
Helmet: Thine eyes are lost for tears, old man.

---

671 5.8.43. *my poor*: my poor man.
672 5.8.49. *hoary head*: Cf. Leviticus 19.32 (KJV).
673 5.8.55. *blooded*: bloodstained.
674 5.8.59. *been*: be. Cf. note 5.7.3. This survived late as a literary form because of its impact on iambic pacing. Whereas *be* can be either hard or soft, *been* is invariably hard, determining meter.
675 5.8.63. *rescide*: cut, cut out.

Thomas: Nay, lord, you ne fear me.
   Fall back fall edge, you are my helm.
   I weep but for Plantagenet, my lord.
   It is for all Plantagenets I weep.   69
      Crying, **Thomas** *goes.*

ACT 5, SCENE 9

The king's pavilion, Ambien Hill, above Market Bosworth, the night of August 21–22, 1485. **King Richard** *lies on a cot.* **Spirit**, *or a hologram thereof, stands in shadow, dressed as a gardener, its face concealed.*

Off: The light of fires. Sfx: Armourers hammering.

King Richard: *wakes, grabs up his sword*:
   Who's there? Stand to it, ho! How a tumult speaks,
   as sour-voic'd as Tower ravens, and as black.
   The very night doth chill for cold, for fright.
      Ha, th'expectant air prológues th'induction
   to tomorrow's end. O, to be beforehand with the eye,
   to eye what lives, which fortunes won or cast,
   and O, to claim the epilogue at the last.
      Sweet iron, stern tool to strew the tainted field
   with gobbets of the sudden dead, thou look'st too purely,
   art too cold, to be address'd to anger's heat
   and vengeful spleen.   10
      Besides, the grounded moiling in my head is noisomer
   than all the din of armourers assailing steel. No coal so hot,

---

676 5.8.67. *Fall back fall edge*: Through thick and thin.
677 5.9. *Stage Direction: grabs up his sword*: In fact the king is thought to have used a battle-hammer, a more effective weapon, perhaps, but not one with much symbolic significance.

no edge so keen as pangs the head doth forbear, who,
casting the worst, strains so to thwart the tide of conscience 678
as it soon must slip away. How long to think? 679
to cling to failing resolution, trow? Whether will my essence
be best pleas'd to bear out crack'd? Or loose and go?
    Sees **Spirit**: What monstrous prodigy is that?
That carries a form constraineth matter too. 680
But does it live? Or doth this mannishness well forth   20
of nether brain, as now unplumb'd?
Challenges: Be you of faerie, fiend or flesh?
Will you not speak? You think I see you not.
If I stand here I see you. Speak! 681
Spirit: I am the darkness in thee, lord.
    I am — thy soul of light.
King Richard: Who dare bear a contubernial visit to his king? 682
Spirit: The shadow of his king.
King Richard, *aside*: For want of sun nor flame it cannot be a shade:
    This speaks a living wight. *Speaks*: Be uncover'd in presence!   30
Spirit: Thou look'st to find my face. I tell thee,
    'tis none otherwise than every mother's child's, and thine.
    Corrupted. Purified.
King Richard: A' would beseem familiarly to the king, quotha!
    As who should guise him to a gardener. 683
Spirit: All kings return to earth.
King Richard: Say at last. I'd know. Be you *vif or mort*? 684

---

678 5.9.14. *casting the worst*: forecasting, expecting the worst.

679 5.9.15. *How long to think?* Plays on the expression *to think long*, suggesting impatience with an expectation delayed.

680 5.9.19. *form constraineth matter*: Everything requires a form, hence a form defines some 'thing'. Cf. 4.1.105, re. *species*. The original Aristotelian notion was worked to death by the Scholastic school of philosophy.

681 5.9.24. *If I stand here…*: There is no *if* about this expression. It implies: It is precisely because I'm standing here that I can see you!

682 5.9.27. *contubernial*: Literally, sharing the same tent. After Chaucer, *The Parson's Tale*. *Contubernial* staged a nineteenth century come-back in letters from British officers overseas describing regimental life under canvas.

683 5.9.35. *As who should guise him*: As if one would disguise himself.

684 5.9.37. *vif or mort*: among the living or the dead. In late medieval art, the living were depicted talking with skeletons, often three of each, giving rise to the phrase *'les trois vifs et morts'*.

Spirit: How thou perceivest me soe'er, I am.
King Richard: How are you that disputes with me this?
Spirit: I am to teach sans voice of word. 40
    Fain too am I to satisfy thee with thy doom.
King Richard: What is my doom?
Spirit: Whatever it may be.
King Richard: Give me the morrow. How I crave the day.
Spirit: There lacketh power to dispose.
    Notwithstand past acts redound to present time,
    tomorrow scorns today; and shall,
    till every atomy and moment of eternity
    is shed abroad and gather'd in.
    Bet were thee that thy several wills 50
    made common suit against the careful hour. 685
    Thou canst not gull the still point.
King Richard: Cáre it was did urge infected passion to rash acts ...
Spirit: In recompense, care taketh not but fear.
King Richard: ... empanell'd deaf regard
    to justify intemperate deeds ...
Spirit: Moreover, thinking on it only self, 686
    doth urge more strife unthought-on.
King Richard: ... until at length insensate fear slew doubt
    with blameless blood.
Spirit: Doubting is the price men pay for wisdom; 60
    reality the price they pay for dreams.
King Richard: He is no dreamer that, despite of bloody cost,
    attach'd the throne in price with safety. 687
Spirit: Thou sayest;
    and saying, sitt'st in judgment upon thyself.
    Wherein I do commend thee to the resolutions of thy wills.

---

685 5.9.51 *careful*: full of care, anxious.

686 5.9.57. *it only self*: Itself. In common with other words, such as *how/so/ever* (in 5.9.38), *itself* was sometimes split (*tmesis*) to enclose other words. Usually, in the case of *itself*, the addition was a simple adjective. Cf. *Cymbeline*, III.iv.159: 'Woman it pretty self'.

687 5.9.63. *in price with*: suggests an obligatory, or contractual, means to an end. *Sáféty* may retain a hint of its French trisyllabic pronunciation.

Whether hadst thou rather win this only day?
Or gain eternity? The question's plain.
Comes in the morrow-light. I go. 70
Spirit *vanishes.*
   Lights: *Dawn breaks.*
   Sfx: *A flourish, horses, drums.*

Enter **Norfolk** *(formerly* **Howard***),*   688
with **Ratcliffe, Catesby** *and* **Forces.**

Norfolk: Best fortune to your highness
   may the morrow with it bring.
King Richard: We would, brave Norfolk,
   that the even blessing lights on you.
Norfolk: The foeman's forces stir, his scourers hurry home,
   their war-like blood determines of condemnéd fight.
King Richard: By how much they betray us, by so much must they die.
   Their sudden time, be now! Give order:
   Trumpets sound up points of war! Long day has pass'd 80   689
   wherein the Tydder may forswear his treachery.   690
     Sfx: *Horns sound points of war.*
     Forces *remove the king's cot.*
   Do we but let those live sufficient while
   to rue the foul-adviséd night
   they quaff'd their cups of courage off.
Norfolk: Your battles, in meanwhile, zealously attend.
   Twice arm them, lord. Bind their resolve.
   Gird these with mighty words against the day.
King Richard: My own true Northern men,
   beyond that tongue can tell, ye wot it well,

---

[688] *Stage Direction*: Even before Gloucester's coronation on July 6th, he had raised John Howard (on June 28, 1483) to the rank of duke of Norfolk as a reward for his support.

[689] 5.9.80. *points of war*: military signals sounded on horns. SOED defines the phrase, improbably, as 'warlike exercises'.

[690] 5.9.81. *Tydder*: The spelling, and perhaps the pronunciation, used by Richard III in proclamations against the largely unknown Henry Tudor.

I love you as myself that stand with me the day. 90
We get of Tydder by two souls upon this hill
to each scabb'd Welsh, scald Breton, pelf,
the trash of the hedgerows as they are.
But withal, though we take odds, despise them not.
Trust to have sport at them, ne rely not upon the victory,
which will get our undoing, but the rather to take it, aspire.
    I plight ye an assurance,
wherewith the fire may course through every vein
to strength the arm, instil resolve into the blood.
Who marshal here the day hath double right: 100
We are God's will, His chosenest weapons
wherewith t'indict the pain of treason.
Ye prove allegiance here unto your king,
by that unto your hearths, and that ye love.
Norfolk: I would repay your grace's favour with my service,
    — if it chance, my life. Give me to lead the head.
King Richard: That lesser men deem bloody, desperate work,
thou dost demand of me as boon. Worthy Norfolk,
draws breath no more truer friend than thou.
The parlous favour thou dost ask is thine. 110
    Exeunt **Norfolk** *and the* **Main Force**.
    Sfx: *Battle is soon heard.*
Good friends, set hard your face as flint.
Clum each the fight no whit less keenly than his edge.
Stifle them in reeking death, do;
look our enemies be drown'd in their own gore.
Lést there be that weary in well doing, mark:
The mightier onset that we give today,
the more remains to you King Richard's peace hereafter.

---

[691] 5.9.91. *get of*: have the advantage over.
[692] 5.9.104. *by that*: and therefore.
[693] 5.9.112. *Clum*: Seize, v. By the nineteenth century *clum* was restricted to Hampshire and Dorset dialects.
    § *edge*: edged weapon, sword.
[694] 5.9.116. *onset that we give*: attack that we make. *OED* does not find the military sense before 1631.
    However, this usage goes back at least to Daus, in 1560.

Set at them! To! Do we set on ...
Forces *cheer*: Long live King Richard, ho!
    Exeunt **King Richard** *and* **Forces**.

Enter **Henry** *and* **Jasper Tudor**, *with* **Forces**.
Enter a **Scout**, *meeting them.*

Scout: With hateful ire the armies shock.   120
    Our battles onward go. Although they press us grievously,
    the earl of Oxford's men shove Norfolk at the hill.
Jasper Tudor: Yet do they tire.
    For all their valours, they have human hearts.
    Except we bring them helps, they are to fail.
Henry Tudor: How chance Lord Stanley comes not in?
    And Sir William holds his redcoats back.   695
Jasper Tudor: They lie aloof. Richard holds Stanley's son
    in hostage against the part of his kinsmen.
Henry Tudor: Haste we to bring them in at last!   130
Jasper Tudor: Beware from them, boy. For lack of manners   696
    cannot these by honourable argument be won.
    The brothers hang their honour at their arse.
Henry Tudor: Me rather had, my eyes might view
    four thousand arses than one front!
    If Stanleys take our part, the day is won;
    if they oppose against us, w'are undone.
    To horse! We'll parle wi' Stanleys,
    or to quiet them, or to bring them to us either.
    Exeunt **Tudors** *and* **Forces**.

Enter the **King**, **Ratcliffe**, **Catesby** *and* **Escort** *as may be.*
Enter a **Scourer**, *meeting them.*

---

[695] 5.9.127. *redcoats*: Perhaps the first use of this word as applied to a body of soldiers was c. 1520, when the *Song of the Lady Bessy* described Sir William Stanley's forces as 'Ten thowsand read coates'. Dr. Hanham (p.133) cautions that 'It is clear from "The Song of the Lady Bessy" that the Stanley family later created for themselves a kind of private historical apotheosis which bears little resemblance to fact'. Certainly that number is exaggerated.

[696] 5.9.131. *manners*: morality (Bacon).

Scourer: The Tudor, my liege, unsettled by adversity, 140
 voids aside, intending to the Stanleys' camps,
 and with a strong power at his back.
 It seems to me he'd ally the Stanleys to his treason.
King Richard: Stanley will not stop of tendering
 his brother's treason, and his own.
 Treachery wi' those was ever good friends.
 Come all, we'll in, to finish as we find.
Ratcliffe: We are but number'd to your meinie;
 the Tudor's train is some score strong.
King Richard: Make no matter for 't. 150
 Stay, those that take not stomach against the fight.
 Who love me, come! W'are put to lottery.
 And though my blood at last reek o'er the foe,
 yet shall I die as I have liv'd, alone, untouch'd,
 a virgin soul. Whatever Providence intend, prevail!
  Sfx: *Trumpets.*

Enter the **Tudors** *and* **Forces**. *All fight.*

Voice 1: W'are overpow'red, my liege.
Voice 2: Fly the field, my lord, or we must fail.
Voice 1: A horse! A horse! Some bring the king a horse!
King Richard: I will not budge a foot.
 I'll rather die the king of England. 160

Enter **Forces***, shouting*: Stanley! Stanley! Stanley!

King Richard: Treason! Treason! Treason!
  King Richard *is killed.*
   Ratcliffe *is killed,* **Catesby** *captured.*
   Many fall; the living fight off.
   Sfx: Battle continues, off, fading.

Enter **Spirit** *as epilogue-speaker,*
finding its way among the dead to stand above the body of the **King**.

EPILOGUE

Spirit: That Was Once King, with thee was slain   697
    the spired buds of maz'd imaginings.   698
    The time hath been, when thy flower was crush'd.
    Time is, that thy bitterest fruits endure.
    Ghost, thy time without time is now;
    forthy, list till nobler wills   699
    than such that brought thee low.
    To the audience:
        Vouchsafe me speak to innocence unborn   170
    how came the ending so to evil pass.
    Our tale was written of an island of tormented souls,
    which, setting off the common weal, sought several wealths,
    for and to bring the less evil upon their parts.   700
        Reflect upon this litany of little ills
    grown great beyond design. You shall mind echoes
    of base judgments, fearful slaughters,   701
    savage, heinous and unhuman acts.
    You shall beweep the lot of innocents, brought low sans ruth.   702
    You shall bewail prudence, brought to give way to advantage;   180   703
    brought again to harbour rash designs.

---

[697] 5.9.163. *was*: A form frequently used in the plural during the sixteenth and seventeenth centuries. See Ind.1.53.

[698] 5.9.164. *spired buds*: sprouted seeds. *Spired* was used in the sixteenth and seventeenth centuries to describe sprouted seed, particularly barley, which, having germinated, was useless for brewing. *Spired* here therefore combines both the senses of germinated and spoiled. Though never itself figurative, it is attached here to 'buds', which has had figurative application since 'a bud of ambition' (1579).

[699] 5.9.168. *forthy*: for which reason.

[700] 5.9.174. *for and*: and in addition, moreover.

[701] 5.9.177. *fearful slaughters*: slaughters induced by fear.

[702] 5.9.179. *sans ruth*: without pity.

[703] 5.9.180. *brought*: induced.

> Quoth Bernard how that hell is full of good desires.   704
> A doubtful enterprise is through and throughly folly's way.
> Who will such things affect, of lust, of longing or affrights,
> need know their venture shall become his proper ens,   705
> uncheck'd, above their several parts;
> which men infirm of conscience may not turn,
> but if to carry to their end,   706
> impell'd to be impal'd on grief.
> *Stoops to take the crown:*
> Suffer me unloose the coronal doth pin thy brains.   190
> How doth unwisdom gild this fillet in false wise.
> Now to let it lie amid a thorn bush:
> Than whereamong no place so seemly beéth as a briar   707
> to rest the wheel and wind her up again;   708
> for in the upshot is this golden hoop transform'd
> into the anguish'd crown of thorn,
> which doth inhere in all whose legend claims   709
> the yellow thorny flower of *Planta genest*.   198 710

---

704   5.9.182. *Bernard*: St. Bernard of Clairvaux. Attrib.

705   5.9.185. *his proper ens*: its own creature; something that develops a life or impetus of its own; a distinct and independent entity.

706   5.9.188. *but if to*: except to.

707   5.9.193. For clarity's sake, sound this as *briar*, although it should be pronounced *brere*, a monosyllable from Chaucer to Spenser, and persisting in the U.S. South. Shakespeare uses the modern form in *All's Well*, IV.iv.32. Webster's continues to give a softer phonetic value than *OED*.

708   5.9.194. *to rest the wheel and wind her up*: The wheel is both the crown and the Wheel of Fortune, hence the feminine pronoun. *Wind up* conveys a dual sense: to energize, as in clockwork; and, to involve or to implicate.

709   5.9.197. *inhere in*: abide in (something, as an essential, though perhaps intangible, property). § *legend*: history, record.

710   5.9.198. *planta genest*: the broom plant, from *genista* (Virgil). Several reasons have been suggested for the nickname Plantagenet, first given to Geoffrey, count of Anjou (d. 1151). It was applied to the English royal house centuries later, in 1460, when Richard III's father, Richard duke of York, claimed the throne as Richard Plantagenet.

To the audience:
    And there be more to tell, let it o'erlive,
resounding in your brains. For we are out.   200
Our voice is still'd; our fury spent;   711
Our tale ran out his course.
Mortality, fare well.   203 712
Spirit *vanishes with the crown.*
    Curtain.

---

711 5.9.201. *fury*: poetic 'rage' (*OED*).
712 *fare well*: fare well or farewell? Ambiguity is intended.

THE MERCHANT SCENE

INTRODUCTION

THE 'MERCHANT SCENE' FOLLOWS. I wrote it in 2006, eighteen years after laying down the first 'final' draft of *Dark Sovereign*. Director Nathaniel Merchant asked for a bridge, and this is it. Not all tragedy need be tragic. This scene brings light relief.

Nate Merchant believes that Richard III was a reasonable man and a benign king. The creature whom William Shakespeare invented as Tudor propaganda is not credible. Nate, a director of opera and theatre working in New York, asked me for something that would explicitly express Richard's loyalty to his brother, King Edward IV, and the Yorkist cause. I saw no editorial reason to refuse and plenty of room to agree: we seem to see the person and policies of Richard in a similar light. The 'Merchant Scene' fulfills its mission through Richard Gloucester's dialogue with his varlet, Thomas. This scene is not numbered. Directors can play it where it seems to fit, within reason.

This is not the scene to which Professor John Meagher refers in his 'Comments about *Dark Sovereign*'. That is Act 2.1, the first of the Richard and Thomas dialogues.

Robert Fripp
November 2007

Middleham Castle, North Yorkshire, 1471–'72. Night.
Enter **Thomas**, *varlet to* **Gloucester**.
He looks around through the tube of a rolled letter. The wax seal is broken.

Thomas: What a curiosity is writing!   713
    What curiosity a man must find to fathom it.
    These kind of scratching sparrows' feet are quite past me!

Enter **Gloucester**.

Thomas *discovers* **Gloucester** *through the rolled letter*:
    Hah! Your grace, this letter is rode a great gallop from the South.
Gloucester: A great gallop methinks that betokens
    a false gallop of news. Of whence, Thomas?   714
Thomas: Of or Araby, or London.   715
Gloucester: The seal is torn out!
Thomas: Devoured, I doubt not, by a hungry rat.
Gloucester *takes the letter gingerly*: Who is the author?   10
Thomas: He is your cousin Harry, duke of Buckingham, your grace.
Gloucester, *aside*: Aye, a ravening rat!
    Thrusts the letter back at **Thomas**:
    What matter-subject does my cousin write?
Thomas: Your grace knows that I cannot read.
Gloucester: Lack of learning seeleth up thine eyes;
    but withal it stoppeth not thine ears.   716
    What do my letter'd scullions say?

---

⁷¹³ *curiosity*: a desire to know; thus, a lust for education.
⁷¹⁴ *false gallop*: poor writing, bad verse. Freq. in Shaks., following others.
⁷¹⁵ *Or ... or*: The word 'or' precedes both alternatives. Freq. in the Period and Shaks.
⁷¹⁶ *thine*: Thine was falling out of use, but lingered as the standard possessive form before words starting with 'h' or a vowel. Hence Ben Jonson's 'Drink to me only with *thine* eyes' (1616).

Thomas *makes a show of remembering.*
Clutching the letter, recites the contents by heart:
Hm. Harry, duke of Buckingham, to our royal and virtuous cousin,
Richard, duke of Gloucester, fairest greeting.
I am moved to write this present, 20
praying that you take my letter to the best.
Cousin Gloucester, be not foreign from us while the queen,
her brother Rivers and her sons withal do drain the sap from out our veins
and pill the treasuries of England.
Though thou scorn London and the court, 717
yet do you embrace our cause! Your brother the king is blind
in the wickedness his queen effects this twenty years.
Gloucester: Who is so blind as he *will* not see!
Thomas *recites*: Cousin, do you join with us
to put the Woodvilles in deservéd durance! 30
If Elizabeth prevail, we, who been the true tree that is York,
shall be pluck'd down to death or exile.
But whitherward our words? That you keep silent bids us ask:
Do northern tempests waste our urgence far abroad
upon your blasted hills?
Or doth your mind as armour flect our sense? 718
Repair to London, cousin.
Speak truth to perfidy for those who love you.
Gloucester: For those who love me! For those who rather love themselves!
I that am young in years am old in hours of service. 40
I am to Edward shield and general captain
in the office of a wall against the Scot. 719
But these would have me hole the wall, lay down my arms,
quit vigilance, invite invasion.
Is England so phantastically king'd, that I

---

717 *Though thou scorn* ...: *Though* formerly took subjunctive tenses, as here. Usage was changing during the Period. Shaks. uses both subjunctive and indicative tenses.
718 *flect*: deflect, turn aside.
719 *Scot*: The word, being singular, implies the king of Scotland, James III, a reign marked by turmoil stirred by rebellious nobles rather than determined campaigns against England.

— while Scotsmen ravish English wives —
must haste to London, there to save my brother from his queen?
Psha! His fool's bell is soon rung doth war two fronts.
Buckingham, Hastings, Howard, Stanleys — *and* the mess of Woodvilles:
Pox of their power, the hollow profit of their court!   50
Let them writhe their necks like eels in a tun.   720
I piss against their politics — saving for the kingdom
cleave to Edward's line of life, and eke his line.   721
Though it be comfort-killing, yet the Border is my stage,
and I shall order myself in the play I have in hand.
(He offers to depart)
Thomas, *calling after*: Lastly... Duke Harry writes a privy business.
Gloucester: *My* privy business: Whereof I am the last to know;
wherethrough the tongues of stable-grooms and ostlers
pay their lord a privy nip.   722
Is it for this moment apt?   60   723
Thomas: O, apt, sir. Fit and apt.
Gloucester: Recite my private business, do!
Thomas *recites*: Your brother George, duke of Clarence,
our loyalst friend against the queen, would seize my Lady Anne.   724
Duke Harry writes: He means to sever from you her inheritance.
Gloucester *snatches the letter. Tries to find the place*:
Writes he for gospel, Thomas?
Thomas: Aye, your grace, for gospel.
Gloucester: Wherefore rouse our men at arms!
Thomas: Belikely they lie with their whores.
Gloucester: Then bid them fix their blades in feller foes.   70   725
To horse!

---

720 *Writhe ... tun*: get themselves in a stew (like eels slithering over each other in a barrel). Eels from the Thames were a favourite London dish. Hence Gloucester, no lover of the South, uses this simile.

721 *saving for ... eke his line*: My only concern is that the kingdom attach to Edward through his long life, and the lives of his heirs.

722 *pay ... a privy nip*: have their private joke behind my back.

723 *for this moment apt*: Is it important at this moment? Does it matter right now?

724 Cut this reference if Clarence has already been executed!

725 *feller*: more terrible.

Thomas: The whores?

Gloucester: To horse!

Thomas: Fare we against the Scots, your grace?

Gloucester: Drowsy-headed monkey, we ride south.
   *Thrusts the letter at **Thomas**.* Post we sans stop to London!   76
   They go.

A SCENE BY SCENE SYNOPSIS

Induction 1: Two Murderers debate whether to kill the two little princes in the Tower of London. The stronger will prevails, and the uncrowned King Edward V (12), and his brother Richard duke of York (10) are murdered in their bed — perhaps.

Induction 2: The character of Rumour asks the audience to consider whether the previous scene depicted fact or rumour. She takes us back thirteen years, returning us to the winter of 1471–2, when the action of *Dark Sovereign* begins.

ACT I

Act 1.1: Lady Anne Neville mourns the death of her betrothed, Edward of Lancaster, Prince of Wales. Yorkist leaders killed Edward during or after the battle of Tewkesbury. Now, with both her father and husband dead, she is in law *une femme seule* (a woman alone) without a male protector. She owns half of the greatest estate in England, but this is claimed by her brother in law, George, duke of Clarence, by virtue — he claims — of his marriage to Lady Anne's elder sister.

Richard duke of Gloucester, who is younger than his brothers King Edward IV and Clarence, seeks Lady Anne's hand in marriage. As the wealthiest heiress in England, their match would bring advantage to both parties. The youngest son needs wealth; the lady needs a powerful husband to regain her estates.

Lady Anne neither forgets nor forgives Richard Gloucester, who was among the Yorkists who killed Edward of Lancaster at Tewkesbury just months before. But if she is to escape her plight, she must set aside her hatred of Gloucester and overcome her predicament by marrying him for his power.

Act 1.2: George duke of Clarence bitterly opposes his brother's claim to Lady Anne. The matter becomes the talk of London when the dukes' retainers battle to possess her. The eldest of the three brothers, King Edward IV, must postpone sailing to France with an army, being forced to call a special council meeting to resolve his brothers' quarrel.

Act 1.3: Truth, Rumour's identical twin, describes the outcome of the royal brothers' quarrel. At first, the audience believes her to be Rumour.

Enter Queen Elizabeth Woodville, shadowed by Rumour. Truth and Rumour dissect the queen's character before disappearing at the approach of the queen's brother, Anthony Woodville the earl of Rivers, and the queen's elder son by her first marriage, Thomas Grey, marquis of Dorset.

Rivers, Dorset and the queen stress the imperative of keeping the young Prince of Wales, the future Edward V, safe from the intrigues of London and from opinions that run counter to the Woodville family interests by bringing him up at Rivers' estate in the Welsh borders.

Truth and Rumour describe the bizarre execution of the duke of Clarence.

ACT 2

Act 2.1: Gloucester returns to his stronghold of Middleham in North Yorkshire to be greeted by his varlet, Thomas. Enter the duchess, Anne, formerly Lady Anne Neville. The duke and duchess worry that King Edward IV has become a pawn to serve the insatiable ambitions of his queen and her family, the Woodvilles and Greys. This discussion sets the scene for the faction fight that dominates the play.

Act 2.2: King Edward IV lies dying in his fortieth year. The king, aware of the bitter schism his policies have created between his queen's family and the 'old nobility' tries to force a deathbed reconciliation. His action comes nineteen years too late: only the force of his personal authority had prevented civil war from erupting long before.

Privately, Hastings stresses the importance of keeping power in the hands of the old nobility (Gloucester, Buckingham, Hastings, Howard *et al*). Only by doing so can they humble the Woodvilles and the Greys, who used the queen's power and influence to abuse their privilege, running England and Wales as their private fief for almost twenty years.

On the other side of King Edward's deathbed, the queen's two sons by her first marriage take the opposite view. Factional tension builds while the king lies dying.

Act 2.3: Hastings sends a letter to Richard Gloucester in Yorkshire, informing him of his brother's death. Gloucester plans to travel to London, promising Anne that he will make every effort to thwart Queen Elizabeth's grasp for power. The influence the queen holds over her son, the boy-king Edward V, assists her in this.

Act 2.4: The queen, in mourning, convenes a meeting of the royal council at Westminster. Hastings and Howard hotly oppose the queen's and River's plan to bring the young king to London at the head of a Welsh army commanded by Rivers. Bishop Russell mediates. Compromise is reached on the numbers of men in the parties' respective forces. In a second compromise, Gloucester is named Chief Counsellor to King Edward V.

Act 2.5: Gloucester, now in York, meets Humphrey Percival, a secret envoy from Duke Harry of Buckingham. Percival relays Buckingham's urgent message that, for the sake of the old nobility, Gloucester must assume the role of Protector to the king, thereby blunting the Woodvilles' grab for power.

ACT 3

Act 3.1: Gloucester and a henchman, Ratcliffe, meet Harry Buckingham at Northampton. Gloucester asks Buckingham's motives for offering his support.

Act 3.2: The young king, Edward V, escorted by Rivers and retinue, stops at Stony Stratford. Rivers turns back to Northampton to greet the two dukes in the name of their nephew, the new king.

Act 3.3: Rivers meets the dukes, and the evening is spent drinking, without rancor. Rivers retires, whereupon Buckingham urges Gloucester to seize him while he sleeps, thereby depriving the king's party, and the Woodville faction, of effective leadership. After a soliloquy on his moral dilemma, Gloucester decides to act. The dukes seize Rivers, and start after the king.

Act 3.4: The dukes meet the young king and seize the leading members of his retinue. Disbanded, his military escort is ordered back to Wales. Whether the king becomes Gloucester's prisoner or his ward is left an open question.

Act 3.5: Hastings and Howard, hearing the news in London, celebrate Gloucester's success. They encounter several low persons trying to drum up recruits for a Woodville 'army', a sign of strife to come.

Act 3.6: The queen flees to the sanctuary of Westminster Abbey with her family and baggage. Servants steal her baggage.

Enter Dorset, who announces that his search for support has yielded few allies.

Enter Archbishop Rotherham, who hands the queen the Great Seal of England, in effect resigning his office of Lord Chancellor. The queen berates him.

Act 3.7: Hastings persuades Londoners to relinquish arms and refrain from civil war.

ACT 4

Act 4.1: Buckingham hints that Gloucester should seize the throne. Before Gloucester can challenge him, Duchess Anne enters. Buckingham withdraws. Privately, Anne presses the same course of action on her husband. Gloucester concedes that his only hope of avoiding ultimate downfall is to claim the throne.

Act 4.2: A lawyer, Catesby, is astounded when Gloucester asks him to sound out Hastings on the prospect of Gloucester claiming the throne. Hastings, a staunch supporter of the young king (although hostile to the Woodvilles) vehemently opposes the notion, which Catesby puts to him as if it were a current rumour.

No sooner does Catesby leave than an agent from Thomas Lord Stanley tries to persuade Hastings to flee London with Lord Stanley, saying that his master, Stanley, has had a dream that the morrow bodes ill for them both.

Act 4.3: Hastings and Stanley attend a Council meeting at the Tower. Gloucester, accusing Hastings of treason, has him beheaded. Stanley is wounded during this incident, and Rotherham and Bishop Morton seized, breaking the power of those who have shown themselves most loyal to the young King Edward V — and, by implication, to the Woodvilles' cause.

Act 4.4: A crier gives the official explanation for Hastings' speedy execution. A group of Londoners disputes it.

Act 4.5: Gloucester tries to overcome remorse at Hastings' death. His Id, represented by a dwarf, Incubus, tries to persuade him to destroy the little princes, whose continued existence is the only bar to Gloucester's accession. Gloucester settles for a legal remedy, declaring his brother Edward's children bastards.

Act 4.6: Buckingham presses the octogenarian archbishop of Canterbury, Cardinal Bourchier, into service to remove young Richard duke of York from sanctuary in Westminster Abbey. The archbishop denies the boy sanctuary on the grounds that he has committed no offence requiring it.

The queen surrenders her son to the archbishop, entrusting her child to his office. She flees, weeping.

Act 4.7: Gloucester orders Ratcliffe to ride north to oversee the speedy execution of Rivers, Richard Grey, and others of King Edward's household.

Act 4.8: Buckingham tries to persuade the aldermen of London to petition Gloucester to accept the crown.

Act 4.9: Grey, Vaughan, and Rivers go to execution at Pontefract Castle.

ACT 5

Act 5.1: Gloucester enters Act Five as King Richard III. Truth and Rumour debate his personality. Ratcliffe arrives to tell the king of rebellion in the southern counties.

Act 5.2: Bishop Russell, pressed into service as Lord Chancellor, appears with a scribe, Bede, and dictates his account of the times. Russell describes the nature of the southern rebellion, and the fact that an obscure pretender to the throne, Henry Tudor earl of Richmond, now leads the opposition to King Richard's reign. Russell tells how Henry Tudor's fleet was turned back by a 'ten day tempest', and how Buckingham was taken prisoner and brought before a court at Salisbury.

Act 5.3: King Richard refuses clemency to Buckingham, who is led to execution.

Act 5.4: Henry Tudor and his 'court' in exile assemble at Rennes Cathedral to vow the destruction of King Richard. As the price demanded by other factions for their allegiance, Henry Tudor swears to marry Elizabeth of York, the eldest daughter of King Edward IV and Elizabeth Woodville.

Jasper Tudor, Henry's uncle, explains Tudor motivations.

Act 5.5: Russell, once more dictating to Bede, states that Queen Anne is near death; and that Richard's and Anne's only child and heir, Prince Edward of Middleham, is dead. This, almost on the first anniversary of King Edward's death, is taken as an ill omen on Richard's reign.

Act 5.6: Queen Anne, dying, seeks the love and comfort of King Richard, who, beset by stresses and grief, is in no fit shape to give it. The queen dies on the day of a total solar eclipse (March 16, 1485), leaving no heir, her death a second ill omen on King Richard's reign.

Act 5.7: Henry and Jasper Tudor, with forces, land in Wales.

Act 5.8: King Richard's varlet, Thomas, in a 'dialogue' with a helmet, questions the fate of the princes in the Tower, and mourns the apparent downfall of the House of Plantagenet.

Act 5.9: On the night before battle at Bosworth, King Richard is visited in his tent by Spirit, who seems to offer a choice between mortal death in this world by way of atonement, and death of the spirit in the next.

Battle is joined. In a gallant but ill-considered attack on Henry Tudor's escort, the king's bodyguard is outnumbered and the king dies fighting bravely.

Epilogue: Spirit delivers the epilogue.

QUOTABLE QUOTES

ON MONEY: DS IND. 1.18
   Money makes an able sexton:
   A's oft employ'd to bury the corpse of Conscience.

ON THE LAW: DS 1.1.169
   The law's a sword, an iron thing, and cold.
   She cuts no deeper than the might of him who would uphold her.

ON POWER: DS 2.5.97
   Power, Percival! Power is a fickle mistress; vicious are her parts.
   Like to a pleasing strumpet, Power slaves who thinks to hold her.
   I can live without it.

ONE USE FOR A CLEAR CONSCIENCE: DS 3.4.23
   If Conscience virtue has,
   'tis that she bindeth up the weak to aid the strong.

ON COMPASSION: DS 3.4.132
   Compassion's Nature's fools' cloth: [*C. is the uniform of Nature's fools*]
   Never it shall be the stuff of Nature's politics!

ON DECISION-MAKING: DS 3.3.147
   Speaks Reason to my Will?
   or doth proud Will to Reason speak?

ON DESTRUCTIVE ANGER: DS 3.7.20
   Heat but engenders ire, the which, consuming up,
   doth render good with ill, nobility of soul with base,
   and so an end.

ON GRIEF: DS 2.4.7
    When day droops into night, who then can light a brand
    so great 'twill show the hórizont? Nay, my lord.
    The face, the breath, the voice, the touch of hands,
    the quick, the very certain countenance of life
    rebuke our fond imagin'd vizard of eternity.
    Had heaven wept good measure of my grief
    the earth had wash'd away.

ON FICKLE FRIENDS: DS 3.6.160
    Never a friend so leaden sober
    but his voidance was not instant silvern;
    his brain as suddenly beblest of more excuses
    than his shirt had fleas.

ON SORROW: DS 2.4.24
    Sorrow, like refiner's fire, yields best remembrance,
    true, and undefiled.

ON REPENTANCE: DS 3.6.70
    True repentance is the hasty path from sin.

A DEATHBED APPEAL FOR LOVE: DS 5.6.41
    Deny me not of love; an' if thou must, mask thy disdain.
    At least fast echoes from thy passion on me till we part.

A DESIRE FOR VENGEANCE: DS 3.3.219
    Dearth reward the doing of it; death revenge the act;
    the Devil pick the scraps!

ONE DEFINITION OF OLD AGE: DS 5.8.9
    Ah me, when youth seems yesterday,
    when yesterday's forgot, this then is age.

ON THE SLEEPLESS CARES OF KINGSHIP: DS 1.2.33
    Endue our mind with that affair, which,
    ringing in our night-stopp'd ears,
    doth murder care-bestriding sleep.

ON THE SEDUCTIVE POWER OF WOMEN: DS 1.3.62
    If chastity be sorcery
    there's many a woman's a witch
    for many's the man bewitched withal!

IN PRAISE OF SILENCE: DS 5.8.3
    Do you hear it, sir? Do you hear it?
    Why, the blessèd silence! Hark!
    There is glory in silence. What's naught is all.

A VARLET'S LAMENT: DS 2.1.62
    On my grave they'll 'grave the epitaph...

            He fetch'd.
          And he fetch'd
       Until God did him fetch.
     Here lies Thomas, fetch'd up,
      His old life fetch'd again.

KING ARTHUR: SURVIVING PIECES

BY THE TIME I FINISHED writing *Dark Sovereign* in 1988 I had mapped out scenarios for two more plays. I started writing one of these, based on Sir Thomas Malory's *Le Morte d'Arthur*, careful to discard the part of his book covering the romance between the Cornish knight Tristan (Tristram) and the Irish princess Iseult (Isolde, or Yseult). Meanwhile, *Dark Sovereign* was meeting such resistance from the Shakespeare establishment that I could not see another project justifying my time and energy, so I finished three scenes and abandoned *Arthur*.

My second proposed play fared better. My notes on the life of Eleanor of Aquitaine eventually took shape as a book. Eleanor dictates her memoirs in *Power of a Woman. Memoirs of a turbulent life: Eleanor of Aquitaine*, 2007. (I can report that I wrote Eleanor's 'autobiography' in modern English.)

What remains from my manuscripts of *Arthur* (working title) begins with an experiment. I never used four-stressed-syllable alliterative verse in *Dark Sovereign*, but I did intend to put this Anglo-Saxon metre into the mouth of Taliesin (with an apology to Welsh readers for using Saxon prosody). Taliesin would have been my narrator throughout *Arthur*.

A stop (cesura) figures near the middle of each line in the first part of the following passage. Purists take this further: a masculine cesura follows a stressed syllable; a feminine cesura follows an unstressed syllable. There are other distinctions, but that is enough for now. Apart from the cesura, the vocabulary in Taliesin's introduction to *Arthur* meets the same rigid etymological standard as the text of *Dark Sovereign*.

Alliterative verse forms the spine of most Old English poetry. That includes *Beowulf*. Common in many ancient verse forms, alliterative verse was most prevalent in Germanic languages. In Britain it survived into Middle English. Around the end of the fourteenth century the Pearl Poet used it to write *Sir Gawain and the Green Knight*. William Langland may have been the last English poet to pen alliterative verse, in *Piers Plowman*.

Without more ado, here is Taliesin's introduction to *Arthur*. A bard would shout the formula of words on the opening line to quiet a hall:

TALIESIN'S INTRODUCTION TO ARTHUR

                  Unstop your ears!
                The tále-téller   Táliesin, Welsh bárd,
           unbúrden'd would bé   of an old Brítish tále,
     which, swóllen with shádows   and shádes forth of the pást,
      Doth yet fly with his fáme   to the fúture, past déath.

Time in his age doth ránd and téar,   doing off trúth for táles,
      Till bárds, truth-béaring   bríng forth hístory;
  Touching stríngs, playing stóps,   speaking Stóry as tíme no more knows.

        Now Tíme silence télls: trúth fáils.
         So Táliesin tákes it up   his tále to sáy,
           With súch blunt stóry   as séeled eyes shall ópe,
      Whereat your sháfts of síght   shall sée the dark pást again.
                 Déath's dúst   I dóom to líveliness.

[*Taliesin's pace quickens, changing to dactyls.*]

When forests were darker,
When mountains stood higher,
When dewfalls were rivers,
When valleys were mire;
When castles were hilltops,
When fog thick as milk droop'd in air
And the Ancient of Days was yet young;
Then Uther Pendragon was king of the English,
Whose lust to Igrain — that was wife to
The duke of Tintagil — begat on her body
An infant whose name was called Arthur,
For he was the glory of men
And the doom of his age.

[*Taliesin quickens again, to running iambs.*]

The duchess warn'd her lord from Uther's lust,
Whereon they fled Pendragon's court, to Cornwall,
Where the duke ensconc'd his wife, Igrain,
Within the massy fortilage, Tintagil,
Whilst himself held Castle Terrabil.
Now, after them came Uther's dreadful host,
To bear Gorloís down and seize Igrain.

But budg'd Tintagil not. King Uther now,
For anger and for lust fell passing sick,
Till that Sir Ulfius, (a noble knight,
That loyalst was, and truest to his king,)
Ask'd him cause-why he was with care forspent.
Which being told, Sir Ulfius took horse,
And spurring hard came on a beggar old
Beside the road. He ask'd the way to Merlin.
Quoth that fiend-sired ancient: 'I am he'.
Sir Ulfius bade Merlin turn him back
To render to the king what help he might.

King Uther for his part told him his plight;
Agreed most freely of rewarding Merlin well
Should he advance a winning stratagem.

The wizard got him to his magic arts, and,
Casting omens, came again to Uther,
Telling him that on that selfsame night
His force should war the Castle Terrabil:
The king the whilst should to Tintagil hie,
And wait his time.

''Tis written in the entrails', Merlin said,
'That ere Arcturus show the midnight-hour
Tintagil's ghost shall from his flesh depart'.

Quoth Merlin to the king, 'Stay your desire
Until the magic hour! Go in, then. Lie with her.
Speak not a word lest she discover you.
This starry night, O king, do only this,
And you shall get upon Igrain a son'.

What needs Taliesin specify his book?
Tintagil issued out of Terrabil
And on a bloody-facéd field was slain.
King Uther *after* lay with fair Igrain,
But rising before dawn he stole away.
Thérefore the life of Arthur gotten was
Not in adultery, but rather death.

Time passes, and the fair Igrain,
At even-dusk a wife, at dawn a widow is
— Yet young with child!

Time passes, and King Uther
To the fair Igrain is wed.

Time passes, and Igrain is wonderf'ly amaz'd
To learn the seed she bears is Uther's blood.

Time passes, and Igerna's time is come
Wherein she should bring forth her newborn son.

Child Arthur was no sooner born but ta'en,
For Merlin henc'd the babe, unchristen'd still,
Unto Sir Ector, who, by his good faith,
Had sworn to bring him up as 'twere his own.
Thus Arthur from a boy not knew his line,
But he was ever spoken Ector's son,
The younger brother of Sir Kay.

Thereafter was King Uther seldom whole,
But plagued with sickness, war and other strife
Whereof he lay him down at last, to die;
And in the face of Merlin, and his lords,
Claim'd Arthur, his young son — whose life,
In's life, the king had never joy'd —
should thenceforth to the lion throne ascend,
and lord on England.
Thus much Taliesin's tale.
Begins our play.

I recycled 'Taliesin's tale' a long time ago, building a short story around it. It now forms the spine of *The Cottar's Tale* in my forthcoming *New Wessex Tales* series of nearly forty short stories.

CAROL BURTIN FRIPP, HER VERSE

Spell the words formed by the initial letter on each line. This style was popular in the 1590s.

Could I the impress of thy love rehearse,
And set in lame syllabs thy moving force,
Rewarding thee by turns with my poor verse,
O, then I should with better skill endorse
Love's ardor, suiting words with thy sweet worths.

But all my art shall never captive thee
Vntil Time equals love and poetry:
Retiring that, of our mortality;
This guarding, to preserve that was our knot
In words shall tarry till eternity,
Nor been forgot, though empires rise and fail.

For thy life's gift to me, gift I thee this,
Returning thee this mirror to thy flame.
In loving lines, transform'd be love to bliss,
Professing qualities may justly claim:
Profound in life; in time to come, sublime.

How shall I tell thee? 'tis but thou alone
Effects my joy, holds my heart's hand in thine,
Renews past love against each present day.

Vaunt in my love, as I increase in thine,
Excell'd in nothing else our world can give.
Render her perfection, Muse! Do on each line
See you take heed to set my Carol down.
Exhort me evermore to sing her praise.

RSPF for CBF, on our anniversary, 1991

BOOKS BY ROBERT FRIPP
(Robert Stephen Parker Fripp)

For reviews and synopses: http://robertfripp.ca/ Books

THE BECOMING
(John Hunt Publications, U.K. 1998)
Sixty essays explain the science and wonder of our cosmic and organic origins.
An allegorical creation myth accompanies the essays.
John Fowles wrote the foreword.

LET THERE BE LIFE
(Paulist Press, HiddenSpring imprint, U.S.A, 2001)
An updated edition of *The Becoming* for North America.
John Fowles wrote the foreword.
61 line cuts, library stock.

DESIGN AND SCIENCE: THE LIFE AND WORK OF WILL BURTIN
(Lund Humphries, London; Ashgate Publishing, N.Y., 2007)
Richly illustrated. Traces the career of designer Will Burtin who pioneered several design fields.
Co-author, R. Roger Remington.

POWER OF A WOMAN. MEMOIRS OF A TURBULENT LIFE: ELEANOR OF AQUITAINE
(BookSurge.com, Shillingstone Press, 2007)
Eleanor of Aquitaine dictates her 'autobiographical' memoirs
See http://eleanor.robertfripp.ca/ (*temporary*)

Spirit in Health
(Shillingstone Press, 2009)
Spirit in Health explores non-technical, spiritual healing cultures in ancient Animist societies. The book follows their progress as some healing techniques are adopted into modern medicine.

New Wessex Tales
Thirty-seven short stories set in Thomas Hardy's Dorset
(Work in progress)

To contact Robert Fripp
www.robertfripp.ca
Also try: http://eleanor.robertfripp.ca/ (*temporary*)
416-481-7070 x29, at The Impact Group, Toronto

CPSIA information can be obtained at www.ICGtesting.com
Printed in the USA
LVOW060330300911

248458LV00002B/5/P